Praise for *N*

Damn! Kally rips your heart out, shreds it to pieces, and then ties it all back together with a sexy red bow. I love her wounded heroes. Then she weaves in hot sex just to keep you on pins and needles. One of the best books I've read in a truly long time!

~ J.M. Madden, author

~ ~ ~

Thank you thank you thank you for writing Ryder's story! And thank you for doing so much justice for PTSD survivors! Reading his trek into the city the first time and into the mall made me feel…Very *not* alone. You understand us. You get us. Thank you. Reading about his healing journey gives me hope and keeps me going.

~ Victoria Bagosy, a reader's post on Facebook

~ ~ ~

Kallypso Masters has a way of making every day problems that people face come to life in her writing. It comes to life in a way that helps you understand yourself and other people in your life going through some of the same issues her characters are going through. And *Nobody's Lost* is no exception.

~ Chipmunk251, a review

~ ~ ~

Firstly, I have to say that when I see the name Kallypso Masters, it is an automatic purchase. This saga is one of my all-time favourites. I was not disappointed by the latest addition to the saga. Every book I have read by Kallypso Masters has touched my soul. The way the author layers the storylines is amazing… Well done, Kallypso Masters. I cannot wait for more.

~ Erin Lewis (Maimeo's Angels), a review at MI Bookshelf

Rescue Me Saga
Reading Order

For the most part, the books in this series are not stand-alone novels. Please read in order.

However, *Nobody's Lost* could be read as a new entry point to the series.

In a saga, of course, characters recur to continue working on real-life problems in later books, so Megan and Ryder, the main couple in this book, will return in *Nobody's Dream* and subsequent books.

The first six Rescue Me Saga titles are available in e-book and print formats:

Masters at Arms & Nobody's Angel (Combined Volume)

Nobody's Hero

Nobody's Perfect

Somebody's Angel

Nobody's Lost

Nobody's Dream

kallypsomasters.com/books

Kallypso Masters will be working on more books that will include characters from the Rescue Me Saga, but some will be in spin-off series (including a trilogy with three romances featuring Mistress V. Grant, Gunnar Larson, and Patrick Gallagher). As much as she loves engaging with her readers, Kally writes by inspiration and follows the dictates of her characters, so she cannot write to deadlines or predict whose story will come next. Be sure to subscribe to her newsletter so you can be sure not to miss any release announcements!

As of this writing, next in the series appears to be ROAR, a story about Kristoffer Roar Larson and Pamela Jeffery. You met Pamela very briefly in Chapter 18 of *Somebody's Angel*, but have yet to meet Gunnar's relative, Kristoffer. Stay tuned!

Nobody's Lost

(Fifth in the Rescue Me Saga)

Kallypso Masters

Nobody's Lost
Fifth in the Rescue Me Saga
Kallypso Masters

Copyright © 2014-2015, Kallypso Masters LLC
Print Edition
E-book ISBN: 978-1941060094
Print ISBN: 978-1941060100

Original e-book version: December 9, 2014
Original print version: January 22, 2015
Last revised for e-book and print: May 18, 2015

ALL RIGHTS RESERVED
Edited by Meredith Bowery, Jacy Mackin, and Ekatarina Sayanova
Cover design by Michelle Preast
Cover image licensed through Getty Images;
Image graphically altered by Michelle Preast
Formatted by BB eBooks

To discover more about the books in this series, see the *Rescue Me Saga* section at the end of this book. For more about Kallypso Masters, please go to the About the Author section.

Dedication

This one is dedicated to all of my patient and supportive readers who stood by me during my recent battle to overcome cancer. I know with your prayers and encouragement I beat it much more quickly than anyone expected.

Thanks especially to the members of my Rescue Me Saga Discussion Group, a secret group on Facebook, who were there to brainstorm ideas for this story, helping me find Megan and Ryder and bring them together.

And to my author friends who agreed to join me for my first KallypsoCon without having a clue what I had in mind. (Because my instructions were vague—fun, relaxing, and intimate!) Thanks, Lexi Blake, Eliza Gayle, Annabel Joseph, Kennedy Layne, Red Phoenix, and Cherise Sinclair for giving so much of yourselves that weekend. And to all the readers who traveled near and far to be there. We certainly had no idea what it would take for *me* to be there only three weeks post-op, but all of you provided the best-ever healing medicine, enabling me to start writing *Nobody's Lost* just two weeks later, something I probably wouldn't have been able to do without that special weekend.

Acknowledgements

As always, no book happens in a vacuum. There are many to thank for helping me bring you this latest installment in the Rescue Me Saga.

My editorial team—Meredith Bowery, Jacy Mackin, and Ekatarina Sayanova—for working so quickly, sometimes in the midst of a major holiday week, to help me polish this book. They help me continue to improve and grow as a writer with each book I put out, large or small. Of course, I'm always changing something *after* my editorial team and subject experts sign off on a book and that invariably leads to new errors. So, as always, all typos and errors are solely *my* responsibility (and if you find any, please report them to Charlotte Oliver at charlotte@kallypsomasters.com).

My awesome beta readers—Margie Dees, Kathy Holtzclaw, Kellie Hunter, Kelly Mueller, Ruth Reid, and Lisa Simo-Kinzer—who read through the entire book (some of them more than once!) and helped me fix both major and minor (but important!) problems.

I'd like to extend a special thanks to Iliana GK, a new beta reader who took on the challenge of reading *Nobody's Lost* without having read any others in the series. She let me know that it truly is an enjoyable standalone read for those new to the series. She also provided great insights to help me improve several major scenes, especially the kink ones.

My proofreaders who all find my typos and errors—just not the same ones as each other—Alison K., Eva Meyers, Christine Sullivan Mulcair, Gilda Mary Sacca, and Lynde Shaw. Special thanks also to Angelique Luzader who shared some crucial revisions for the print version.

Toymaker and Mr. Sayanova who read over my BDSM scenes to help point out problems and make them Safe, Sane, and Consensual.

Top Griz for his expertise on weapons, military, and Marine Corps references—including how to remove a Marine's dress blues. And, as always, for helping me tune into Master Adam more clearly.

Ruth Reid and Ekatarina Sayanova for confirming that I nailed the psychological aspects of Ryder's deep, deep pain and survivor guilt.

My Facebook friends and fans who, even before I realized this would be the next book in the series, helped me brainstorm ideas to help me better understand Megan, Ryder, and many other upcoming characters. I pose countless questions in my Rescue Me Saga Discussion Group on Facebook, as well as on my Facebook timeline and author page and they always come through for me. You always are there to help me out when I need you!

One of the discussion group questions was to ask readers to find me the perfect stock photo for the cover of this book and Stephanie Henderson found the perfect Ryder and Megan for the couple in my head (except that we had to add a touch of gray to Ryder's hair).

Another question asked in the discussion group was to pick a first name for Wilson from Masters at Arms and Erin Miller came up with Ryder. Lots of other names were suggested, but that was the overwhelming favorite from the poll we took in the group.

And to whoever put together the information on vision quest rituals and purification lodge ceremonies at several Web sites (especially Barefoot's World). This and other sites helped me take Ryder on the journey into his soul. I also learned from watching videos like the one produced by the Salt Lake City Tribune "Trib Talk: The importance of sweat lodges to Native American veterans," as well as "Introducing the Sweat Lodge," produced by GRYPHON Media Productions. It's encouraging that the Veterans Administration acknowledges the importance of these Native American traditions in helping our wounded heroes find spiritual and emotional healing.

The Kallypso's Street Brats who always entertain me with their pimping exploits. And to my Masters Brats (fans) the world around. Without you all telling all your friends about my books, I never would have reached so many readers.

My awesome new administrative and personal assistant, Charlotte Oliver, who helped keep me sane through so much activity and so many trials this year. She had everything under control when I had to check out of my writing world those first three weeks after surgery. I'm especially grateful to her for making my first KallypsoCon come together just the way I envisioned it and hoped for—only better.

Thanks to Leagh Christensen and Lisa Simo-Kinzer for keeping my online groups hopping and everyone informed of what's happening in my unpredictable life.

Author's Note

As I said on the dedication page, this book came about in large part because of my love for my readers. For those who might not follow me in social media and aren't aware of what happened, let me explain. In September, just about two months before *Nobody's Dream* was supposed to be released, I was diagnosed with uterine cancer. Five days later, I underwent a total abdominal hysterectomy and am now happy to say I'm cancer free. For anyone facing similar surgery, I highly recommend the HysterSisters web site at www.hystersisters.com!

But the surgery was more debilitating than I imagined. While I anticipated having physical issues, when I sat down to work on Luke's book five weeks after the operation, I quickly realized I was not going to be physically or mentally able to accomplish that feat this fall. After spending a day crying about disappointing you and not giving you a fall release as promised (although I know most understood), I started writing *Nobody's Lost*.

This story poured out of me in a matter of five weeks. I had no idea Ryder was hurting so badly, but am happy to bring him and Megan together—and give you an unexpected installment in the Rescue Me Saga. Even if it's not the one you planned on, it is now very much a part of the saga and I can see I couldn't have finished *Nobody's Dream* without first telling this story. (So maybe it wasn't just post-surgical issues holding me back, but a muse who knew this story had to be told first!)

Please enjoy reading this newest novel in the Rescue Me Saga. It very much is part of the series for those who are reading in order. However, because so little is known of these two, I wrote it in such a way that it also can be a new entry point for someone who hasn't read the other books yet. It is my hope they will then want to go back and read the earlier books—but at the very least I hope they will continue forward with Megan and Ryder as they will appear in later books in the series including *Nobody's Dream*.

Thanks to all of my readers who have always rallied around me to support my writing, wherever the muse and characters took me. We writers aren't easy to understand, and I'm sure some of you are wondering how I could write an entirely new novel instead of just finishing one that's already so far along. I can't really explain it other than, with fewer subplots and timeline issues to wrangle into place, this one was much more manageable.

Enjoy *Nobody's Lost* and the journey with Megan and Ryder. I've already begun working on *Nobody's Dream* again. Now that I'm feeling stronger and healthier than ever, I hope to bring you *Dream* within the next few months.

Here are some web sites that can help if you need to talk with someone.

Crisis and Suicide Prevention Services (United States):
www.suicidepreventionlifeline.org

For military-service related PTSD, the Veterans Administration or any veterans group.

I'm also very impressed with and appreciative of the work done by these organizations for veterans and their families:

Hope for the Warriors:
http://www.hopeforthewarriors.org/

Save a Warrior:
http://www.saveawarrior.org/

Snowball Express (for the children of the fallen):
https://snowballexpress.org/

Prologue

Fallujah, Iraq, 15 November 2004

Ryder Wilson enjoyed talking with Lance Corporal Grant. She was young, but sure as hell knew her shit when it came to advanced satellite communications.

His recon Marine unit had been on this rooftop in Fallujah for hours, waiting for something to break and to go after the insurgents who had terrorized this part of the city for the last few days.

Too damned quiet. Sergeant Miller suggested they eat in shifts while they could. He was informing Damián Orlando of the SITREP while Ryder spent time getting to know the Marine newly attached to their unit.

Didn't usually find women Marines assigned to combat units, although the cease-fire they were under meant they probably wouldn't have any direct engagement. He hoped not anyway.

"So where are you from?" Grant asked.

"Born and raised in New Mexico. Albuquerque. How about you?"

"Army brat. I've lived all over and then some."

"That why you enlisted?"

Silence dragged out before she responded. "I guess so. Pissed my dad off that I didn't choose the Army, but I had something to prove to myself. I just hope I'm still in when women Marines are allowed to serve in combat."

"Not so sure that's a good idea."

She sat up straighter and glared at him. "Why not? I can perform just as—"

"Grenade!"

Orlando's voice jarred them from the conversation. He and Sergeant Miller were hurtling across the rooftop in their direction when the sound of an explosion threw Ryder against the wall he'd been leaning on. His ears rang from the blast. They were under fire.

Momentarily dazed, Ryder tried to remember what he had been doing, but his focus shifted to protecting Lance Corporal Grant. She was his responsibility and shouldn't be in the middle of this shit.

"Get behind me," he said, picking up his rifle.

"Sergeant Miller and Orlando have been hit." Ignoring him, she moved toward the two fallen Marines, and he followed.

"Madre de Dios! No! Sergeant, don't you fucking die!"

Orlando was lying under the body of Sergeant Miller. *Holy fuck!* Ryder and Grant reached the body at about the same time and lifted their Sergeant off Orlando with reverence and speed combined.

"Corpsman up!" Ryder called. Once they had set Sergeant's body down, they returned to check on Orlando.

Jesus, no. His foot dangled by what looked like some skin and meat alone. Where was Doc? Grant grabbed Orlando's hand and spoke to him. Ryder had never seen so much carnage in all his years serving in the Marines.

Ryder moved so Doc could assess the situation and keep Orlando alive.

"Keep his head down!" Doc ordered, and Ryder moved to his head where he placed one hand on the young private's forehead and another on his shoulder. Ryder filled Doc in on what had happened, but the mention of Sergeant's name had him glancing over at the man's head.

So much blood.

The hiss of an RPG made it clear the attack was still under way. Ryder realized he hadn't done his damned job. He radioed their immediate need for artillery and air support with their preplanned fire coordinates.

Doc shouted, "Let's get him off the roof!"

"Sure thing, Doc!" With Doc's help, he and Grant lifted an unconscious Orlando onto a litter…

*　　*　　*

Just after midnight

Ryder rolled over in bed, drenched in sweat. His heart pounding, he gasped for breath. Fucking nightmares. He laid his arm over his eyes, but the images came back in living color. Vivid, but different than the one the other night.

Blast.

Brains.

Blood.

Sergeant Miller's lifeless body. Damián Orlando's foot blown off. Doc D'Alessio nearly killed.

Jesus, I fucked up that mission. While he was shooting the shit with Grant, all hell broke out for his unit.

His cell phone buzzed. *Not now.* He didn't want to speak to anyone until he had time to regroup. Tossing the sheet aside, he sat up. A beer. That ought to take the edge off.

Before he could open the door to the fridge, his landline phone rang. Whoever it was could leave a message. He wasn't talking to anyone tonight. Even if it was Marcia. He could call his sister back in an hour or however long it took to regain control of himself.

The answering machine kicked in, and he waited for his sister's voice.

"Wilson. Pick up the phone. Adam Montague here."

How the fuck did Top have his phone number? He must have been the one calling on the cell, too.

Had Orlando mentioned to his former master sergeant that they had run into each other a couple of months ago on a Patriot Guard ride in southern Colorado? He had known it was a bad idea to go, but the man being buried had served with him in Kosovo. To lay low during his funeral would have been disrespectful, and he damn well wouldn't let any asshole activist protester disrupt his buddy finally being laid to rest.

Another brave and hurting hero's fucking suicide.

Other than the Patriot Guard Riders, Ryder had severed all ties to those who survived the past and had hoped Orlando would respect his request not to say anything to the others. He wanted to put all that behind him.

The nightmare from the mayhem on the rooftop in Fallujah told him he wasn't doing a very good job of that, though. He reached for the phone.

"Yes, Top. Sorry. I was…in the head."

"Glad I waited. How're you doing?"

"Great. Got myself a nice place in the Jemez Mountains. Nice and quiet."

Nobody bothers me, and I sure as hell don't bother anyone else.

"Sounds good." Top paused a moment. "Listen, Wilson, my sister is staying at our brother's place in Albuquerque. I have no fucking clue what's wrong, but when I called a little while ago, she said the police were there. Also said she'd call me back when they left, but I haven't heard a thing. Patrick's out of the country, and I'm worried about her."

"Sorry to bother you this late, but would you mind running over to make sure she's okay? It would mean a lot to me knowing someone I trust has taken a look around."

Go into the city? All those people? Adrenaline kicked in, and Ryder's heart began pounding.

A mission. His master sergeant hadn't given him orders in nearly eight years.

Someone I trust.

The desire to live up to those words and help the man who had brought him and nearly every man home from their deployments outweighed Ryder's penchant for drowning in his own shit.

"Sure, Top." He reached for a pen and pad of paper. "What's the address?" The neighborhood was more familiar than he liked. Ryder also jotted down her name—Megan Gallagher. Must be married since they didn't have the same last names. Why wasn't her husband looking in on her?

But Ryder would help where he could. She was Top's sister. That's all that mattered.

After also taking down a couple of phone numbers where he could reach Top, he said goodbye and tucked the paper inside his jeans pocket before returning to the bedroom to grab a long-sleeved flannel shirt and his leather jacket. It got colder than a witch's tit when the sun went down here in the high desert. Riding a Harley without a windscreen didn't help.

But he preferred to detach it when he rode alone. He couldn't stand being cooped up in a car or truck either. Needed to be able to breathe—and have an unobstructed view of any potential threat. Usually, his treks were on mountain roads and small highways, limiting the danger.

Not like tonight. The lights of the Albuquerque valley spread out before him as he headed south on I-25. He couldn't avoid the city this time.

Still, he wished he was alone back at Carlos's house in the mountains. Being around people wore him down quicker than the road.

Only because you asked, Top.

A man didn't turn his back on his Marine family, ever—no matter how fucked up he was. He hadn't been in a real city in nearly two years. If he needed anything he couldn't acquire for himself, his friend Carlos usually took care of it. But Ryder prided himself on being self-sufficient. He might be totally useless as far as holding a job went, but he didn't take handouts.

If he'd truly gone off the grid, Master Sergeant Montague never would have found him. But he kept a phone because of his sister Marcia in Santa Fe. Maybe he'd tracked him through phone records. But didn't he say he'd just heard from his sister about some trouble? Had he already known Ryder's number? No answers came as the lights of the valley grew brighter.

Fucking city. God, he hated being around that many people.

Just let me keep it together in front of Top's sister.

The last thing he wanted was for his unit to find out how badly he was handling the aftermath of his years in service. He'd tried going to the VA, but they were too far away—in miles and philosophy—to be of much help.

Hell, why was *he* so screwed up? He'd come home. In one piece, even. Look at Orlando. He'd adjusted well to his amputation, at least from what Ryder could tell from their brief meeting during the Alamosa PGR procession. If he hadn't seen the man's foot blown off by that damned grenade with his own eyes, Ryder would never have guessed Orlando wore a prosthesis.

Why couldn't Ryder put the past behind him like everyone else in his unit had done?

Chapter One

M egan Gallagher surveyed the makeshift studio she'd set up in her brother's condo only a couple of weeks ago. She balled her hands into fists. How dare someone break in and steal her property?

Some welcome to New Mexico.

Her brother had invited her to stay with him this summer after she graduated from USC in Los Angeles. She wanted to build a strong portfolio before deciding what to do next with her MFA. Well, looked like she'd be going computer shopping tomorrow. She couldn't postpone it because she needed to finish editing the photos she'd shot this past week for some clients who answered her local ad.

Two of Albuquerque's finest had left ten minutes ago after taking her report. As soon as she came home from dinner and saw the garage door open when she'd most definitely left it closed, she'd called 911 and waited for them to check the premises before going inside. They'd asked her to see what was missing. As far as she could tell, nothing but her computer, but she'd told them her brother would have to take inventory of his possessions after he returned Sunday or Monday.

Her studio props and lighting equipment stood where she'd left them. No street value on those, she supposed.

Brother dear needed to improve his security system, although breaking into Fort Knox might be simpler considering all the numbers she had to push to open the garage door.

Why hadn't the alarm gone off during the break-in?

She doubted anyone would be arrested and brought to justice, but felt better for reporting the crime. At least Patrick's fireproof safe was secure. It held her more expensive cameras and the external memory drive where she stored photos not still in her online cloud backup. Patrick's weapons were in there, too.

Thankfully, she took her digital SLR wherever she went. The heavier cameras in the safe were used more often for her studio work. She'd just leave them there.

No sense trying to call Patrick about this. He said he'd only be in Italy briefly before flying to Pakistan with someone he was co-piloting for. The man went to great extremes to build up his flight hours.

The thought of staying here tonight didn't hold as much appeal as it once had. Her sense of security had been shattered by the thieves. What if they returned for more? Suddenly afraid, she went to the bedroom and retrieved her own pistol, prepared to take on any intruders.

In the kitchen again, she opened the garage door from the box on the kitchen wall, but her cell phone buzzed before she could go into the garage. She glanced down at the caller ID.

Adam again?

Oh, crap! She'd forgotten all about him.

She'd met her long-lost half-brother for the first time last Thanksgiving. He'd called her while the police were here, and she'd forgotten to call him back to let him know what had happened. Did Marines come with internal radar or something? Or had he been calling to let her know how his wife Karla was doing?

He'd worry more if she didn't answer, so she returned to the kitchen and dead-bolted the interior door before accepting the call.

"Megan, is everything all right? What happened?" The concern in his voice was palpable.

She cleared her throat, knowing her silence would only stress him out more. "I'm fine. Some asshats broke into Patrick's place and stole my computer."

"Well, f—." She smiled hearing him reroute his mouth around the expletive she knew had almost spewed out. "You need to get out of there, but stay put a little longer. I've sent someone to check on you."

Without even knowing what the problem was? The man didn't let any moss grow under his boots.

"Are you armed?"

She smiled again. "Patrick made sure I knew how to use a weapon before I went to college."

"You didn't get too rusty while on campus?"

"No. Went to the firing range regularly."

"Good for you. I'm going to stay on the phone with you until Wilson shows up."

She guessed she ought to be thankful he hadn't sent in a platoon of Marines. Still, knowing someone was on the way did make her feel a little less scared.

"How's Karla doing?"

"She's fine. Tired mostly. We just took four days to drive back from a Memorial Day weekend wedding in San Diego County. Remember Damián Orlando?"

"Yes." Adam treated him like a son. One of his beloved Marines.

"Anyway, Karla's trying to get some shut-eye. It's not easy these days."

"I can imagine. Give her a hug and kiss from me. I hate to take you away from her tonight."

"Oh…well, she'll sleep better if I'm not in the bed with her." His voice sounded funny, but she smiled as she remembered taking some special photos of Karla a few months ago when the family came together in Denver for a weekend. He was in for one heck of a surprise, but they had turned out beautifully. Still, Megan regretted she would never—

"How's mom doing?" Adam interrupted her thoughts, thankfully. He had only just found their shared mother again after spending decades on his own from the age of sixteen.

"Going as strong as ever. She's glad the weather's improving so she won't be cooped up inside as much." Being wheelchair-bound kept her mother from traversing Chicago's snowy streets, but her attendants made sure she had regular outings. Megan had never known her mom to feel sorry for herself. And, having been paralyzed long before Megan had been born, she had never thought anything odd about having her mother confined to a wheelchair.

While Adam talked about the wedding he'd just attended, Megan looked around to see what else she should pack in her SUV. The safe provided more security for her equipment than she would have inside her SUV or a hotel room. The thieves hadn't tried to break into the safe, either, according to the police. No, she didn't really see much of anything she needed to take with her. Just the overnight bag.

But would she really only be away from the condo one night?

She sighed. "Uh-huh." She should be listening to the phone conversation, but her mind was too rattled to focus.

How long would she have to wait around for Adam's Marine to show up so she could send him on his way? No doubt in her mind that he would come, though. At Adam's wedding, she'd witnessed how much the men and women who served with him adored the retired master sergeant. Any of them would move heaven and earth to please him.

With any luck, the Marine would quickly see she could take care of her own problems and leave.

*   *   *

The roar of the hog's engine lulled him away from giving in to the anxiety nipping at his heels like a rabid dog. He had memorized the woman's address and merged onto I-40 as he headed toward the Sandias. She lived in one of the older neighborhoods in the foothills there. Couple of miles farther.

The sound of a long-range rifle split the air. *Sniper!*

Ryder ducked and tried to take evasive maneuvers into another lane. No, wait. That wasn't a rifle. A fucking car must have backfired. Thank God the highway was nearly deserted at this hour. He could have gotten himself or someone else killed.

Maintain control. You're okay. No one is gunning for you.

He repeated those phrases for the duration of the fifteen-minute drive to her exit. The quiet residential streets helped him relax somewhat, but there were too many fucking places for insurgents to hide with all these houses and condos.

No one is aiming for you. Get a fucking grip.

Barely two o'clock in the morning. No doubt he'd piss off some of the older residents in this wealthy neighborhood. Easing off the throttle, he slowed and rounded the corner onto the street where he'd once lived. Impossible to keep a hog quiet, so he gave up.

The houses began to look familiar. Not much had changed since he lived here as a teenager. He passed by the place his mom had owned and tried not to stare. He'd lived there with her and his sister until she lost the place. Ryder married Sherry at nineteen, and his mom moved into an apartment about the same time Marcia relocated to Santa Fe. Like him, his sister preferred the beat of her own drum.

A few years later, unable to find steady work, he joined the Marine Corps. Maybe he'd just wanted to escape from family problems.

How'd that work out for you?

His mom died while he was in the Corps. No chance to reconcile.

He loved his Marine family, but, man, he'd sure gotten himself fucked up over there. Big-ass wuss. Couldn't be around people more than a few hours now without shutting down or running away.

Just keep your focus on Top's sister—then get your ass home.

Three blocks later, he pulled into a cul-de-sac and parked in the driveway beside a luxury townhouse. Why was the garage wide open? The BMW motorcycle parked in the corner sure didn't fit the mental image he had of Adam's sister. Must be her brother's.

Ryder eased his helmet off and retrieved the knife from his boot. A month in the psych ward at the VA hospital and he'd voluntarily surrendered his sidearm and shotgun to Carlos. Last thing he wanted was to have one of those night terrors lead to him blowing his brains out. So many veterans had lost that battle…

Not that he couldn't use other means, but if he was going to do it, he'd make sure he succeeded with one try.

Even without a sidearm, he could cause a lot of damage to an insurg—no, intruder—with his Bowie. Carlos's people had taught him well.

He heard a woman's voice coming from inside the house. He relaxed a bit. Probably Adam's sister. Her voice sounded younger than her forty- or fifty-something age.

"Megan Gallagher? Ryder Wilson out here. Your brother Adam sent me to check on you."

She said something he couldn't hear and then yelled, "Speak loudly. Adam's on the phone and wants you to confirm you are who you say you are."

"No worries." At least she didn't let just anyone inside.

She spoke into the phone and listened before relaying the message to Ryder. "Adam asked me to ask you where the two of you first met."

"Kosovo. I was a replacement for one of his recon Marines."

Apparently, Adam gave her the go-ahead to let him inside. "Okay. Talk to you later. Love you, too."

The still night air was split by the sound of a deadbolt unlocking, and the door opened slowly.

"Sorry. My brother taught me to be careful."

"Megan Gallagher?"

She nodded and extended her hand in greeting.

Holy fuck. The woman standing before him was years younger than Ryder had expected. How much younger was she than Top?

Her dark auburn hair spilled over her shoulders, long and thick. A man's hands could get lost in those curls. She didn't look anything like Top, who had dark hair and Lakota blood. She looked more Irish or maybe Scottish.

He couldn't make out the color of her eyes in the dim light, but imagined they sparkled with life and humor. A tiny nose sprinkled with freckles and full, red lips adorned the most beautiful face he'd ever seen.

Man, what would it be like to kiss her? He hadn't kissed a woman since his ex walked out on him five years ago.

Shit. What was he doing thinking about kissing her? This was Top's sister. Top's *little* sister! His master sergeant would have his hide if he did anything inappropriate with her.

God, he hoped he didn't fuck up this mission. He needed to redeem himself in Top's eyes.

"Close the garage door before anyone gets in."

Chapter Two

M egan stared back a moment longer than prudent before pushing in the code. The man had a lethal air about him as though a deadly current vibrated beneath his skin. *Of course, he's a Marine.* But what struck her was the vacancy in his eyes that hadn't been noticeable in Patrick's or Adam's.

Lost.

"What happened to bring the cops in?"

"A break-in."

"You sure you didn't just leave the garage door open by mistake?"

"No. I definitely closed it." *No doubt about it.*

"If you didn't lock the interior door to the house either, they could have just walked in without having to disarm the system at all."

"I *said* I closed the garage door." Megan folded her arms in front of her. "The reason you found it open was that I was about to leave to check into a hotel when Adam called. I was distracted."

She couldn't get a read on whether he believed her yet. Maybe she could send him on his way soon.

Be nice, Megan. The man's come here to check on you in the middle of the night, for Pete's sake.

"Please, come in." Standing aside, she waved him inside.

He wore a weathered leather jacket as black as his hair. His jeans looked as if they'd been through a shredder at the knees. Had he rolled his bike at some point? He didn't seem the type to buy fashionably stressed jeans.

She'd done a double take at the gleaming Harley he'd left parked in her driveway. Man, what would it be like to take a ride on that machine? Much sexier looking than Patrick's BMW. Nothing beat the rumble of a Harley Davidson. Of course, no way would Megan ask this stranger for a ride.

The man—whose name escaped her already—had hair cut short, but not a high and tight. A bit of gray made her fight the urge to reach out and touch his temples and glide her finger down his sideburns.

Whoa, Megan!

What was the matter with her? She hadn't thought about touching a guy since college when she'd decided she simply preferred to focus on building her career rather than involve herself in relationships that could only end badly.

He probably had earned every one of those gray strands through multiple deployments. Patrick came home with a few himself, and he was still in his twenties.

Megan held her hand out to him. "I'm sorry. Let's start over. I'm Megan Gallagher, and I'm terrible with names." Her self-deprecating grin charmed him.

He accepted her hand. Firm grip, but he didn't try to go he-man like and crush her hand. "Ryder Wilson. I served with your brother in Fallujah. Well, in Kosovo and Kandahar, too, before that."

What Megan had learned about some of the horrors Adam's units had suffered made her want to wrap him in her arms and offer comfort along with her appreciation. "Thank you for serving. I know that's lame, and you probably grow tired of hearing it from those of us who didn't have the guts to do what you did. I can't imagine the sacrifices you and those who served this country have made. And your families, too." Most people forgot about the families left behind during long and continuous deployments.

He shrugged. "Just doing my job." His gaze darted behind her and down the hallway. "Top—*Adam*—said you'd had some trouble. What happened?"

She recognized the familiar Marine nickname for master sergeant that Ryder used. Rather than go into the story yet again, she decided to show him the evidence—well, the lack thereof, actually. "Follow me." She turned away and led him down the hall to the doorway of her makeshift studio and pointed inside. "The scene of the crime. My computer tower used to sit on that desk."

"That's all they took?"

"Well, this is my brother's place, so I can't be sure. The safe wasn't tampered with, and the TV and other electronics are still in the media room." She sighed. "My computer's probably already been resold and the hard drive reformatted by now."

"Doesn't make sense."

He doesn't believe me.

Why did that bother her? She had to admit to being as perplexed as he was. The police officer even suggested perhaps she had left it somewhere else.

"The police couldn't find any broken windows or jimmied doors. *All* were closed and locked. Whoever came in bypassed or usurped the security code at one of the outside entrances, which are a lot more complicated than the one in the kitchen. I already checked to make sure I still have the remote in my purse."

"Was it a sophisticated system?"

"By my standards, it was at least complicated."

"Have you called your brother—Patrick, I mean?"

She shook her head. "He's out of the country. Won't be home until Sunday at the earliest."

"Show me the alarm system."

She led him farther down the hall to Patrick's bedroom. "Here's the main panel."

"Damn. What's he worried about having stolen?"

Megan shrugged. "Told you it's complicated. I guess he wants to protect his media equipment."

"But you said nothing was taken except for your computer."

"True. It's a mystery to me."

Ryder walked down the hallway toward the front entrance she'd never even used. "I'm going to take a look around outside. Stay here."

He moved like a jungle cat. She wondered what it would be like to photograph him. Not good at taking orders or being idle, she followed him. She wanted answers, too.

He glared at her before pulling out a penlight from his pocket and surveying the area inside and out. "No visible signs anyone tampered with them. Whoever broke in possessed some sophisticated communications knowledge."

"That's pretty much what the police said."

He gave her a pointed look. "Do *not* follow me. I mean it this time." The man didn't like being disobeyed. "Open the garage door when you hear me knock four times." He waited for her to go back inside. When she didn't, he prompted, "Why don't we close this one before we let in any more dirtbags?"

"I didn't let in the first ones. They *broke* in." He nodded, but she doubted he believed her. At least he'd given her something to do.

"I'll meet you at the garage door, Ryder."

She closed and dead-bolted the door before returning to the kitchen and opening the interior door so she'd hear him. A few minutes later, she heard four knocks and gave him access into the garage. He rolled his Harley inside before she closed the door for what she hoped would be the last time tonight. She'd show him she hadn't left it open earlier without thinking.

Megan waved him into the kitchen. "Listen, it's been a crazy few hours around here. I need a drink. Can I get anything for you?"

"Coffee. Black. Thanks, ma'am."

No way was she going for coffee herself. As she prepared a pot for him, she no longer felt the need to move to a hotel tonight. With both of them armed—he with a deadly looking knife and she her Smith & Wesson .40 caliber pistol—they should be able to fight off anyone who tried to break in again.

"I'll stand watch while you get some sleep tonight, ma'am."

She sighed. "Ryder, first off, my name is Megan. Second, no one is after *me*. It was a random break-in. Theft of one computer. End of story. I've only been here a few weeks. They probably thought they were getting some of Patrick's expensive equipment or some government secrets or something."

"He works for the government?"

"Private contractor, actually. I don't know much other than that."

"Explains the top-notch civilian security system. I still don't think some kid looking for drug money did this. Why they didn't clean out this place is confusing as hell."

"I guess you're right." Her hand trembled as she reached for a brandy snifter and a bottle of Courvoisier. She poured until the snifter was more than half-filled.

"We'll know more after a few days."

What? A few days? The man already had a disturbing effect on her. One minute, he ticked her off because he didn't believe her. The next he had her face flushing and nipples peaking because he exuded some kind of sexual pheromone or something.

Did humans have pheromones?

She tossed her head back and drained the snifter in two swallows.

"Whoa! Go easy with that!"

She set the empty glass on the counter and squeezed her eyes shut, trying to block out the burning down her throat and watering in her eyes. The potent drink's warmth spread through her belly. How did her brother drink this stuff? She preferred margaritas, but he didn't have a machine for them. She coughed to clear her throat before turning around to face him.

"It's been a hell of a night. That's going to help me sleep."

Rather than lie awake fantasizing about a man sexier than sin keeping watch over me.

*   *   *

Damn, he didn't mean to scare her. But she wasn't taking this as seriously as she should be.

"Do you think your brother can come home early?"

"No. He was flying to Pakistan on a humanitarian-aid mission with a new friend of his. Then they have to fly back to Italy to pick up the couple who flew over with them. Do you know Marc D'Alessio?"

"Doc?"

She nodded.

"He was my Navy corpsman in Fallujah." *I nearly got him killed.*

"Patrick is co-piloting for the guy flying Marc and Angelina to Italy." She furrowed her brows and cocked her head. "When's the last time you saw Adam?"

"He retired following my last tour. I left the unit not long after."

"You must be one of the few Marines he served with who didn't show up for his wedding last December."

Ryder shuffled his feet. He hadn't heard about the wedding, but that had been a rough month for him. He wouldn't have been in any shape to show up in polite society for something as special as Top's wedding.

"Sorry I missed it." *Not really.* He was glad no one had found him to send an invite. He'd worked hard to stay under the scope since his discharge. But Megan didn't need to know that.

Guarding her was not going to be an easy assignment, either. He hadn't spent much time alone with a woman since Sherry left him. He'd topped a few women at a private dungeon in Santa Fe one night, but only because Carlos dragged him up there.

Last thing he wanted or needed was another woman in his life. How many nights had he slept on the couch before his ex walked out, afraid he would hurt her during a night terror? His inability to be a husband anymore probably was the main reason she'd called it quits. That and she didn't want to live holed up in a fucking cave in the desert, which was how she'd referred to the place he'd chosen to hide away from life.

His refuge.

Jesus, let me just finish this mission so I can head back there.

The demons lurked on the edges of his consciousness. He couldn't keep them at bay forever. Last thing he needed was for Megan to report back to Top that he was in desperate need of a shrink.

She placed a mug of steaming coffee on the counter between them, and he removed his leather jacket. She stared at the Marine emblem ink on his forearm. He'd been drunk and on shore leave in Istanbul when that became his first and last tat back in 1998.

He noticed a trembling in her hand. "You don't have to worry about anyone hurting you. I won't let anyone near you."

"That's not what I'm worried about."

He waited, but she didn't elaborate. He needed more answers from her. "Is there someone who might have wanted to hurt you by disrupting your life? A thwarted lover, maybe?"

"Sorry to be so boring, but I have no enemies or jilted lovers. I can't imagine anyone having it in for me or wanting revenge, and Lord knows no one would be jealous of me." She met his gaze. "Even if there had been some former lover, what would he want with my computer? I'm a photographer, but I don't take *those* kinds of photos."

He wondered what she did photograph, but clearly the woman had no clue how beautiful she was if she thought no one would be jealous.

"You don't believe me."

He shrugged. "Doesn't matter."

"It matters to me." She glanced at her empty glass before meeting his gaze again. "I hate to disappoint a conspiracy theorist, but I've been solely focused on earning my master's in fine arts and making plans to start my career. No time to date anyone on a serious level. I haven't been in love since my high-school sweetheart, and we broke up in college."

"I can remember what it's like to be that age. Intense...emotions."

"Well, those *emotions* ended long ago. Besides, my big brother scared him so badly on prom night that he couldn't do anything—intense or otherwise—if he wanted to."

"I imagine Adam would make guys toe the line around you." One thing was certain, Ryder wouldn't cross that line. Was he afraid of Adam? Maybe. But what he feared most was dishonoring himself in front of his master sergeant.

"Not Adam. I've only known him for about six months. He's actually my half-brother. He disappeared from my mother's life until last Thanksgiving.

No, I'm talking about my other brother, Patrick. He was a pilot in the Marine Air-Ground Task Force and is working on his commercial pilot's license now."

Ah. A Marine. Regardless, Ryder needed to find out who this old boyfriend was and have him checked out.

Megan held up her hand. "Before you form a posse to search for my last boyfriend, he's now happily married to one of my best friends, and they have three kids."

A shadow of pain crossed her eyes. She wasn't being completely honest with him. Perhaps she still had a thing for him.

*   *   *

Something I could never give him.

She stared at her empty snifter, but decided she'd had more than enough. Her lips began to tingle as numbness set in. She hadn't slept in more than twenty-four hours, not that she hadn't gone longer during her college days. Dealing with the break-in left her exhausted, more tired than she ever remembered being.

"I think I just want to sleep for a day or…three."

"Do you think it's a good idea for you to stay in Albuquerque with these perps on the loose? Come morning, maybe we can get you to a friend's house or something."

"Leave town? I can't do that."

"Why the hell not?"

"I don't know anyone here but Patrick, and I *refuse* to give some petty thieves that much control over me. Besides, why prolong the inevitable? My first order of business is to buy a laptop that I can keep locked in the safe at night—or whenever I don't have it with me."

He ran a hand through his hair before he shot her a pleading look. "Megan, I've been charged by your brother—Adam—with making sure you are protected. I can't reassure him of that if you stay here where you're an easy target if they *haven't* already gotten what they wanted."

He seemed more concerned with disappointing Adam than with pissing her off. If he thought her a less formidable foe, he needed to be enlightened.

"I'm sure whoever broke in has what they wanted—my computer was top of the line. You are under no obligation to stay, not even tonight."

"I'm going to protect you until we know for sure you're safe or your brother tells me to stand down."

"That *could* take days."

He sighed. "Don't worry, Megan. I'll keep you safe until Patrick returns."

Safe? Up to a point, maybe. But this man did things to her no other had done in a very long time. Honestly, not even her old boyfriend had turned her body on the way this man did with a simple glance.

Damn it, she'd put her life on a course for success and wasn't going to let her residual hormones mess that up.

Chapter Three

J	*esus, don't let this be the third biggest mistake of my life. I fucked up so many times.*

"I have a spare bedroom at my place in the Jemez Mountains." Man, he'd kill to be back there right now. He could protect her more competently with fewer people around.

I can breathe there.

Megan shook her head, releasing her scent into the air—something spicy, classy, yet understated like the redhead standing next to him.

"Out of the question. I don't even know you."

"You're part of my Marine family. I would never do anything to dishonor myself before Top or any member of his family." He ran a hand through his hair. "Look, ma'am, no way am I going to let your brother down."

Her displeasure with him was evident by a raised eyebrow. Probably didn't care for being called ma'am by someone only eight or ten years older, but the formality helped him remember she was off limits.

She retrieved her cell phone from her pants pocket. "I'm sure he's still awake worrying. Let me call Adam and ask him to let you off the hook."

He placed his hand over her fingers before she placed the call. "My mission is under way. He expects me to use my judgment and skills to see that you're safe. At the moment, I'm not convinced you're out of danger, no matter how you play it down to him on the phone. I won't lie to Top." *Not about this, anyway.*

Their gazes locked for a long moment before she set the phone on the counter. "You win. If Adam is anything like Patrick, he's not going to back down." She sighed. "But I'm not moving into your house, not even overnight. You can barricade the doors if you want, but I'm sleeping here. Alone."

"I can stand guard outside if that makes you feel safer."

She nibbled her lower lip, and he felt the first stirrings of a hard-on in longer than he could remember.

Fuck that shit.

Top's little sister. Hands off, grunt.

"I don't want you sleeping outside. But I wouldn't feel right giving you Patrick's room. I can let you take the sofa, if you'd like."

"I won't be sleeping."

"But you've probably been up all night, same as I have."

"I've stayed awake longer than this while on guard duty. I'll be fine."

"Ryder, just how long does Adam expect you to shadow me?"

"Until the mission is completed and the objective achieved—or Patrick returns. I won't sugarcoat the situation, and I won't leave you in any kind of danger."

"But I'm not in danger."

"You sure?"

"I told you, I have no enemies."

"Give me the access codes to the security system and go get some sleep." She wrote them on a piece of paper that he pocketed in his jeans. "Call out if you need me. Rest assured no one will harm you on my watch, Megan."

"Thanks. I do appreciate you coming on such short notice like this. I hope your wife and family don't mind."

He tensed, not wanting to reveal more about himself than she needed to know. "I live alone."

"You wouldn't have a little sister, would you, Ryder?"

"What?" Had his mind strayed from the conversation? Wouldn't be the first time he'd tuned out a woman.

"Just wondering if you have a sister, because my brothers are just as protective as you are. Maybe it's a Marine thing."

He glanced down at the floor. "I have one older sister. She lives up in Santa Fe."

"Well, I'm glad you're going to stay, because I really didn't want to go to a hotel."

Ryder nodded. "I'm going to check the perimeter. Pleasant dreams, Megan."

*   *   *

Megan watched him walk out of the room, his body ramrod straight. Did the man even know *how* to relax?

Well, *she* did. This night had been exhausting, and she wanted nothing more than to crawl into bed and zone out for a few hours. She contemplated having another belt of cognac to help achieve that, but decided against it. First, she'd try lying down and closing her eyes. If that didn't work, she'd resort to alcohol or sleep aids. She didn't like taking drugs or anything that impaired her mind or judgment, not after having to rely on so many of them just to keep the pain at bay for so many years. Never again.

Before going to her room, she made up a bed for Ryder on the sofa. Surely he'd realize soon how ridiculous he was being about all-night guard duty and would at least take a nap.

Stretching out on her bed, she pulled the sheet and summer bedspread up to her neck and curled onto her side. Every time she closed her eyes, thoughts of her missing computer bombarded her. She couldn't wait to get to the computer store.

Megan turned on her other side and reached for one of the paperbacks on the nightstand, flipping the light on before settling back on her pillows. Maybe if she read a few chapters, she'd become tired enough to sleep. She might even replace the mayhem in her life with that of the protagonist's in this fascinating mystery novel by her favorite author.

Her mind strayed a few times to the erotica site she accessed from her iPad when she craved a little self-induced stress relief, but the last thing she needed was any more sexual stimulation tonight. That potent man patrolling Patrick's condo right now exuded enough sexiness to keep her in fantasies the rest of her life.

An hour later, she realized the book had the opposite effect to making her sleepy. She'd replaced the male protagonist's image in her mind with one of Ryder Wilson. No more sleepy than before, she picked up the latest issue of one of Patrick's boring news magazines. When she heard a knock on her bedroom doorframe a few minutes later, she jumped.

"Megan?"

"Come in."

The door opened. "Sorry, but I saw the light on and wanted to check to make sure you were okay." He glanced at the magazine now lying on her chest. "Can't sleep?"

She set it aside. "Not a wink. My mind won't shut down." She tented her knees, keeping the covers on. "Any sign of trouble out there?"

"All quiet. Can I get you anything?"

She shook her head. Seeing to her needs was above and beyond his mission.

Ryder's gaze darted from her to the floor in front of him and back. Megan motioned toward the foot of the bed. "We might as well get to know each other a little better if we're going to be under forced confinement for a while. Have a seat."

"I don't think that's a good idea."

"What—the having a seat part or the getting to know each other better part?"

"Both, actually. I don't think your brothers would like hearing about a major lapse in protocol on my part, like sitting on your bed while you're in it."

She grinned. "Ah, a cautious man. Well, brothers be damned, if you won't sit here, we can go into the kitchen and brew some coffee or cocoa or something. Then you can tell me more about Adam."

He furrowed his brow. "You really should try to get some sleep. You've been through a lot in the last few hours."

"Short of taking a sleeping pill, I don't think sleep is going to happen. The sun streaming through my windows shortly is going to make that even harder. Unless you blindfold me."

His brown eyes smoldered before he stared at the floor again. She'd embarrassed him. Well, from what she'd read and heard, people dabbling in kink were more common these days than anyone knew. The media was all over it. She'd been reading an article about it when Ryder knocked. Not that she'd tried it herself or had any desire to give up control at that level to a man. But having a man under *her* control might be fun to try.

Oh, she'd let him squirm long enough about the blindfold. "I meant blindfold me with my sleep mask. To block out the sun, of course."

The relief in his gaze surprised her. Did he think she was flirting with him? She'd never bothered developing such wiles. What man would want damaged goods or a wife who could never…

Don't go there, Megan.

"What was Adam like when you knew him in service?"

"He was a senior SNCO." Marines had so much jargon and apparently her confusion showed. "Sorry, staff non-commissioned officer. We were both enlisted men. I was a corporal, several ranks below Top. We didn't pal around or anything so there's not much I could tell you, even *if* I wanted to."

And clearly he didn't. "So, then, what was he like as your master sergeant?"

He visibly relaxed and leaned against the doorjamb. "The best there is. He gave it to us straight and wouldn't ask us to do anything he wouldn't do himself or hadn't already done many times before. He put his life on the line to get all of his Marines out of every engagement."

"I know it killed him that he didn't succeed."

His eyelids narrowed. "Did he tell you about Kandahar or Fallujah?"

"No. At the wedding, I overheard snippets of conversations throughout the house as I was taking photos. Fallujah was where one of his business partners—Damián Orlando—was injured." Ryder nodded. "That's all I know. A wedding isn't the place to discuss the gory details of war, but given how many military personnel were present, there had to be some."

The light in his eyes dimmed as though the windows to his soul had just been slammed shut. "The details of his combat history are something you need to discuss with him. He'll decide how much he wants you to know." He reached for the doorknob and began to pull it closed as well. "I'm going to take another look around."

Ryder left before she could say another word. Great. Now she was even less sleepy, wondering what he wasn't telling her. It must have been a nightmare in Fallujah. She knew even less about Kandahar.

Megan tossed the sheet and bedspread back and went into the bathroom. After a long, hot shower, she dressed and went in search of Ryder.

The smell of eggs cooking assailed her the moment she opened her bedroom door and ventured into the hallway. When she reached the kitchen, she found him standing in front of the stove as he flipped over the scrambled eggs.

"That smells great."

"I figured since you couldn't sleep, you might like an early breakfast." The skylight showed the beginning stages of dawn. She wondered if he'd been planning to serve her in bed if she hadn't come in here.

He sprinkled liberal amounts of cheese, mushrooms, and chopped peppers onto the surface of the eggs and flipped half of the overstuffed omelet onto the other half. He probably could have eaten the entire thing himself. She'd always been amazed at how much food Patrick could pack away and still never gain an extra ounce.

She went to the cupboard, pulled out two plates, and set them next to the stove. "Thanks for making breakfast. Nothing sexier than a man working at the stove."

Crap! What made her say something like that?

His hand stilled a moment. "No worries."

Needing something to distract herself—and put some distance between them—she fixed four slices of toast and poured orange juice into two glasses. The coffee pot was three-fourths full. He probably planned on drinking the brew to stay awake. She poured herself a mug and refreshed his.

The two of them sat at the bar rather than at the table and ate and drank in silence for several minutes before he set his fork down and looked sidelong at her. "When do you want to go buy the new computer?"

She smiled. "As soon as the mall opens."

"There's no more remote store to buy one?"

"'Fraid not. Only one in the whole city. I'll need to buy new software for programs I don't have digitally and download and install everything again. The sooner I do that, the sooner I can resume some semblance of normalcy."

He nodded and swallowed a sip of his black coffee.

"Where do you live, Ryder?"

"On a pueblo north of here."

"You're Native American?" He didn't have the coloring or features, for sure. She'd have guessed his ancestors were more central European.

"No. A friend from high school let me stay at his grandmother's place when I…returned from Fallujah. She passed away more than a decade ago, but we used to spend summers there as teens when he was sent to the pueblo to learn the ways of his people. Lucky for me, his folks didn't mind having me tag along."

"How interesting that must have been for you."

He narrowed his gaze as if gauging her sincerity but soon relaxed. "Actually, those were some of the best times of my childhood."

So he hadn't had the idyllic childhood she had. "What kinds of things did you learn?"

He took a bite of his omelet and chewed slowly. She thought he was going to evade the question, but he washed the last of his eggs down with his juice and sat back in his chair.

"Hunting. Fishing. Drumming."

"Drumming! My family has a cabin up in the Black Hills that my brother is fixing up, and I spent a couple of summers there. We went to a powwow every summer. Also learned to fish. Didn't really care for hunting, though. Something about those cute furry animals—well, I couldn't kill one."

"We only killed what we needed to survive. It was never about the sport of killing."

"Oh, I'm sure it wasn't!" She didn't mean to guilt him out about it. "I'm just, well, rambling, I guess." She stood and started clearing the dishes from the counter. Together they rinsed and stacked them in the dishwasher in companionable silence.

Setting the last plate in the rack, she turned to Ryder. "What would you like to do until the mall opens?"

He hesitated a moment. "We still have a few hours. You sure you don't want to try to get some sleep first?"

She shook her head. "No, I couldn't sleep a wink after all this coffee. Besides, I'm anxious to see if I can get what I need out of my cloud."

"Cloud?"

"It's where my current work is stored. Like a back-up system in the sky." She grinned at his blank expression. Apparently, he didn't use computers much.

"I'm going to take another look around."

She watched him walk down the hallway and found herself zeroing in on his butt. Never one to ogle a man, her face flushed at the thoughts racing through her mind. Time for a little alone time in her bedroom until they were ready to head to the mall.

Chapter Four

R yder rode shotgun as her metallic blue Ford Escape sped to the mall. He hoped he wasn't making a mistake leaving the condo unguarded. One thing was certain—he'd rather be alone with her there than have to face all those people at the computer store. No way would he let her out of his sight, though. No harm would come to her on his watch.

When he could get some time alone, he needed to call Top and update him on the situation—what he could figure of it, anyway. He wished the woman would let him take her out of the city for a few days. He could protect her so much better at his place.

Whoa there, buddy.

The thought of taking a woman to his place was dumber than a sack of nails. That house was way too isolated for someone used to living where she did. Then again, it sounded as though she had spent some time in the country at her family's summer cabin.

Too soon, she pulled into the parking lot for the mall. Jesus Christ, wall-to-wall vehicles.

"I may have to park out a ways."

He wished she'd been deterred and would give up on the idea of shopping now. "Maybe we should try during the dinner hour. I hear there are fewer people shopping then."

"I'm sure they aren't all headed to the computer store. It'll be fine."

Ryder began scanning the scene for any threats to her safety, but the pounding of his blood rushing in his ears blocked out all use of that sense. Sweat broke out on his upper lip. What if he couldn't protect her from harm?

"Ryder, are you all right?"

Belatedly, he realized she'd found a place and parked. Now, she stared at him and wondered what the fuck his problem was. How could he explain?

"My breakfast isn't setting too well. Haven't eaten like that in a while."

"Oh, I'm sorry! Let's go back to my place then." She inserted the key in the ignition and turned the engine over.

He refused to allow his fears to hinder her from doing what she needed to do. She needed that computer to be able to get back to work.

Ryder reached out and placed his hand lightly on top of her wrist. Soft. He pulled away again. "No. Let's go on in. They'll have bathrooms if I need one, but you need to get that computer."

"Are you sure? I can wait."

He opened his door. "Yes. I'm fine." After exiting the Escape, he scanned the lot, but only saw a dozen or so shoppers either heading inside or returning to their cars.

"You look like you're expecting a full-on attack."

He met her gaze. He was, but wouldn't tell her that. She'd think he was crazy like all the other civilians did.

Maybe he was.

"Never hurts to be aware of your surroundings. Marine training."

She nodded and smiled. "I have two Marine brothers. I understand completely." She started toward the mall entrance again and turned back to make sure he was following. "Sooner we get this done, the sooner we can get out of here."

She winked, and his defenses dropped. Or maybe his big head just deferred to his little head's judgment. What the fuck?

Focus, man. This is Top's sister.

She continued toward the store, her hips swaying in her jeans. He forced himself to keep careful watch over her without ogling.

Ryder followed a few feet behind so she wouldn't become alarmed by the way he continually scanned their surroundings looking for any unusual activity. Once inside the doors of the mall, an assault of sound and movement bombarded him.

He came to a halt as he tried to process the scene.

Shoppers rushing toward them with bags in both hands. *Merchandise. Not suicide bombs.*

Screaming kids heightened his senses, but they weren't solemn like the ones in Iraq.

Don't trust the kids.

No, wait. These kids were just pissed they didn't get what they wanted at the mall. No booby traps. No human barricades—

Then a sound he couldn't mistake anywhere—the hiss of an RPG.

"Hit the floor!"

He rushed toward Megan to provide cover before his brain kicked in and computed that they were near a party store. The sound was the helium filling a birthday balloon.

You're in suburban Albuquerque. No one is aiming for you.

Megan turned and stared at him as if he'd grown a second head. Hoping to regain his cool, he looked at the floor and reached down to pick up an imaginary object he quickly pretended to put in his pocket.

"Found it."

Her brows furrowed, but she smiled again and turned, making her way toward the computer store once more. People passed within barely a foot of her, and he went on high alert again. Too many people. Too many unfamiliar sounds.

Jesus, let's get this over with and get back to her place.

Inside the computer store, a saleswoman entered her name in her iPad, and he surveyed the showroom while waiting for her to be served. While busy, fewer than ten people occupied the store, half of them appearing to be staff members. One quickly recorded her order and headed to the back to retrieve the components she'd requested.

Less than half an hour later, he carried the bag with her new computer to the Escape.

"That was fast."

"They usually are."

"It helped that you knew what you wanted."

At the SUV, they stowed the bag in the back seat. He moved to the driver's door and opened it for her.

"You don't have to open my door." She smiled. "But thank you."

After one more glance around the parking lot, unable to shake the feeling of being scrutinized, he took his place in the front passenger seat.

Ryder breathed a little easier for the first time since they'd arrived at the mall. Before she started the ignition, he suggested, "Let's stop by the hardware store. I'd like to pick up some new locks for the condo. I can work on that while you set up your computer." His nerves were stretched thin. He needed to decompress before he had a full-blown anxiety attack. Installing the locks would give him something to do that would get his head back in the game.

"Sounds good. All I know is the sooner I restore my photo files, the better I'll feel. Maybe we can go out later tonight as a reward for working so hard today."

"We'll see."

When she still didn't start the engine, he turned to meet her gaze.

"Relax, Ryder. We're not in any danger. If you remain on a constant level of heightened awareness, you're going to exhaust yourself."

"I'm fine."

But she spoke the truth. Just this past hour or so had left him drained. How could he effectively protect her if he didn't have the strength to fight off attacks?

Especially the attacks from within.

*   *   *

After they stopped at the hardware store, Megan hurried back to the condo. Seated beside her, Ryder fisted and unfisted his hand repeatedly. She didn't know what had caused his anxiety, but remembered those first months with Patrick after he returned from Afghanistan.

Did Ryder suffer from post-traumatic stress or was he just someone who didn't like being in crowds? The way he expected everyone around them to attack at any moment must be exhausting. She made a note not to ask him to go out during the busiest part of the day again.

She reached across the seat and squeezed his arm, feeling a slight tremor through his shirt sleeve. "Thanks for going along with me. I appreciate it."

"I promised your brother I'd protect you."

Putting her hand back on the wheel, she realized she and Adam needed to have a talk. Did he expect Ryder to be plastered to her side indefinitely?

"I think we both know that whatever the burglars wanted, they got. I don't expect any more trouble."

"Don't you want to bring them to justice?"

She sighed. "Do you have any idea how long it takes to find justice in this world? No, thanks. I'm happy knowing they are out of my life. I don't need anything more."

His gaze lingered on her for a long time, and she tried to ignore the way his stare made her insides turn to jelly. Not easy. The man was so…intense. Didn't he ever lighten up and have fun?

Don't judge, Megan. You haven't been through what he has.

Combat changed people. She'd seen it in Patrick and the few from her high school who'd gone off to serve their country. No one should have to do the things they had to do, but thank God men and women were willing to make those sacrifices.

The rest of the drive passed in silence. She wondered what he was thinking, but decided to give him time to unwind after the shopping trip. Opening the garage door, she pulled in next to his Harley.

Outside the SUV, her hand stroked over its leather seat before remembering what part of his anatomy had been plastered to it. Heat flooded her cheeks. *Don't go there.* She'd never ridden on a Harley. "Maybe we can go for a ride later."

"I don't think that's a good idea."

"Why not?"

He stared at her as if she were clueless. Oh, of course he would be worried about her safety.

"I have a helmet. I ride with Patrick sometimes on his BMW."

"We'll see." He opened the back door to collect their bags.

"Do you have kids, Ryder?"

He shifted his gaze toward her. "No. Why?"

"I just wondered. You're always saying 'We'll see.' Just reminds me of what my dad would say when he hoped I'd forget about whatever it was I wanted."

She thought she saw a glint of humor in his eyes, but if it had been there, it soon disappeared. "I take it you didn't forget very often."

She flashed him a smile. "Never."

He sighed and shook his head, but she definitely saw the hint of a smile before he averted his face. "Maybe we can go for a ride later on, when the day cools off."

She joined him behind the SUV. "That sounds great. Thanks for the offer."

Perhaps a ride in the mountains or desert. Maybe he'd relax if they left the city for a while.

Ryder took the bags from the cargo area and carried them to her office. "I'll start working on the locks while you're busy in here." He left her alone.

The hours flew by checking her computer files after connecting the laptop to the monitor the thieves left behind. At lunchtime, he brought her a sandwich, but she barely paused to eat. Finally, she breathed a sigh of relief when all of her latest work had been restored. She hadn't lost anything.

A soft knock came to the door. "We have about three more hours of daylight if you still want to take that ride."

That he would remind her was surprising, but she saved what she was doing and closed the lid on her laptop. She tried to knead the knot in her right shoulder.

"Want me to work the kinks out first? I used to give a mean neck, head, and shoulder massage."

She nearly came at the thought. "Please!"

His footsteps approached, and she closed her eyes. The T-shirt she wore was so thin she felt the heat from his body against her back as if she were naked.

Stop thinking about getting naked with him.

His hands were heavy and strong as he laid them on her shoulders. Without even beginning the massage, her shoulders tingled. Magic hands.

More lightly than expected, his fingers and thumbs probed the muscles of her shoulders. When his thumb pressed into the knot on the back of her right shoulder, she groaned, and his movements stopped.

"Did I hurt you?" His voice sounded more husky than usual, probably from being silent so long as he concentrated on her massage.

"God, no. You just homed in on where I hold most of my tension. Keep doing that."

Ryder didn't move immediately. She grinned. He probably was berating himself for touching his master sergeant's little sister in such an intimate way. The man really did take his responsibility to her brother seriously.

No surprise. Adam's Marines revered him.

When he did begin to work on that knot, she groaned again. *So good.* Her head lolled to the side to give him better access.

"Feel better?"

"Yes—but please don't stop." *Not yet.* The next sound from her mouth was more of a moan, and she blushed. Sounded as though she was turned on, but truly she just loved what his hands were doing. Her nipples hardened, and she was thankful he couldn't see them. Maybe she needed to put an end to this.

Soon.

"You're very good with your hands." Her voice sounded a little husky now, too.

"My wife used to enjoy massages, too."

She patted his hand to stop him. Dear God, she was getting turned on by a married man. No wife would be this understanding of a man's loyalty to his military buddies. He had mentioned earlier he lived alone, but even if separated, they were still married.

"Isn't she going to miss you if you spend too much time here with me?"

His hands stopped. "No. She left me years ago. We're divorced."

Megan swiveled around in the chair, breaking the contact with his hands. "I'm so sorry. I didn't mean to pry."

She saw the hurt in his eyes, but he tried to shrug it off. "You didn't pry. I wouldn't respect you much if you didn't ask about her when you thought I was married." His gaze dropped to her chest, and her face grew hot. He could see her nipples and had to know the effect his hands had on her.

Being a gentleman, he quickly met her gaze again. "Unfortunately, I couldn't give her back the man she married after I returned from my last deployment." He shrugged. "It happens."

She nodded. "I know Patrick couldn't make it work with his old girlfriend after he came home, either. I guess a lot of relationships are casualties of long and multiple deployments. How many times were you sent over there?"

"Three since 9/11, but I also served in Kosovo. That's where I first met your brother."

"Were you planning on a career in the Corps?"

"Initially, but missed it by a long shot. Didn't reenlist after Fallujah. Eight years was plenty."

"Well, thank you for the many years you served. I know I couldn't have made it eight minutes." A silence ensued that told her that this conversation was over.

Megan picked up the laptop. "I guess I'd better lock this computer in Patrick's safe and get ready if we're going to ride tonight."

She heard the relief in his voice that she'd changed the subject. "Sure thing. I'll wait for you in the garage."

"Be there in ten minutes."

Chapter Five

Ryder's HD Road King was in top-notch condition, but he needed to keep his hands busy, so he tinkered with the engine while he waited for her. What the fuck was he thinking giving her a massage like that? Touching her had him firing on cylinders long blocked. Good thing he didn't explode.

The sight of her hard nipples nearly caused him to turn tail and run so she wouldn't notice his hard-on. Thank God she turned away first.

He didn't know how old she was, but she couldn't be much more than twenty-five. Hell, he'd be thirty-eight in a couple of months. What the fuck was he doing getting turned on by someone so young and innocent?

Worse yet, how could he turn her on? He was a fucked-up Marine.

This ride was a bad idea on so many fronts. He probably should just tell her there was something wrong with his bike and escape from having her sweet body plastered against his for the ride up to Gilman Tunnels he had planned for them.

It would be just his luck, though, that she'd pull out her tool box and fix it. He wouldn't put it past the woman to know how.

When she entered the garage, he didn't make eye contact with her. While he continued to inspect his bike for the ride, she walked over to the shelf in the corner.

Next thing he knew, she stood next to him in black leather pants and boots with her patriotic helmet, emblazoned with the American flag and a bald eagle, held against her hip by her wrist. As his gaze roamed up her body, he saw what appeared to be a tank top peeking out from a leather jacket.

He moved quickly past her chest to meet her gaze. "You're more than a casual rider."

She grinned and took his breath away. "I don't get to ride often, but if you or Patrick roll your bikes, I'm not getting road rash."

"I've never rolled a bike."

She glanced at the holes in the knees of his jeans. "Well, good. Then this will just keep me warm when the sun goes down."

Practical and resilient. He liked those traits in a woman.

Hell, Top's little sister wasn't a woman. She was a girl. Besides, he had no plans to be messing around with her.

"Grab the door remote and let's ride."

The sooner he got this over with, the better. Maybe he should take her over to the other side of the Sandias. They could ride to Madrid and then double back. Shorter trip for sure.

But no. After nearly a day in the city, he needed the special peace that only came from being in the Jemez Mountains. Ryder mounted the bike as she opened the garage door with the remote.

"Do you mind if I bring my camera? I promise not to slow us down, but I'd hate to be without it when we get off the bike to stretch."

"No worries." While she ran back inside, he got off the bike and opened the right-hand saddlebag. Minutes later, she stowed her camera case before donning her helmet.

The woman was too hot for words.

Fuck. She's Top's sister. Hands off, grunt.

At least she'd be seated behind him where she couldn't feel his hard-on. He walked the bike out of the garage and waited for her to close the door and stow the remote. He didn't look forward to having her crotch pressed against his back for the next hour, but too late now. He mounted the bike and waited for the inevitable.

Placing her left hand on his shoulder, she mounted the bike before wrapping her arms around his waist and plastering her entire torso against his back.

Sweet Jesus, what did I ever do to deserve this kind of torture?

He rolled the throttle and shouted over the noise, "Hang on, Red."

Red? Where had that come from? Still, it fit her personality, as well as her red hair.

The bike eased down the drive and onto the cul-de-sac. Through her neighborhood, he took it slowly, but as soon as they reached the interstate, he flew. Her arms squeezed harder at his waist. His cock throbbed. Eventually, the rumble of the motor numbed his thighs and eased his hard-on.

As they left the overpopulated valley and Albuquerque's city limits, the landscape changed in a flash. His body relaxed as the desert enveloped them. Cool air touched his kneecaps where he'd ripped his jeans for that purpose, and he flipped his visor up and took a deep breath. He'd been cooped up less than a day in the city. How much longer would he need to be there to watch over Megan?

He hadn't been able to reach Adam this morning, but had left him a message to let him know she was safe. He'd try to call tonight for further orders.

When he came to the stop at Highway 4, he pulled over to the shoulder and pointed ahead of them. "Let's stop so you can take some photos."

The first sign of the red rocks always took his breath away. This evening was especially beautiful with white puffy clouds against a deep blue sky and even a patch of green grass in front of the rocks.

She dismounted first and removed her helmet while he pulled out her camera case. After retrieving her camera, she ran across the road to snap photos, as if afraid he wouldn't give her enough time.

Ryder took off his helmet and ran his hand through his hair. He watched her shoot the formation from all angles. When she crouched down to the ground, the outline of her ass in the form-fitting leather ramped up his guilt level at having the hots for Top's baby sister.

She came back smiling. "Thanks for stopping. This is one of my favorite places to shoot, but I've never seen the colors more vivid than today."

Megan placed a kiss on his cheek and picked up her helmet. The skin where she'd kissed him burned to life, and he rubbed it when she wasn't looking, trying to disperse whatever strange kinetic energy had been in the simple press of her lips.

Before he put his own helmet on again, she leaned close to his ear and whispered, "My brother's bike rides well, but I love the rumble and vibration of your Harley."

His groin tightened at her husky voice and the suggestion in her words. But she didn't mean them the way he interpreted them.

Focus, man. "We'll head up Highway 4 a bit and then take the Gilman Camp Loop. You're going to get some great photos up there."

Seeing some of his favorite places through her eyes energized him like nothing had in a long while. He rolled the throttle and eased into traffic then gunned the engine as he raced to the turnoff. Daylight was fleeting. He wanted to be sure she had all the time she needed to take photos of the tunnels, mountains, and Rio Guadalupe.

They weren't far from his place, but it would be dark soon. *Hold on!* He hadn't planned on taking her there anyway. He sighed. No, tonight they would return to that boxy condo in the city.

Live in the moment. He didn't want to think about going back yet.

The time he'd spent with Carlos at his grandmother's had taught him a lot about that philosophy. Forget the past. Stop worrying about the future.

Sometimes easier said than done.

* * *

Megan watched the breathtaking scenery fly by as they rode up the mountain road. Patrick had told her about the tunnels and this old logging road, but she hadn't ventured out here. Usually she was on her way to Bandelier or some other site any time she had visited him.

The evergreens against the deep red earth stole her breath away, but the sky mesmerized her. Every now and then, she caught a glimpse of a river down below as they climbed the narrow road. When he slowed down and eventually cut off the engine, she removed her helmet and peeked around him to see a tunnel. She'd always enjoyed taking photographs through windows and tunnels. They made great frames for the view that lay beyond.

Ryder was sweet to accommodate her need to grab her camera and take photos. She hoped they turned out well enough to sell as prints in a gallery.

"After you take some shots here, we can ride up to the next tunnel where there's some interesting road art you might like to see."

"Absolutely! But I'd rather stretch my legs."

She started walking until he tugged at her arm, slowing her down. "You walk at a city pace."

"Guilty as charged. Grew up in Chicago."

She started up the hill through the first tunnel again, and soon he grabbed her hand, forcing her to match his pace. "It's not a race. Time to slow down and smell the roses."

The heat from his hand made her palm tingle, but she ignored it and forced herself to focus on the speed of her steps. She looked ahead, not finding much of interest in the darkened tunnel.

Until Ryder stopped.

"What is it?"

He stared at some faded graffiti on the tunnel wall then pointed at the initials RW. "I've been coming here since I was sixteen. Left my mark all those years ago."

"What, no girlfriend you were in love with?"

He shook his head. "No. She came along when I was seventeen."

"Your ex?"

He nodded.

"High-school sweethearts. I'm sorry it didn't work out."

Ryder shrugged. "A lot of my buddies had marriages fail. Military spouses become used to living on their own and handling things without you. Hard for them to make the adjustment to share responsibilities when you come home." His gaze remained steadfast on his initials.

Megan wondered if that was the only issue he and his ex struggled with, but it was none of her business. She squeezed his hand, pulling him back to her.

"Show me what you were talking about on the other side of the tunnel."

"It's after the next one." He began walking again, and she held onto his hand. Anyone happening upon them would think they were a couple.

Would Patrick and Adam approve if she got involved with a fellow Marine?

Whoa. Who said anything about a relationship? You only met him a day ago.

"You seem lost in thought."

She shrugged. No way did she intend to tell him her real thoughts. "Just thinking about my overprotective brothers."

"Why didn't you get to know Adam growing up?"

"Long story. He ran away at sixteen when…well, his dad died, and Mom married my dad and moved to Chicago from Minneapolis. Took decades for her and Adam to find each other again, in part because Adam changed his last name to her maiden name, Montague. Their reunion happened last Thanksgiving. But I had heard about my wonderful, missing older brother my whole life. He was larger than life to me."

"He *is* larger than life. Best there is."

She smiled. "Thanks. I'm kind of fond of him, too. What was he like to serve under?"

"Stern, but fair. I knew him before his wife died. He changed a lot after he lost her."

"I don't think he ever expected to find love again."

"Most people aren't so lucky."

"Do you think you'll ever marry again?"

"Hell, no. I'm not the marrying kind."

"But you were married once."

"That was before. I'm not that man any longer. Wouldn't inflict myself on anyone, much less a wife."

Talk about a gauntlet. "Women are stronger than you think. Don't assume all of them will run at the first sign of a challenge."

He continued to walk without responding. She hoped he would give her words some thought. Any woman would be proud to have such a brave hero as her partner.

If *she* were the marrying kind, she'd certainly have him on her short list.

They exited the first tunnel, and she heard the rushing of the river down below them. Leading him to the guardrail, she peeked down the ravine while moving her camera into position.

After snapping a few shots of the river and the red-rock hills beyond the gorge, she reached for his hand. "Help me over and let's go down for some closer shots."

"That's awfully steep."

She flashed a smile at him. "You need to lighten up, Ryder. Play a little. Come on."

She climbed to the other side of the guardrail, but he didn't accept her help in return. He simply stepped over as if it was nothing. He didn't appear to be taller than five-eleven, but seemed to have the legs of a man much taller. Funny that her walking pace was faster since his legs were considerably longer.

They found a bit of a path to follow. Probably one that animals used. She couldn't imagine this being a popular hiking trail. Once at the bank of the river, she set her shutter speed slower and propped her elbows on a boulder to try and steady the camera as she took some frames of the water. The slow speed would show the movement of the water, giving it a white, flowing appearance in the photo.

After several more shots at varying speeds, she stood and looked around. "It's gorgeous down here."

He nodded, but seemed too lost in thought to speak.

"I haven't been down here in decades. Carlos and I used to hike here when we came to stay with his grandmother." He pointed toward the tunnels. "She lived on the other side of that hill on an old Indian service road."

"That's where you live now?"

"Yeah. She passed over long before I went on my last deployment. The house was vacant, and Carlos said I'd do him a favor by living there and keeping an eye on the place. I think he wants to use it as a vacation home or maybe retire there someday. But he knew I needed a hand up. I do maintenance on the place instead of paying rent."

"I can see why you love it out here. And why it's so hard for you to spend time in the city."

"You like it out here. Why don't you stay at my place? There's a second bedroom, of course."

Megan grinned as she stared down at his boots. Her face flushed warm at the thought of sharing his house out here.

"I'm sure you'd have lots of time to work on your photo editing. You might even build a new portfolio of nature shots."

She was tempted, wondering what the morning light would be like up here and what flora and creatures she'd find on walks around his place.

"We'll see." She smiled at him, taking pleasure in giving him back a bit of his own non-commitment medicine. But the idea intrigued her. Since the break-in, the thought of getting away sounded better all of the time. But she didn't know if it was a good idea.

"Hey, take off your boots and socks. Let's go wading." She placed her hand on his upper arm to steady herself as she shed her own shoes and socks. Rolling up her leather pants to her calves took a little more work, and she belatedly realized she'd given him a good view of her leather-encased butt while bent over at the waist to do so.

"Do you know how cold that water's going to be this time of year?" His voice sounded a little husky.

"But it's so warm in the sun."

"Most of that water comes from snow runoff. It probably never is truly warm, but certainly not this early in the summer."

"Oh, come on! Have a little fun!"

She found a safe place for her camera and waded into the water. "Oh my God! You're right! It's freezing!"

"Told you."

A look of longing convinced her Ryder needed to let down his guard and play. Careful to miss the camera, she reached down and splashed a few drops of water on him. "I'm going to splash you until you come in with me. Might as well control how wet you get."

He shook his head and unzipped his boots, sitting on a rock by the bank to remove them and tuck a sock inside each one. "I'll be nicer than you were and be careful not to mess up your fancy leather outfit. I'd hate to see it ruined."

Did he like seeing her in leather? She grinned.

When he hissed as he entered the cold water, she reached for his hand. "Come on. Let's wade out a little bit."

"The river's not too high now, but promise me you won't walk blindly into a river or arroyo without paying attention. Flash floods from storms many miles away are a problem here."

She nodded, but sensing no sudden wall of water about to descend on her, she stayed put and bent over to look for minnows. "Oh, look! A tadpole!"

She pointed it out to him, but when she glanced up, she found him focused more on her butt until caught looking, and then he turned away. She grinned. Maybe the man was more interested than he let on.

When she could no longer feel her feet, she started for the bank. "Let's head back up as soon as my feet dry a bit." They sat together on the bank, and she pulled out her camera, taking more photos of the water, as well as their feet against the red rocks.

After they donned their shoes and socks, she stood and picked up the camera. Climbing the hill was tricky as she tried to keep her camera from banging against the ground. Ryder suggested she hold the camera with one hand while he pulled her up holding her free hand. The man was wicked strong. He must not be very idle. She wondered what he did for a living, but was too focused on hauling her ass up the hill to ask. Jeez, was she ever out of shape.

He gave her one last pull at the crest, and they stood side by side. She gasped for breath and felt sweat trickling down her neck. Man, leather was not the thing to wear when hiking up a hill.

When she could form a sentence again, she asked, "Where to next, Ryder?"

Chapter Six

Ryder tried to ignore the breathiness of her voice and the way her chest heaved as she attempted to catch her breath the last few minutes. The last half hour had been a test of his self-control as he'd been treated to the sight of her leather-encased ass on a couple of occasions as she bent over. The way the outfit molded around her breasts, too, was equally distracting.

Stop looking at her breasts, asshole.

He needed to get back on the bike and take her back to the condo. But first, he'd promised to show her something on the other end of the second tunnel. "Ready?"

She nodded, and he took her hand. He told himself it was to help her over the guardrail, but he'd enjoyed walking through the tunnel holding her hand earlier. He hadn't spent companionable time with a woman in…forever.

Megan was comfortable to be with. She didn't act silly or play games. The real deal.

He liked her. A lot.

But not in *that* way. More like a sister.

Then why are you noticing her ass, breathy voice, and heaving chest?

The admonishing inner voice sounded a lot like Carlos.

Oh, shut the fuck up.

Sometimes being honorable and doing the right thing got in the way of his baser needs. All he had to do was remember who had sent him on this mission, though, and he'd stay on the straight and narrow.

The sunlight waned as they walked out of the second tunnel. The timber operation died in the first half of the last century. Now the road was popular with locals and adventurous tourists. Ryder avoided the area during July and August when the road became congested with too many people, but right now, it was just the two of them.

The wind picked up, and he heard the squawk of two or more Steller's jays. He often hiked here during the winter months to just sit and listen to the birds and watch for other wildlife. Helped him some, especially when he'd had a rough night. Carlos's Pueblo elders had taught both boys how to become one with the Universe.

"It's so serene here."

Megan felt it, too.

He smiled. "I still feel close to the Great Spirit here."

"I can see why."

Sherry had never wanted to spend time outside of Albuquerque. Megan was the first woman he'd brought out here. For some reason, that made him happy.

"Oh, look at these!"

Her eagle eye homed in on the rusty nails and bolts that had been pounded into posts at the side of the road to form representations of wildlife. The posts had been intended to keep cars from going over the embankment to the river below, but someone decided to decorate them with fanciful doodads.

Megan spent the next fifteen minutes photographing each one from every angle. Her excitement over the simplest things ignited a spark of life inside Ryder in places he thought long since dead. He hoped she'd show him the photos after she downloaded them off her camera. He wondered if she was any good at what she did, but if she had earned her master's studying photography, then she must be.

"Do you ever put any of your pieces in galleries?"

She stood and smiled at him. "Not yet. I was thinking earlier this evening that I might have captured some that would make great gallery pieces."

She scrutinized him a moment and lifted the camera to her face before snapping a couple photos of him.

"Careful. You don't want to break your camera."

She giggled. "You make a wonderful subject."

"Not for a gallery, though."

"Oh, no. Those are just for me."

Without warning, she leaned toward him and pecked him on the cheek. His heart pounded hard before he convinced himself he wasn't under attack. Not the kind that would warrant his fleeing anyway.

"Thanks for bringing me here, Ryder, and for sharing one of your special places with me."

He cleared his throat after it tightened with emotion. "It's nothing. You needed to get away as much as I did."

The thought of returning to her place in the city unsettled him and ruined the moment. "I guess we'd better head back. This isn't a good road to be on after dark."

She took his hand, and they started for the bike. He didn't slow her down this time, because the sooner they re-entered her world, the better. He'd be able to keep up his defenses against her more easily there than out here. Maybe he'd adjust better tonight than he had over the last day.

They donned their helmets, and when she straddled the seat behind him, he leaned back into her body before catching himself and sitting up straighter. She wrapped her arms around him.

"Ready to ride when you are."

Jesus, don't think about riding her.

He rolled the throttle and sped off down the road heading back to hell on earth. Okay, he exaggerated. While he hated being in any over-populated city, the number of perils there paled in comparison to the streets of Fallujah.

After he pulled into the garage and closed the door, he breathed a little easier. At least in here he only had one other person to worry about.

No doubt he would worry until he completed this mission.

"I'm going to try and get some more work done before I turn in. If you want anything in the kitchen, help yourself."

"Don't you want anything to eat?"

"Oh, I'll grab something later."

Well, at least now he knew what he needed to do. The woman didn't know how to take care of herself. She'd sat at her computer for hours without even taking a bathroom break earlier today. She must love her work, but that couldn't be healthy. Didn't computer screens emit some kind of rays that could cause health problems over time?

Forty-five minutes later, he knocked on her office door.

"Yes?"

He cracked the door and peeked inside. "Time for a break. Dinner is about to be served."

She turned to him with a puzzled expression on her face as if he'd just spoken Serbian to her, and then she gave him the sweetest smile.

"You didn't have to do that."

"I know. That's why I enjoyed doing it."

He crossed the room to pull her chair away from the desk and held out his hand to her.

"My. What service." She stood and stared into his eyes, seemingly as lost in the moment as he was, before glancing down. Was she blushing?

Back off, Ryder.

He took a step back before he noticed the photo on her computer screen. Him. His eyes had lines he didn't remember, but he didn't spend a lot of time staring in the mirror. And where had all that gray come from?

"I didn't realize I'd gotten so old."

"Men age gracefully. I love that shot. Your guard was down. There was almost a twinkle in your eyes."

He looked closer before backing off. Twinkle, hell. He was probably turned on by the woman standing in front of him at the time. Of all the photos she'd taken, he hadn't expected her to be looking at that one. She snapped the candids before he'd known what she intended to do. Before he could glance away. The man staring back at him looked lost more than anything.

Fucking lost.

"After you." He indicated with his hand for her to precede him from the room. When she would have gone to the kitchen, he took her elbow gently and steered her into the dining room. Shit. He had set the lights a little too low and, using the dimmer switch on the wall, bumped up the brightness some. This wasn't a romantic dinner for two. Last thing he wanted was for her to read anything into this other than having a meal together.

He pulled out her chair and seated her. He had already set the table and poured a glass of red wine for each of them, giving it time to breathe. She or her brother had good taste in wine. He and Sherry used to drink wine at dinner, back before he left the Marine Corps. "Feel free to enjoy your wine."

"You make me feel like a princess or something."

Okay, now that wouldn't do.

"I'm a Marine whose big sister taught him manners."

A light dimmed in her eyes, and the smile left her face.

Fuck.

He hated that he came across sounding as though he didn't care about her. He just didn't want her to think he cared in *that* way.

"I'll be right back with our dinner."

Time to retreat to the kitchen and move past this awkward moment. As he plated their dinner, he heard soft music begin playing in the dining room.

Shit. He could have done without mood-setting music. What did she expect to happen tonight?

This was fucking dinner!

He placed a piece of freshly made fry bread on the corner of each plate and carried them into the dining room. "Here we go. Time to chow down." There. Maybe that would help convey the point of this meal. He took his seat on her right side.

"It smells delicious. When did you make a food run?"

"I haven't left the place. You know I wouldn't leave you alone. I made it from what you had on hand."

"From what you found in my *brother's* kitchen? I haven't had time to stock the pantry as well as I'd like yet, but his cooking skills are minimal. Worse than mine even."

"Yeah. I took inventory and found cans of tomatoes with green chiles, corn, and black beans, not to mention frozen chicken and other meats in the freezer. I remembered eating lots of dishes like this when I stayed with Carlos's grandmother. It won't be as delicious as hers, but I'm sure it'll be edible."

She picked up the piece of bread. "You even made bread?"

"Fry bread. A lot simpler than yeast breads in the oven. I've made fry bread lots of times, so I had that recipe in my head."

"Oh, I've seen stands at the side of the road where they are selling fry bread. I just never stopped to try any." She took a bite and closed her eyes as she chewed and swallowed. "Oh, my gosh. That's incredible! I could get spoiled if you keep cooking for me. I've been staying here for weeks, but as you might have guessed, we don't spend a lot of time in the kitchen. Patrick and I tend to eat on the run."

"I do think a trip to the grocery store might be overdue."

"Ugh. I hate that even worse than cooking."

He enjoyed cooking. Yet another solitary pursuit, but he found some kind of satisfaction in being creative with ingredients. He rarely cooked with a recipe. His sister had taught him as a kid how to be self-sufficient and make do with what they had in the cupboards. Mom usually came home late and didn't quit working until well after dark.

She picked up her fork and smiled before stabbing a piece of chicken. "But I love to eat."

He was anxious to see what she thought of his meal. True, the kitchen didn't boast a lot, but he'd found plenty he could use to make a simple New Mexican dish like this one.

She took a bite, and he waited. Again, she closed her eyes and chewed slowly. The sensual way she enjoyed food turned him on. Okay, anything Megan did had that effect on him, apparently.

She swallowed, opened her eyes, and smiled with approval. "That is the most incredible thing I've ever put in my mouth."

Don't you fucking dare think about what else you want to put in her mouth.

His cock didn't get the message and strained against his jeans. Why was he responding to her like a teenager? Thank goodness the table hid his erection.

Swallowing a bite of chicken, he agreed it tasted pretty good.

"Oh, I forgot. A toast." She lifted her glass and held it toward him. "Here's to new friendships and many, many more delightful meals together."

Jesus, get me through this dinner and evening unscathed.

Chapter Seven

M egan wondered why Ryder had become so stiff with her again, but decided nothing would spoil her enjoyment of this dinner. She could quickly get used to having someone see to her needs like this.

Careful what you wish for, girl.

Sure, she'd had a fabulous day with Ryder, but she had no business thinking about anything long-term. Friends, yes. She very much enjoyed being with Ryder, but they lived worlds apart.

He belonged out in the mountains of the high desert. Her photo had captured the way his face relaxed and he exuded a sense of belonging when they were at the tunnels that made it abundantly clear that the rigid man seated beside her now wasn't comfortable in her world.

She needed to put an end to his misery and call Adam.

"I sent Adam a text and told him everything was fine here. You will probably hear from him soon, letting you off the hook. I know you probably want to get home."

The expression on his face was anything but one of relief. Had she insulted him by calling an end to his mission, as he called it? While having him here to cook for me was wonderful, she didn't intend for this occupation to go on endlessly. Perhaps they should talk about something else until she heard from Adam. Odd that he wouldn't respond more quickly. She hoped everything was okay.

"Tell me what you do, Ryder."

"Do about what?"

"How you make your living?"

He glanced down at his plate and scooped up a bite of tomatoes and beans, but didn't eat it. His demeanor changed.

She reached out to place her hand over his. "Sorry. None of my business."

He stared at her hand but didn't say anything for the longest time. She pulled away. "I used to do maintenance at a local hospital. When I came back from Fallujah, I couldn't get my act together. Missed a lot of work."

"I'm sorry. Were you able to transition to something else?"

"Not really. I…prefer spending time out in the mountains. Alone." He grinned. "Not much call for mountain men these days."

"So you're self-sufficient."

"I suppose so."

"You even hunt your own food?"

He nodded. "Carlos and I learned to hunt with knives. It's a challenge making yourself one with nature so that the rabbit or snake just happens upon you and never knows you're there."

"Wait a minute. You eat snakes?"

He grinned. "I guess it's an acquired taste."

She laughed. "Well, at least you didn't say it tastes like chicken."

"No, it pretty much tastes like rattlesnake."

"Rattlers? Are you crazy?"

He sobered. "A little."

Oh, surely he didn't think she meant literally crazy. But trying to change her words would only make him think she meant that even more. She took a quick swallow of her wine. "I'm not that adventurous with food. I have eaten escargot."

"A little too upscale for me."

Great. Now she'd come across as elitist.

Just eat, Megan.

She did just that, and silence ensued as they finished dinner. She'd wanted to learn more about him, but hadn't gotten very far. The man enjoyed his privacy. No big surprise. He lived alone in the wilderness.

"After I clean up the dishes, I think I'm going to catch a few winks. But I want you to yell for me if you need me."

"You cooked. I do dishes." She paused a moment. *Oh, why not?* "What do you like to do for fun?"

He stared at her as if he didn't comprehend the question. "Fun?"

"Hobbies. Sports. Activities."

"Does hunting count?"

"I suppose so, unless it's how you put food on your table. Then it seems like a job."

"I guess it's a little of both. Sometimes I'm able to catch enough to share with the elders at the pueblo who aren't able to hunt for themselves any longer."

"Are you very active there?"

"Active?"

"You know, tribal councils. Festivals."

"I'm not a tribal member. Just a guest."

"I see. But you seem to do a lot for them."

"No, they're the ones who've done a lot for me. They respect veterans and gave me a place to regroup when I just couldn't take the world any longer."

"Has it gotten better for you out there?"

"Some. I'm here and haven't gone nuts. That wouldn't have happened even a year ago."

How had Adam lost one of his Marines? He had to keep tabs on them and their families if he'd managed to round up so many of them for such a rushed wedding. She'd overheard some of the conversations at the reception about what he meant to so many of them.

So how had Ryder fallen through the cracks?

"When was the last time you heard from Adam before he called you the other night?"

"A while."

His evasive answer told her what she needed to know. "How did he find you after all these years?"

"I've tried to figure that out. I think if he knew my number he'd have called to check on me earlier. I'm sure he does that with his Marines. But my guess is Lance Corporal Grant. That woman could track anyone through a computer and government or public files. Orlando might have said something, but I didn't tell him where I live. I ran into him at a Patriot Guard Riders funeral a couple months back."

"Patrick goes to PGR events, too, when he can."

"Anyway, if I had to place money on it, I'd still say Grant. She probably found where I'd been to the VA Hospital."

"Old injury?"

A muscle tensed in his jaw. His piercing stare made her so uncomfortable she sat back in her chair, taking her wine glass with her.

"No. Psych ward."

She took a deep breath. Tears burned the backs of her eyes. "I'm so sorry. Did they help any?"

He shrugged. "Not sure there's any hope."

"Never give up. They're going to figure this shit out one of these days, but if you ever need someone to talk with, I'm here."

"Don't promise that to a combat veteran unless you're ready for a call at all hours, even three in the morning."

"I *said* I'm here. I don't make promises I can't keep. I've been there for those three a.m. night terrors with Patrick."

"Beg pardon. I guess you know more than most civilians. You get tired of the platitudes after a while."

"I know how to listen. I won't judge. I know you guys went through hell over there. The women, too. Combat has changed. Everyone deployed overseas is affected in some way. Patrick spent most of his time in a plane, but I think there was a friendly fire incident."

"Fuck. Sorry. Those can be some of the worst to put behind you."

"He found a program out in Malibu that turned things around for him pretty fast. If you ever want to try it, let me know, and I'll get you the contact info."

"That's all right. Being anywhere near Los Angeles would cause more harm than it would do good. Besides, I'm doing a lot better now."

"When's the last time the nightmares came?"

He stood abruptly and picked up his empty plate and wine glass. "I'd better get these to the kitchen and clean up my mess."

The way his hand held the wine glass made her wonder what his hand would feel like on her breast. A momentary image of her and Ryder in a passionate embrace in her bed caught her by surprise. Her face flamed hot.

What the heck was the matter with her?

She followed him to the kitchen with her own dirty dishes and shooed him out so she could wash them. "I made up the sofa for you last night. Why don't you go rest a while before you drop?"

He didn't argue. Probably wanted to put some distance between her and her questions. She'd only been making conversation. Hadn't meant to pry. Okay, maybe she had a little. While loading the dishwasher, she thought about the day she had spent with Ryder. They had enjoyed many companionable moments. A few times, some tension interfered, but she was learning where he was sensitive so she could avoid those areas.

On her way down the hall, instead of stopping immediately in her office, she peeked into the living room where he lay stretched out on the sofa. He appeared to be asleep. She supposed he hadn't lost the knack for falling asleep the moment his head hit the pillow.

*   *   *

Ryder stretched out on the couch again. Sleeping on the floor would probably be better than this, but he'd make do. How much longer could Top possibly want him here? After adjusting the pillow cushions to his liking, he curled on his side. He didn't like a lot of covers. They tended to tangle up around his feet when he slept. What if he needed to make a quick escape?

Ryder closed his eyes and heard Megan approach and stand in the doorway, but he pretended to be sleeping. He'd already warned her not to touch him while he slept and doubted she could see much from half a room away.

She said Patrick was the same way about being touched while sleeping. Ryder wondered what veterans' program he'd found that helped him deal with his post-traumatic stress. Was he able to have a successful marriage? Megan hadn't mentioned anything about him having a wife or family. Did he still have nightmares? Trouble holding a job?

Probably not if he was off to—where did she say? Europe?—Italy, to be exact. Pakistan, too. The man must have a screw loose. Ryder wouldn't go near that part of the world again. But her brother must be doing well financially—although there was every indication the two came from money to start with. Ryder envied Patrick for being able to deal with the past and move on, though.

With a place to live that provided for his needs and only himself to worry about, Ryder didn't want or need money. He just wanted a fucking night's sleep without being reminded of the nightmares of the past.

Well, he hadn't had one last night. Of course not. He hadn't slept. So far, he didn't have a lot of trouble with triggers and living nightmares while awake, although that helium machine sure took him to a bad place briefly this morning.

His demons crept in relentlessly whenever his defenses were down. Like when he was asleep. Jesus, he was tired. Getting no sleep could weaken his ability to keep the demons away, too.

His phone vibrated in his pocket. So much for sleep now. He pulled out the phone and checked the screen.

Adam.

He bolted up and answered. "Yes, Top."

"Report."

He briefly flashed back to Fallujah, hearing Top give the same command after an IED exploded near their caravan. Only this time he wasn't checking on Ryder's whereabouts or safety, but his sister's.

"No problems since the break-in."

"She have any idea who did it?"

"No. She's convinced it's just some random thing. Maybe she's right, but someone disabled a sophisticated security system to get in here. I plan on keeping an eye on her until your brother returns."

Silence.

"How secure is her place now?"

"New locks and deadbolts on the doors. I'm staying at the condo to keep an eye on things."

"Glad you're there."

He trusts me.

No way would he blow it again with Top by messing with his sister.

"I don't think they'll be back, though. They seemed to have found what they wanted."

"Regardless, if you can stick around a few more days, I'd feel better. Didn't even know I had a sister until a short time ago. I don't want to lose her now. I know if Patrick was there he'd have things under control. I owe you one for doing this for my family."

Ryder wasn't sure if he meant Top's family or the Marine family. Well, maybe that was the same thing. "No worries. You don't owe me anything, Top. I'm happy to help. Had some down time anyway." He wouldn't admit his unemployed status. No fucking way. But he'd shared that with Megan. Would she tell Top?

"If my wife wasn't about to deliver, I'd have gone down there myself."

"Glad I can be here to help. Good luck to you and your wife." At least he and Sherry hadn't brought kids into their marriage.

After a pause, Top asked, "So you two are getting along okay?"

What was he asking? "Sure."

"Good. She's feisty at times. Strong-willed. Independent."

Yeah, I noticed.

"Knows what she wants and goes for it. Reminds me of my wife. Keep her safe."

"Will do, Top." Or he'd die trying.

"Thanks."

The call ended as abruptly as it had begun. So he wasn't relieved from this mission yet, even though there wasn't a whole lot he could do without an enemy to take out.

Megan entered the room as he was putting his phone back in his pocket.

"Let me guess. Adam."

"Hmm? Oh. Yeah." He sat up on the sofa and tossed the sheet to the side.

"I guess he couldn't just call and ask me how things were going. Did you convince him no one is after me still?"

"Not exactly."

She leaned against the door. "Why not?"

"He just wants to be sure. He cares a lot about you. Neither of us wants to see anything happen to you."

"I surrender."

"What?"

"I'm not going to fight either one of you. If you have nothing better to do than sit around and wait for someone to attack me, then have fun. I'm going to bed."

She turned and walked away. He wished she wasn't angry at him for doing his job, but tough. He wasn't here to please her. He was here to protect her.

And to make up for the things he'd screwed up in Kandahar and Fallujah.

*   *   *

He stared at the ceiling. Without any lights on, the room remained fucking bright. Not like at his place where, once the lights were off, it became pitch dark. Every now and then, he heard a car pass in front of the condo. Someone several blocks away set off a car alarm.

How did anyone fucking sleep in the city?

He slid his feet off the couch and onto the floor as he sat up again. Maybe he'd just take a walk around and double check the locks on the windows and doors. Not that he hadn't checked them all twice at least.

As he passed by Megan's closed bedroom door, he heard a familiar buzzing sound. Ryder remembered the sound from happier times with his wife. A vibrator. Probably a Hitachi like the one he and Sherry had used.

The image of Megan lying naked in bed, pinching her nipple while using a vibrator on herself just about made him come in his jeans. He forced himself away from her door to do what he'd set out to, but all he could think about was the look of pleasure on her face when she came.

After checking the garage and heading back down the hall, he tried to walk as quickly as possible by her door. Her mewling sounds told him the tension was building up to what would be one hell of an orgasm. Ryder tried not to think about her nipples pebbling.

Or the hardness of her clit as the vibrator sent tremors through her body.

Sweet Jesus.

Not that he could think of anything else.

He forced himself away from her door and back into the living room. Lying on the couch again, he tried to banish the images of Megan pleasuring herself from his mind, but damned if he could. He removed his jeans and stretched out again, but soon found himself reaching for his hard-on and stroking it. He didn't need a magazine or a movie. All he needed was the image of Megan, her vibrator stroking her clit. Perhaps a finger or two rammed up inside her...

Harder than he'd been since making love to his ex before his last deployment. The sticky, warm cum spilled over his hand as he came for the first time in longer than he could remember. He reached for the sheet and cleaned himself up. Laundry detail would be on his agenda in the morning. He didn't want Megan knowing he'd jacked off on her couch. He wadded up the sheet and tossed it on the floor.

His eyelids grew heavy as his body relaxed into the cushions. Maybe he could sleep a bit tonight after all.

*   *   *

Megan pressed the Hitachi to her clit again, her pelvis jolting upward as she imagined Ryder's mouth on her nipple. The scratchiness of his five-o'clock shadow only heightened her senses. A moan escaped, and she glanced toward the door. Closed. She pulled the powerful vibrator away from her most sensitive spot and let it rest against the opening of her vagina.

So empty. Not that she'd ever been filled, but tonight, she had never felt so empty.

Oh, Ryder.

She closed her eyes and let the feelings engulf her. As a teen, she'd read books and seen movies and imagined finding that perfect man to be her first and only lover, but the older she got, the less she thought that time would ever come. She chose quality in the life she had over what *might* be someday.

But her chosen path was a solitary one. How had this man ignited feelings she'd thought she could so easily suppress? Her battery-operated boyfriends were a pale substitute for the sexy man sleeping in the living room. So not fair. But if she came on to him, he'd probably run as fast as possible to his hideaway in the mountains.

Not wanting to postpone her orgasm any longer, she moved the Hitachi back to her clit and nearly moaned aloud with need as she rode the wave up and over in a mad rush.

Oh, oh, oh!

And done. Too fast, but she needed this. Now.

Coming quietly wasn't her preference, either, but she'd never be able to face Ryder over the breakfast table if she thought he'd heard her masturbating in her bedroom.

After slowly returning to earth, she sat up and unplugged the toy. A quick trip to the bathroom to clean it, and she stored it in her nightstand drawer before crawling back to bed. Her hand moved to her erect right nipple and pulled. Man, she still wasn't satisfied. The thought of Ryder nibbling, biting, pulling on her nipples just made her want to come all over again. Most times a good orgasm with her vibrator would last her for days, even a week.

Megan would never manage to sleep tonight, despite how little rest she'd had over the past two days. She picked up the book on photography techniques from her nightstand. Normally, this would entertain her for hours, but after a few pages, she caught herself about to nod off. Rather than fight it, she shut the book, set it on the far side of the bed, and closed her eyes. She curled onto her side and surrendered.

"Take cover!"

Chapter Eight

M egan's eyes shot open, and she bolted up in bed. Ryder? Had someone broken in again? Why was this happening? She reached for the nightstand drawer and moved her vibrator aside to retrieve her much more lethal handgun. No way was she going to let either of them be hurt.

One thing Patrick had made sure of before she was nineteen was that she knew how to fire a weapon. She probably would have learned sooner, but their mother wanted no guns in her home. They understood after learning of the incident that put their mother in a wheelchair and took her first husband's life.

She listened for more from Ryder, but heard only silence. The blood rushed in her ears as adrenaline surged through her body. Was he okay? Needing to check on him, she crept to the door and opened it, thankful it didn't squeak. Taking the pistol in both hands, she swept the hallway, but saw no one.

"Report!"

Oh, Ryder. A sick feeling gnawed at the pit of her stomach. Less concerned about being under attack from outside forces, she relaxed her arms. Inching toward the living room, she scanned the room quickly to be sure. Ryder was under attack from within. He was in the throes of a nightmare—or night terror.

He thrashed on the sofa, bare except for his black boxers. Sweat glistened on his skin from the streetlight shining between the open blinds. Past experience with Patrick had taught her not to approach or touch him.

"Ryder. Wake up. You're dreaming."

The muscles in his arms and chest strained as the battle raged on in his mind. His head turned toward her, and his brow furrowed as if in pain. Had he been injured?

She approached, but as instructed, she didn't touch him. "Ryder! I said wake up. *Now!*"

He jolted awake and bolted up, grabbing for the knife on the coffee table and starting toward her.

Her heart beat wildly. "No! It's me. Megan Gallagher. You were having a nightmare."

He halted and stared at her. Setting the knife back down, he ran his hand through his hair. "Sorry I woke you."

"Don't you dare apologize. I'm just glad I was here to put an end to this one. No one should go through those alone."

He stared at her as if he wanted to disagree, but relaxed his body instead. "Go get some sleep. I'm okay now."

"It might help to talk about it."

"Hell, no." He met her gaze. "No offense, but it's over. I'll just take a look around to make sure everything's secure."

He started toward her again, but she didn't move to let him pass. "*Is* it over, Ryder? How often do you have the nightmares?"

He gave her another defiant stare. "Not as often as I used to."

Clearly, he wasn't ready to talk about them. "Offer still stands. And it's three-fifteen, by the way. I told you, anytime you need to talk."

Was the plea in his eyes Ryder wanting to open up to her. Or did he just wish she would get lost? Whichever, it disappeared in a flash.

"I appreciate the offer. But no worries. It's over."

She wondered how many times he would have to say that before he started to believe those words.

"You just keep telling yourself that, Ryder. I hope your words come true someday."

She returned to her bedroom, closing the door and putting her handgun away.

With no chance of sleeping again anytime soon, she spent the next two hours reading the photography book, actually able to focus on the pages this time, before deciding it was time to go to her office and edit some more photos.

When she opened the door, her senses were assaulted by the smell of bacon and coffee. She sure could get used to having a man around who liked to cook, although she was going to gain a ton if they kept eating like this. Maybe they could make a trip to the farmer's market rather than live off the unhealthy choices in Patrick's freezer and pantry.

Actually, after giving it a lot of thought since Ryder's nightmare, the time had come for her to regain control of her life.

Ryder needed to go home.

*　　*　　*

Megan witnessing his nightmare reminded him what bad news he would be for someone like her. Her world was light and fun and normal. His was…well, a freaking nightmare at times.

He poured another mug of black coffee. The first two hadn't done anything to clear the cobwebs from his head after the dream. Tired. He hadn't run on so little sleep in a long time. Out of practice. The dryer buzzed, and he took one more quick swallow before heading to the laundry room to retrieve the sheet he'd washed after soiling it last night fantasizing about Megan.

Hell, what was he thinking being with a girl like Megan? She deserved someone—

"The coffee smells great. How are you doing this morning?"

Before he could make it through the kitchen with the sheet, he came face to face with her again. Jesus, so beautiful. She wore shorts and a tee, and her legs, though not particularly long, were spectacularly perfect. Muscular calves and thighs that could probably squeeze a man in all the right places.

"You run?"

She looked back at him after setting the coffee pot back on the warmer. "From what?" Before he could clarify, she grinned. "Just teasing. No, not a lot. Sometimes it just helps me feel better."

"You aren't going to go running this morning, are you?" He wasn't sure he was ready to face the potential threats she would encounter. At least she didn't sound like a habitual runner who had to stick to a schedule. Less predictable for predators.

"No. I'm dragging today. Dressed for comfort."

She sure seemed perky despite him disturbing her sleep last night.

"Let me go fold this sheet, and then I'll scramble up some eggs."

She set her mug on the counter. "No, let me help. I used to do this with my dad." She took the sheet from him and found two ends. "Now, you find the other two." He did so and held it up, but when he realized it was twisted, he switched corners at the same time she did, resulting in yet another twist.

"Dad sure made this look easy."

They worked at straightening out the sheet for a moment. She referred to him in the past a lot. Did he ditch his family, too? "Where is he now?"

Her sweet smile faded. "He died more than two years ago."

"Jesus, I'm sorry. Awfully young for you to lose your dad."

"Well, I still have so many wonderful memories, and I'll admit I talk to him every day and almost feel he answers sometimes. Luckily, my mom's going to live to be a hundred and ten. Nothing can keep that woman down long."

Resilience. Megan must have inherited it from her mom.

With arms outstretched, she started walking toward him. Their hands met and lingered a moment before they both reached for their new ends and repeated, coming together again. Her body's heat radiated through the sheet to him. She stared into his eyes longer than made him comfortable.

"Have you ever thought about kissing me?"

Now his fantasies of her were hitting him while wide awake. At least he was pretty sure he was awake and had just imagined Megan talking about kissing her.

"Well, have you?"

So she'd actually asked that question? "No."

Liar.

The twinkle in her eyes faded, and he could kick himself for being the reason.

"Sorry. I sometimes don't think before I talk."

When she moved to turn away, he threw the folded sheet on the table and reached for her arms.

"Okay, I lied. I've thought about that and more. A lot more. But we can't go there."

Her breathing grew shallow, and when she opened her mouth to let in more air, she only made him want to kiss her more than ever.

"Stop doing that."

"Doing what?" The breathlessness in her voice made him hard.

Breathing.

Bewitching.

Being.

God forgive him, but he needed this.

He moved his hands to the sides of her face and lowered his mouth to hers. The first touch of their lips sent electric shocks through his body. More. He needed more. Faster than he should have, he forced his tongue between her lips. He'd been starving for this kiss since the first night he met her.

She groaned and tilted her pelvis into his.

Sweet Jesus, don't do that to me, girl.

Her arms wrapped around his waist—either to keep her balance or draw him closer—before her tongue sparred with his. Another groan, this time definitely his. Where was he planning to go with this? There could never be anything between them. Leading her on to think there could be wasn't his style.

He broke away, and both of them fought for breath.

"I'm sorry. I shouldn't have done that."

"But I wanted you to. It was everything I'd hoped for and so much more."

The desire within him nearly broke down his defenses. He'd never wanted anything more, but she deserved someone who could live in her world. He was marking time until he could get as far away from this place as possible. He needed to go back to a time when life was simpler. Live off the land. Take care of himself.

Home.

Megan went to the stove and pulled a piece of bacon off the paper towels. Watching her eat turned him on as much as kissing her.

"Now, if you'll excuse me, I'm going to skip the rest of breakfast. I need to pack."

He placed a gentle, but restricting hand on her arm. "Going somewhere?"

She flashed him a beautiful smile. "Yes. Your place."

"Beg your pardon?"

"Well, you've invited me to go there several times now. I said, 'We'll see.' And now I've decided it's a wonderful idea. Can you be ready in two hours?"

He nodded, unable to speak.

Home. He was going home.

With Megan.

Holy fuck.

He watched her turn and walk toward the hallway, her ass bouncing with each step. After that kiss, this might be the worst decision he'd ever made. Well, in retrospect, he didn't actually make the decision at all. She did.

But he could manage things better once he returned home. Survival variables would be off the table. He wouldn't let this situation spiral out of control. He was in charge of carrying out this mission to protect her. She couldn't call the shots—although she'd been doing that since he'd met her.

Once they arrived at his place, they would play by *his* rules.

Why did an image of Megan submitting to him flash in front of his eyes?

Hands off, grunt. She's Top's little sister.

A shout from down the hall took him away from his thoughts. "Get the lead out! An hour and forty-five minutes left."

Damned bossy woman.

But this time he would obey. The sooner he cleaned up in here and packed what little he'd brought with him, the sooner he would be heading home.

*   *   *

Megan grinned as she packed her smallest suitcase. She figured she might be out there for a few days. Then she would insist that Adam call off this silly mission and let Ryder return to his own life again.

Her lips still tingled from where he had kissed her. She'd been kissed before, but never as thoroughly as by Ryder. She touched her fingertips to her lips and smiled.

But her smile faded as quickly. Could she allow something to blossom between them? She hadn't been honest with him, never dreaming until last night that she would feel such a strong attraction to the man. Her secret wasn't something she blurted out to everyone she met. Heck, no one but Mom knew. She hadn't even told Patrick. He'd been deployed when she made her irrevocable decision.

She'd been twenty-four. Headstrong. Having suffered with the debilitating pain of endometriosis since she was thirteen—including several days each month where she could barely get out of bed—she chose quality of life over some nebulous dream of possibly getting married and having babies. Not that she hadn't tried less permanent solutions. The third laparoscopic ablation hadn't given her more than minimal relief for her last eighteen months of undergraduate school at Loyola. After nearly flunking out of her first year at USC working on her master's, she'd insisted that her gynecologist do a total laparoscopic hysterectomy, including cervix and ovaries. She'd been on birth control pills since she was fourteen to try to control the pain and also wanted to avoid the side-effects associated with those if she stayed on them too much longer.

Megan just wanted a chance at a normal life and a productive career, even if that meant no possibility of giving birth to babies of her own. She had other options if she ever wanted to have children. She'd just never felt a strong pull to be a mother. Of course she hadn't been attracted to a man long enough for any serious relationship to occur—until Ryder.

Oh, Megan. He kissed you. He didn't propose or ask you to be the mother of his children.

Hoping to lighten up the mood again, she went to her bedside stand and pulled out some of her smaller, quieter toys. At least losing her womb hadn't kept her from enjoying orgasms. She wasn't sure she would have the privacy to use them at Ryder's, but being that close to the man for several more days, she decided it was better to be prepared than frustrated.

Seeing her handgun, she removed it and tucked it in her purse. She had her carry permit. Ryder was handy with a knife, but she didn't feel safe without having her own weapon. Not that she expected any trouble, except maybe for a stray rattler while out hiking or something. God, she hated snakes.

Zipping up the bags, she slung her camera case onto her shoulder and released the handle of her suitcase to wheel it into the hallway. She stopped at her office and made sure the photos she wanted to work with weren't in the cloud. The chance of having an internet connection out there was slim, given the confusion Ryder had when she referred to retrieving things from her cloud.

Megan then packed up her laptop before heading toward the garage. She was about an hour early. Plenty of time to clean up the kitchen. Maybe Ryder would be ready early, too.

When she reached the kitchen, she found it spotless. She left her bags and went in search of Ryder in the living room. His folded blanket lay neatly on the arm of the sofa. The man hadn't left his military ways behind him. Patrick tended to be a neat freak since his days in the Marines, too, especially after a post-traumatic stress episode. She assumed having everything in its place helped them restore order from the chaos in their minds after a nightmare or flashback.

"Ready?"

She turned to find him standing in the hallway. "Yes. I want to stop at the store before we leave the city, though. I'd like to get some groceries."

"There's a good one near my place. Everything we'll need and fewer people."

She walked toward him, and he stepped aside for her to precede him down the hallway. Ryder soon had her bags tucked into the back of her SUV. She set the security system, for whatever good it might do, and pulled out after him. Soon they took the ramp heading for the Jemez. As she followed, she noticed he took care not to weave in and out of traffic so she wouldn't lose him.

The scenery already looked familiar from their ride up here yesterday. After stocking up at the convenience store that served as the local grocery, he turned from the main highway onto one that wasn't as well maintained as the logging road had been. Red dust kicked up from his back tire. She drove slower to keep some distance between their vehicles in case he hit a rut and rolled his bike.

The rock formations and soil surrounding them still had red tinges.

Simple beauty.

She couldn't wait to go exploring with her camera. She'd have to watch for rattlesnakes—probably scorpions, too. So different from her time spent in the wilds of the Black Hills. Of course, there were venomous snakes there, too. None had ever bothered her.

Megan shuddered. She *really* didn't like snakes.

Ryder turned onto an even less maintained road. She maneuvered to avoid some of the ruts. This must be a fun road to drive after a rainstorm. Not. After avoiding what had to be a bone-jarring hole, his bike made a sharp turn, and there stood a one-story adobe house. The reddish tint of the mud made it clear it had been made from local soil.

The unpainted wooden front door welcomed anyone who might happen upon the porch. A ristra of dried red chiles hung from the porch roof rafters. Two small windows on either side of the door completed the façade. Cozy.

A newer addition extended off to the right of the main part of the house with larger, more modern windows. She could imagine his friend's grandmother living in the old section, but until she saw the new addition, she wouldn't have pictured this as his home. Of course, he merely lived here and took care of the place for a friend.

She didn't imagine too many people ventured this far up the mountain, though. Someone had to be looking for the house to find it, and she wasn't sure if she left and tried to come back she could retrace her path.

Vines of morning glory grew up the wall on the left side of the entrance, with hollyhocks shooting up before them. Their blossoms would be gorgeous against the red adobe in mid-summer.

Too bad she wouldn't be here to photograph them.

He indicated with his index finger the spot for her to park, and she exited the SUV. A panoramic view of the valley and mountains stretched out beyond the house.

"What a beautiful place!"

"I agree. I probably didn't appreciate it as a teenager, but it's given me a lot of peace since…since I moved out here."

"I can imagine." The feeling of peace and harmony here was palpable. His friend was a godsend to offer him a place to recover from combat.

"I can't wait to start taking photos." She popped the hatchback. "But first, I guess I ought to carry my things inside."

"I'll get the suitcase and camera case."

Picking up her purse and the two bags of groceries, she followed, noting that he hadn't locked the door when he left. For someone so concerned about her security, he didn't seem to have any worries about his own property or person.

The air in the house was cool. She scanned the room, homing in on the kiva fireplace. Very homey, old-fashioned furnishings from the sofa and armchairs to the bear rug in front of them. She shuddered. How anyone found dead animals or their furs attractive was beyond her.

"I'm going to put your bags in what I call my sister's room, since she's the only one who's ever slept there since I've lived here."

She left the groceries in the kitchen and followed him, grateful he had more than one bedroom here. She didn't want to put him out. Not that the thought of sharing a bed with him didn't send a fleeting image of their entangled bodies passing before her eyes.

Don't go there, girl.

"She visits sometimes from Santa Fe, but isn't due for another trip down here for months. She stays pretty busy up there with her gallery on the Plaza, especially this time of year when she's gearing up for the summer tourists." From his expression, she'd have thought he described the onslaught of a plague of locusts.

"What kind of gallery?"

He shrugged. "Art. Paintings, sculptures—even photographs. Want me to introduce you to her sometime?"

"I'd love to meet her and see if she'd be interested in any of my work. I plan to prepare some images for mounting while I'm up here. I could have a portfolio ready as early as next week."

"I'd be happy to put you in touch with her."

Apparently, he didn't want to go to Santa Fe any more than Albuquerque, even though it was less populated.

She scanned the room, happy to find a desk where she could work. The bedroom was small with tiny windows on two of the walls. She walked to the one she assumed would have the best view. Spectacular. The red hills contrasted against the deep blue sky. Sunrise would be beautiful, too, over the mountains in the distance.

"This used to be Mrs. Chosa's bedroom."

"It's cozy. Warm."

"I didn't change a lot since she...well, since I moved here."

Megan could tell by the emotion in his voice that the woman had meant a lot to him.

"Let's take a walk after you get settled in."

She turned toward Ryder and smiled. "I'd love to. If you'll point out where the bathroom is, I'll make a pit stop, change into my jeans, and be ready in no time." The more covered her legs were, the better. She shuddered at the thought of the creatures out here that would love nothing more than to bite or sting her fair skin.

A few minutes later, she met him in the kitchen as he put away the last of the groceries.

Everything was in its place. She smiled. Ryder had relaxed considerably since he arrived home, but still needed to make sure he maintained order in his environment.

He handed her a bottle of water, and she tucked it into the netting on the side of her camera case.

"Lead the way, Ryder. I can't wait to see more of this sanctuary up close."

Chapter Nine

R yder guided Megan along a well-worn path, one he walked almost daily. When she asked about certain plants, he described them, sometimes telling her about their medicinal and culinary uses. Mrs. Chosa had taught him this and much more.

Sharing his knowledge with Megan pleased him in ways he hadn't expected. Perhaps it made him feel useful again. Not that she needed to know about these things. She had little use for such knowledge in Albuquerque.

Megan paused and did a three-sixty before crouching down and snapping photos of a red and orange spike of Indian paintbrush.

"Is this one good for anything other than beautiful photos?"

"The flowers are edible, but not the leaves or roots, which have a tendency to leach selenium from the ground."

"No thanks. I'll pass."

"We'll avoid those parts, but the flower heads have some of the same nutritional benefits as eating garlic, without the smell."

She seemed to reconsider. "Do you eat the flowers?"

"Sure. In salads."

"Well, maybe I'll try some new things while I'm out here with you." She snapped off two blooms and put them into her pocket.

"Sure you don't want me to find a nice rattler for dinner?"

She jumped up and turned in several directions, searching the ground. "Where is it? I don't hear anything."

Ryder grinned as he watched realization dawn. She turned toward him, fire in her eyes. "You're joking. That's *not* funny."

"You need to face your fear. Besides, I'm here. I'll protect you."

The light left her eyes. "I know. It's your job."

"No, I'd protect you no matter what. You're my guest."

She nodded. "Let's walk some more."

Her mood remained somber. He wasn't sure what he'd said to put a damper on things, but he wanted to return to the way they were a moment ago. Ryder reached for her hand, and she accepted it. They walked side by side where they could, and he preceded her on narrow stretches, keeping an eye out for anything that might hurt or scare her. Man, she was terrified of snakes.

He remembered coming face to face with his first rattler, though, and understood. But after watching Carlos participate in a snake dance once, he'd lost his fear. He still knew to respect the creatures and kept antivenom on hand, just in case.

Another ten minutes hiking and he pointed toward a rock. "Let's sit a minute. There's something I want you to see." Hoping to increase anticipation, he placed his hands over her eyes. "Trust me. I want it to be a surprise."

*   *   *

Ryder's warm hands covering her eyes sent her body aflutter. The heat from his body standing so close behind her only increased her excitement. Her heartbeat raced faster. Her belly turned to molten fire. Her nipples hardened. Thank God he was behind her and couldn't see the effect he had on her.

He inched her along the path. "That's it. Almost there." She remembered seeing an outcropping of rock before he had shut off her vision. The sounds around her magnified. Birds mostly. Wait. Was that something slithering in the dirt? She reached up to move his hands away.

"Shhh. Don't be scared. I'm here. You're safe with me." His whispered words sent a tingle of awareness down her spine.

"I wasn't scared. Just surprised." His words calmed her enough to take another few steps before he stopped walking.

"Prepare to have your breath stolen away."

Her first thought was that he was about to kiss her—again. Oh, she hoped so. Kissing Ryder was her new favorite pastime. Then he lowered his hands, and the valley opened up before her, with more mountains far in the distance. While the view from her bedroom window had been spectacular, being surrounded by the panoramic view without intrusive walls left her speechless.

"Breathe." His whisper in her ear sent a tingle down her spine. True to his promise, he had left her breathless, too.

"I...don't know what to say."

"Shhh. Don't try to speak. Just feel. Experience."

The red ground, mesas, and mountains were dotted with scrubby vegetation. She didn't see a single manmade structure. This must have been what it looked like thousands of years ago.

She knew she would need a wide-angle lens to capture even a tiny bit of this view, but the thought of moving away from Ryder held no appeal. His breathing was slower than hers. He must not be feeling the same current of electricity sparking between them.

Why was she trying to sexualize an innocent scene? He'd just wanted to show her his view from on top of his world.

"Thanks for bringing me here, Ryder."

"My pleasure. Believe me. Thank you for letting me be the one to introduce you to it."

Once again, her thoughts went astray, and she wondered what it would be like to let Ryder introduce her to another wonder of the world. She wanted nothing more than to be initiated to sex by Ryder, but that wasn't why he brought her here. The man preferred no human attachments—and you didn't get more attached than when having a sexual relationship.

Still, the need for his lips on hers, his hands on her—

Megan turned around, her face mere inches from his. "Kiss me, Ryder."

A fire burned hot in his brown eyes before he doused the flame. "I don't think that's a very good idea."

She reached up to frame his face with her hands. "Don't think. Just feel." She pulled his face toward hers and placed her lips on his, tentatively. In an instant, the flames ignited in him as well, and with a groan, he opened his lips, allowing her tongue to slip between them and explore his warmth.

One of his hands that had somehow wound up on her hips—probably prepared to push her away—moved from her hip to her side, skimming upward. She couldn't breathe, but didn't want to break the spell either. When his thumb skimmed the side of her breast, she gasped. Her clit throbbed as if she'd pressed her vibrator on it, and he hadn't even touched her there. Yet.

Rather than pull away, he wrapped his other arm around her waist and pressed her lower body toward his where she felt his hardness against her belly.

Oh, God. This was becoming too real, too fast.

Then why didn't she stop him?

* * *

Megan's tongue darted in and out, teasing him into engaging. He knew he had no business kissing her again, but couldn't for the life of him remember why not.

His fingers grazed up the side of her tank top, and he fought the urge to cup her breast and pinch her nipple. What the hell had set her off like a firecracker? He tried to remember what they had been doing just before she turned and started kissing him. They'd been looking at the valley, one of his favorite places. He hadn't been able to wait to show her—

His hands over her eyes. Had that done it? Would she be interested in a little kink?

She's Top's sister.

He froze then placed both hands on her hips to push her away. Staring down at her swollen lips, he almost lost himself again, but blinked away his inappropriate passion.

"We can't do this."

"Why not?" The hurt in her voice made his heart ache.

"You're Top's sister."

"So?"

"He entrusted me to protect you, not molest you."

"I think I was the one to initiate that kiss. How is that molesting me?"

"I didn't have to respond."

"But you did."

Yeah, did I ever.

He'd have to be a eunuch not to respond to Megan. He took a step back.

She reached out to grab him. "Careful! Don't get so close to the edge."

He turned to see he was only a few feet from the ledge and a very steep plunge. Not feeling particularly suicidal today, he sidestepped away from both dangers—Megan and the fall.

Ryder ran his fingers through his hair, trying to reinvigorate the cells of his scalp, if not his brain. She'd only been out here a few hours, and already he had the hard-on to end all hard-ons. How the hell would he survive a few days with her like this?

"Megan, you're the most beautiful woman I know. Inside and out. But I'm not interested in a relationship, and you're too sweet a girl for anything less."

"How do you know I'm so sweet and innocent? I know what I want. I want you."

"I doubt you've slept with anyone except maybe that boy in college."

She remained silent. The moments stretched out. He hoped she was coming to the realization Ryder was nothing like her former boyfriend.

"I'm not the man you need, Megan."

She squared her shoulders. "I don't *need* any man. But I *want* you."

"What could you possibly want with me?"

Her features softened, and she took a step closer. He fought the urge to step back, but if she came any closer, he would.

"You're brave. You have integrity. You dropped everything to do a favor for me, a total stranger, even though I'm sure it was because a friend, my brother, asked you to help."

"I wouldn't exactly call him a friend. He was my master sergeant."

"He's become good friends with others who served with him. I know he'd count you among his friends if he got a chance to know you in civilian life."

If anything could douse the flames of his arousal, those words could. He turned away and faced the view that usually gave him peace, but now looked desolate, lonely.

"No, I don't think so. I let him down once—no twice."

"How?"

He wasn't going to talk about Kandahar. That pain was still too raw. Fallujah was marginally safer. "We came under fire on a rooftop in Fallujah, and I didn't do my job."

"I'm sure things become chaotic during combat."

"Yeah, but we're trained to focus on our duties—especially during combat. I was supposed to call for artillery and air power, but seeing Sergeant Miller's…" He wouldn't say brains. He just fucking wished he didn't see them whenever he thought about his recurring nightmares from that horrific scene. But once he heard Orlando scream *Grenade!*, his only goal had been to get Grant away from danger. She'd been assigned to his unit temporarily, but—

Megan's body pressed against his, and she wrapped him in a hug. "Please don't beat yourself up. I'm sure you did all you could under the circumstances."

His throat closed up, and he let her hold him but showed no outward sign of weakness.

"Shake it off." His mother sounded in his ears. *"Big boys don't cry."*

He cleared his throat. "My corpsman almost died because I was too busy trying to help Grant evacuate Orlando whose…" *foot had been blown off.*

"Let it out, Ryder. Don't keep stuff like that bottled up. You know Damián and Marc both survived that firefight. Maybe you tending to the wounded was more important than calling for fire power that probably couldn't have arrived in time to keep Marc from being injured anyway."

She was right, but tell that to his guilt-ridden conscience.

He blinked, hoping the wind would pick up and dry the embarrassing moisture from his eyes. Then again, maybe if she saw how weak and hopeless he really was, she'd end her naïve attraction to him.

Ryder turned and took her upper arms in his grip. "I screwed up. I had a job to do, and I screwed it up."

Megan's hand lifted to his cheek and stroked him. Not the response he'd expected.

"If Adam thought you were a screw-up, do you really think he would have called on you to protect his only sister?"

Ryder blinked. That had bugged him from the moment he'd answered the phone the other night. It made no sense. A man died because of him. "Maybe there just wasn't anyone else around on such short notice."

She smiled. "You don't know my brothers. Neither of them would send someone in for them unless they had absolute trust in that person."

Could she be right? Hell, Top *had* sent him onto that rooftop in Fallujah with his best sniper and their communications expert because he trusted him to do the job. Hadn't he? Even after he'd royally fucked up in Kandahar.

"Why do you think Adam doesn't trust you?"

He turned away, staring at the ground instead of the view. "I screwed up on a mission. I'd been trained to do a job, and I fucked up." He closed his eyes. "Excuse my language." His emotions simmered on the surface. Raw.

"When someone in a stateside job screws up, the ramifications are perhaps missing a sale or causing equipment to break down. You had so much pressure on you and in the middle of a war zone no less. Cut yourself some slack, Ryder. No one expects people to perform flawlessly under fire."

"A lot of people were counting on me. Hell, my Marine unit in Kosovo wasn't even involved in any combat situations, so Kandahar would have been—"

Her hand on his sleeve jolted him back to awareness. He needed to keep his distance. "Let's head back, Red. You're probably hungry by now."

He gestured for her to precede him, but she took his hand instead to walk beside him where they could on the sometimes narrow path.

The woman brought out his protective instincts like crazy.

But could he protect her from himself?

Chapter Ten

M egan chopped the bok choy and mushrooms while Ryder prepped the carrots, broccoli, and chicken. Cooking with him was a good change of pace from working at her computer. Editing on a laptop screen also hurt her eyes, so she welcomed the break when he asked if she'd like to help him prepare dinner. While she had been here only a few hours, the man was so easy to be with, it felt as though they'd known each other much longer.

Even so, he drove her insane. Despite her attempts to show she wanted him to look at her as more than his master sergeant's little sister, he kept pushing her away. After their walk this afternoon, she'd complained of a headache just to go to her room and relieve her frustrations with one of her vibrators. She'd never experienced this kind of attraction before.

And there was nothing she could do about it because the man only saw her as someone who needed protection from some very absent foes.

The knife slipped and nicked her finger.

"Ow!"

Before she had time to grab a paper towel, Ryder had her hand under the running faucet with cold water, washing away the blood. Her hand was growing numb, but he continued to hold it under the frigid water.

"I think it's stopped bleeding, Ryder."

When he didn't move or say anything, she turned to him. His eyes had glazed over.

"Ryder. Look at me."

As if a puppet on strings, he slowly turned his head toward her, but his eyes remained unseeing.

"Ryder. It's Megan. I just cut myself. Minor cut. I'm fine. You're here with me in your kitchen."

He blinked and glanced down at her hand again. She pulled it out of the water to show him the bleeding had long since stopped.

His gaze returned to hers, clear-eyed. "You okay?"

She smiled and relaxed, realizing she'd been holding herself so still her arms ached. "I'm fine."

"Let me get you a bandage."

"Just a Band-aid. It's superficial."

He went to a corner cabinet, which apparently served as his medicine cabinet, too, judging from the over-the-counter and prescription bottles she saw inside. He pulled out the familiar box and a tube of antibiotic ointment.

As he ministered to her cut, she asked, "Where did you go?"

"What?"

"You zoned out for a bit when you saw the blood. Want to talk about it?"

"No." He washed his hands and returned to where he'd been chopping vegetables earlier, but it took him a moment to pick up the knife and continue.

"I respect that you want to protect me from the horrors you experienced, but I can handle more than you know if you ever want to share anything."

He glanced her way and stared. "Careful what you wish for, Red. Keep asking me to open up to you, and someday, I just might. You may never look at me the same way again."

Oh, Ryder.

She closed the gap and wrapped her arms around his waist. He was so stiff and unwelcoming, but she continued to hold him. Maybe if he knew she cared—

He laid down the knife. "God damn it! I don't need this!"

Megan held on.

"I don't want you to baby me."

"I'm just holding you, Ryder."

"I don't need to be held and certainly don't deserve to be comforted. The families of the ones who died, they're the ones people should be comforting."

Despite his words, a tiny hole appeared in his armor, and a sob of anguish broke free from him. Megan forced him to turn toward her and held onto him even tighter, but didn't look him in the eyes. His psyche needed space. But his body needed a hug.

Please, trust me enough to let go of what you've bottled up inside.

When she thought he'd continue to stand there like a wooden statue, his arms finally wrapped around her as well, forcing the air from her lungs as he squeezed her. She didn't push him away, though.

"I've got you, Ryder. You're safe. Let it go."

He choked on another sob and then another. "I fucked up. Twice. It was all my fault. Men are dead or maimed because of me. Because I didn't do my job."

Survivor guilt. So many veterans she knew suffered from it. Losing a buddy on the battlefield was the worst thing a Marine could experience.

No man left behind.

But sometimes all they could retrieve was what was left of their buddy's body.

"Tell me about the first time."

"Can't."

"Was it Afghanistan or Iraq?"

The silence dragged out. She waited.

"I can tell you about Fallujah. Iraq."

Apparently, whatever happened in Afghanistan was too painful to speak about yet. She'd give him time. "Tell me what it was like in Fallujah."

"Street warfare. Never knew who the enemy was until it was too late."

"What was your job?" Best not to zero in on the scene he flashed back to, but she wanted to understand more about him—and Adam, too. They had served there together. Usually Patrick didn't mind talking about his job detail.

Ryder was no exception. "I trained in Kosovo to be an artillery fire direction operator, but we didn't see combat on that tour. Basically, I was in charge of calling for air strikes or supporting arms fire missions. By the time we got to Kandahar—Afghanistan—I had advanced to the FIST team, but…"

"FIST?"

"Sorry. The Fire Support Team. In Kandahar, my job was forward observer, calling for fire support and air strikes." He paused. Did he realize he'd revealed something about Kandahar? "I held a similar job by the time we got to Fallujah, just a higher rank."

"Sounds like an important position and one you were well-trained for."

"We worked as a team. Everyone was important to the mission."

"What was the most stressful part?"

He looked away and answered in barely a whisper. "Making sure I knew where all our friendlies were…"

Oh, God, no. Not that.

"Luckily, I never got any of the coalition troops injured or killed."

She relaxed some. He'd just been answering her question. Thank God he didn't have that on his conscience. The guilt would have been unbearable for anyone. She had only to remember how it was for Patrick when he returned home from Afghanistan. So lost.

Ryder squeezed her even tighter. Megan didn't know what to say to comfort him but continued to hug him hoping he would continue to talk. How much more was bottled up inside him? So much like Patrick. She didn't know the half of what he'd experienced either.

When his grip loosened, she took a deep breath. "I'm so sorry you had to go through those things, Ryder. I can't imagine making split-second decisions involving so many lives in the chaos of combat. So much can change in a flash. You aren't the first and won't be the last to make the wrong call."

"It wasn't my first screw-up."

"Tell me what happened," she whispered, although it pained her to hear more anguish from him.

"I don't want to talk about the first time, but when we came under attack in Fallujah, I hesitated in calling for our preplanned fire mission. I was more worried about getting Grant out of there."

Megan remembered talking with Grant at Adam's wedding. One tough woman who apparently wanted to be more like one of the guys if the role she fulfilled in the wedding party was any indication.

While everyone was busy making preparations the day before the wedding, Megan and Grant had found time to talk a little about what it had been like for Adam's unit in Fallujah. The woman even asked if Patrick had any combat-related stress issues and made Megan comfortable enough to share a little about how hard it was for him when he first came home. Grant gave her some tips on how to deal with his PTSD in the future.

"It's normal to take care of your buddies in your unit when under fire, but I didn't think women Marines served in combat situations."

"We were in an observation post during a cease-fire, and hostilities had all but ended. Or so we thought. She'd been assigned temporarily to my unit because of her expertise with high-tech communications. We had a Marine sniper on the roof with us—Damián Orlando. Grant was trying to correlate real-time satellite tactical data on a primary insurgent target's location so he could take him out. Then all hell broke loose.

"My sergeant was killed by a grenade. Nothing I could have done about that, but I put our corpsman in danger by not doing my job. A mortar came in while he was prepping Orlando to be medevacked out. Doc could have died, too, because of me."

Surely someone else could have called for the airstrike when Damián was wounded. Adam had been there, too, although higher up the chain of command. Did her brother blame himself, too? Probably. He certainly took responsibility for everyone around him in civilian life. The man was a protector and a guardian by nature. She wished she could give Adam a hug of comfort to reassure him. She'd do that when she got to Denver this month.

She realized she hadn't heard anything about Karla in a while. She'd call later. Right now, all that mattered was the man in her arms.

"But Marc didn't die. I saw him at Adam's wedding. He looks very fit, in fact."

Ryder pulled away. "I'm glad to hear he's doing well. I never could face him again after Fallujah."

She raised her hand and stroked his cheek, feeling the stubble of his whiskers. "Ryder, you're human. You were put in a position that would leave most of us curled in the fetal position. Please stop blaming yourself for things that didn't go as planned. It was a goddamned war zone."

He stared into her eyes but remained silent.

"You have a lot in common with my brothers, you know. They blame themselves for everything that went wrong, too. Thank God most of you came home, but I hate that you brought the war home with you. All of you deserve to have some peace now. You served your country honorably." She wished she knew what to say to make it right for him. How could she help him release that pain? "What would the Jemez tribal leaders tell you to do?"

"Reconnect with the Great Spirit."

"And how do they suggest you do that?"

"Spiritual ceremonies. Drumming is one way I learned as a kid to reconnect to the heartbeat of Mother Earth."

"When's the last time you drummed?"

He closed his eyes and whispered, "Before I left for Fallujah, I participated in a warrior ceremony that prepared me to go to war again. Carlos had just enlisted in the Navy, so we went through the ceremony together."

"Did you participate in any kind of ceremony when you returned? Something to welcome you home and, more importantly, remove the negativity of your wartime experiences?"

He shook his head.

"Why not? Don't they do something like that?"

"Sure, but I was too busy trying to…save my marriage. And exist."

"Have you talked with Carlos? Perhaps he could arrange some kind of—

"He's been trying to get me to do a purification lodge ceremony and vision quest. I don't know that anything will help at this point."

"Never give up, Ryder. You have people in your life who would be heartbroken if you kept this bottled up inside to a breaking point. Including me."

"You just met me. Why do you care?"

"I…feel a special connection with you." *One I've never felt with any other man before.*

Not able to explain why, she needed to be as close as possible to him. Framing his face, she pulled him toward her as she rose on tiptoes. Her lips brushed his, making hers tingle in a delicious way, but his mouth remained stiff and closed. Her tongue traced the line of his lips. With a groan, he relented and pushed her forward until her hips pressed against the counter behind her. He grabbed her head and held her still in that way, too. His tongue invaded her mouth, and she welcomed this assault on her senses.

Her nipples hardened. She broke away long enough to gasp for a breath.

"Ryder, I want you. Inside me. I'm not promising you anything more than this moment and don't expect anything from you beyond today, but…will you make love to me? Tonight?"

He tried to pull away, and she lowered her hands to his shoulders, not wanting him to leave her frustrated. Again. Neither of them was looking for forever, but right now, they needed each other.

She doubted Ryder could deal with being responsible for another person and knew he would take on the lion's share of responsibility in any relationship he entered into. Just as he held onto his responsibility for the Marines who served with him long after they returned home.

"No strings, Ryder. No regrets either. I know you want me as much as I want you. I've felt how…turned on you are. I feel you now, hard against my belly."

He put some distance between their bodies. "I don't want to hurt you, Megan. You don't strike me as the kind of girl who would sleep around. You need someone who can love and cherish you for a lifetime. I'm not that man. With you, I would feel responsi—"

Megan seethed. Unlike Ryder, she wouldn't hold back. "I'm *not* your responsibility! I'm your friend. A friend who has felt a strong attraction to you as soon as we met." He quirked an eyebrow. "Look, Ryder, I'm not interested in long-term either. Or, God forbid, marriage."

"Why not? You'd make a wonderful wife and mother."

She closed her eyes, the pain of looking into his eyes too difficult. "I'm not… It's just…" She wouldn't explain her fateful decision to him, but gazed up at him again. "Not every woman is looking for marriage and family, Ryder."

He leaned away, widening his eyes. "But you are one perfect woman for some lucky man."

How could she convince him she wasn't looking for a husband? Perhaps actions would speak more loudly than words. She placed her hand on his chest and flicked her thumbnail against his nip and leaned closer to whisper, "You turn me on, Ryder Wilson. No man has ever had that effect on me before. My vibrator has been working overtime for days now."

He grinned. "So I've heard."

Her eyes opened wide. "No way!" Heat rushed into her cheeks.

His callused finger stroked her flushed cheek. "I love how you blush. So sweet. Innocent. But hearing that vibrator the other night surprised the hell out of me."

Oh, God. How many times had he heard it?

Did he just think she was oversexed? "Just know I've been fantasizing about our making love." *Wait. Leave love out of it. Neither of them could handle that.* "I want to have sex with you, Ryder. I can tell by the way you kiss me back and a thousand other gestures that you would be a gentle lover—partner."

She probably should stop, but the words kept pouring out. "I want you beside me, inside me." She wanted to make it very clear going into this deal what he would find. No surprises. No tricks. "I want you to be my first."

The smile left his face. "First—*ever?*"

She nodded. "Yes." First and last, but she wouldn't put that kind of pressure on the man.

He broke away from her and ran a hand through his short-cropped hair. "Jesus, Megan. If your brothers found out I even *slept* with you, much less took your virginity, they'd nail me to the nearest tree."

"Ryder Wilson, I am twenty-six years old! Don't you dare bring my brothers into our bed."

"We don't *have* a bed."

"We will as soon as you admit you want me, too, and drag me into yours." She smiled. "Or if you prefer, we can go to my room."

"Megan, you know I can't deny I am attracted to you. But I'm not here to have sex with you. My mission is to protect you."

"There's nothing you need to protect me from any longer, least of all you. Unless you don't have any condoms." Let him think she was talking about protecting her from pregnancy or STDs.

"I haven't had sex in a while. I doubt there are any condoms around here, but I always practiced safe sex."

"Then we can go to the convenience store and pick up some after dinner."

"I don't have sex with innocent virgins, especially not one whose big brother is my former master sergeant."

"Ryder, whatever happens stays between us. My brothers have nothing to do with it and don't need a report either."

"No, sex is out of the question. If you won't see reason, someone here needs to be the adult."

Now he was saying she was not only a virgin but acting childishly?

She spun away from him. "Excuse me. I'm going to take a walk."

"Megan, you're just going to get hurt if—"

Unable to speak, she waved him away and left the kitchen. How could she make him see her not as his master sergeant's little sister, but as a woman who cared a lot for him and wanted something with him she'd never wanted with any man before? Certainly not marriage. She wouldn't trap any man in that kind of arrangement unless he was fully aware of what she couldn't give him. Friends with benefits, maybe.

Not that they'd done anything more than kiss. Maybe benefits would be wishful thinking on her part.

Outside, she looked left and right and decided it would be best to stick to the beaten path. Critters tended to come out this time of the evening, and she didn't want to have any unwelcome encounters. The only encounter she *did* want was with Ryder, but he refused her.

Megan's face grew warm as she pictured how it must have looked to him with her throwing herself at him. She'd never behaved like that with a man. Why this one? Hormones. She had to blame her screwed up hormones for this.

Obviously having sex with her was the furthest thing from what Ryder wanted. She'd embarrassed the hell out of herself. How was she going to go back in and face him over dinner? God, she hadn't even stayed to help him finish cooking.

Maybe he was right. She *was* behaving childishly. Spoiled, even, although he hadn't accused her of that. She turned around and started up the road again. A movement to her right caught her eye, and she turned to see a large coyote staring at her. Her heart jumped into her throat a moment before she realized the animal probably feared her more than she needed to fear it. If only she had her camera. She'd never been so close to one before.

Megan stood still, not wanting to spook the animal. Its cinnamon-brown eyes seemed a mirror to its soul. She wished she could communicate with it in some way.

"Don't be afraid, Red. I'm here."

She glanced up the driveway toward the house and found Ryder standing there, knife in hand.

"Don't you dare touch that animal!" she whispered with great emphasis, but not loud enough to scare the coyote.

"I won't, unless he attacks you. He's been coming around here for months so maybe he's lost his fear of humans. Still, he's a wild animal and unpredictable."

Her gaze returned to the coyote. "Should we leave some food out for him?"

"No. It would weaken his ability to survive. I won't be here forever. Not to mention the fact that food would attract other animals we may not want hanging around the house. There is a delicate balance with nature out here, and it's best not to upset that."

"Makes sense."

"Walk toward me slowly. Don't make eye contact with the coyote. Just look at me."

She realized staring at the animal probably made him feel challenged, although he didn't seem to want to attack her when she did so. Megan took one step, then another, never quite meeting Ryder's or the coyote's gaze. The animal remained still. Watching. Silent.

When she reached Ryder's side, he wrapped an arm around her. The coyote turned and trotted up the hillside.

"You weren't afraid, were you?"

"No. More than a little annoyed that I didn't have my camera with me."

Ryder chuckled.

"I'm sure you'll have other opportunities if you stay out here any time at all."

"You don't want to send me packing after that scene in the kitchen?"

He grinned. "Do you know how good it sounds for a beautiful young woman to tell a screwed-up, old Marine like me she's turned on by him?"

They began walking toward the house. "Well, it's the truth. I'm not sure I can turn off those feelings. Things might get a little awkward if we spend much more time together."

"Don't you worry. I can make sure things don't get out of control between us."

Oh, is that so?

What if she turned the tables on him and showed him she could exert a little control herself? Maybe Ryder needed to surrender some of the tight control he had on himself to someone else? She'd read about relationships where men and women who were always in control sometimes liked allowing someone else to call the shots, make the decisions.

She wondered if perhaps he was interested in certain forms of kink. From what she'd read in novels anyway, kink didn't have to involve sex.

She wished she had an internet connection to see if what she read about in romance novels and on erotica story sites had any basis in reality, but her cell phone barely worked out here. Ryder didn't have a smartphone she could use to surf the web to learn more.

Well, maybe she could learn by asking Ryder questions. Would he be interested in some non-sexual fun and games like the ones she'd read about on a certain erotica website. Not that she'd needed that site for sexual stimulation since meeting Ryder Wilson.

She intended to make sure the discussions at dinner tonight were very…stimulating.

Chapter Eleven

Ryder marveled at how Megan fit into his world. He'd thought her a pampered city girl, but nothing seemed to faze her. Sure, she probably wouldn't buddy up to a rattler anytime soon, but watching her in silent communication with the coyote had impressed the hell out of him. Most city girls would have screamed and run, possibly encouraging a chase by the coyote. Not Megan.

Now, if only he could get her to stop trying to get into his bed. That wasn't going to happen.

He carried two plates of chicken stir-fry to the table, and she followed with her glass of white wine and his bottle of beer. He preferred having a beer with his dinner, but apparently, her brother preferred wine and harder liquor.

At least the earlier awkward moment seemed to have been diffused. She'd probably only come on to him earlier to divert his attention from his meltdown. Nothing about his post-traumatic stress issues seemed daunting to her, either.

How anyone could be attracted to a man who broke down like that stumped him, though. Definitely had to have been feeling sorry for him.

They ate in silence at first, making him wonder if maybe the scene in the kitchen earlier would cause trouble in their friendship. But Megan managed to get the conversation going again.

"Why did your parents name you Ryder?"

He swallowed a mouthful of food. "You really want to know?"

"Sure!"

"Well, seems they were moving from Idaho to New Mexico when Marcia was about fifteen months old and—"

"No way!" She set her fork down. "You're named for a Ryder rental truck?"

He shrugged and grinned. "Sure enough. Guess it's a good thing they didn't rent a U-Haul."

She cupped her chin in her hand. "I have to hear the rest of this story."

"I'm told I was conceived in the back."

"I thought having another baby would keep your father around, but he planned to leave as soon as we returned the Ryder truck."

He tamped down the memory and tried to make light of the story for Megan. "They left Marcia with Mom's mom during the move. Because they couldn't afford a motel, they slept in the back."

"That's too funny!"

Ryder resumed eating although his appetite was pretty much gone. He enjoyed being with Megan, though. Watching her excitement when she discovered new things brought him a lot of joy, too. He'd forgotten why he loved this place so much until he'd seen it through her eyes.

"Ryder, have you ever tried kink?"

The mouthful of veggies he swallowed at that moment caught in his throat, and he grabbed his beer to wash it down. When he could speak again, he asked, "What did you say?" How long had he tuned out for the conversation to shift so dramatically?

"Kink. You know, bondage, spanking, things like that. Not necessarily as foreplay to sex, but it can be used as a way to regain control."

He set his fork down. "What the hell do you know about kink?"

"Well, I've read some books."

"Like the one all over the news lately?"

She raised her chin in defiance. "Among others."

God save the world from people with enough general knowledge to get them in over their heads. "Listen, there's a lot of misinformation dispensed in those novels."

"But some are well-researched and written by people who live the lifestyle or consult with those who do. Don't worry. I know the difference between what's realistic and what's fantasy, Ryder."

"Do you? Tell me what you've learned."

"That a healthy BDSM or kink relationship involves building a deep trust in each other, open and honest communication, using safewords, negotiating and sharing your hard and soft limits, and always involves activities mutually consented upon between adults."

Time to see if she truly knew fantasy from reality. "Should I get out a pen and paper and draw up a lengthy contract for us to begin then?"

Her frown indicated confusion. "Of course not. I know a written contract in a kink relationship isn't worth the paper it's written on. That's where trust comes in. You need to trust that your play partner won't cry abuse later. It's risky to play with the wrong person because of the societal taboo. There can be serious consequences suffered. That's where verbal negotiations and lots of communication come in." She paused for a breath and smiled. "But a checklist might come in handy. I could list my limits and likes, and you yours."

"I'm impressed you've done your homework. But we aren't drawing up a list, either."

She blushed. "Well, the lifestyle has fascinated me from the moment I read my first BDSM romance novel a few years ago. You have a Dominant and a submissive usually, although there are other combinations. Generally, the Dom or Top acts upon the submissive or bottom, who receives the action."

"Might I ask which of those roles you see yourself in?"

"Oh, the Dominant, of course."

"Is that so?" From what he'd observed of Megan, he questioned her self-assessment, but she wouldn't be the first submissive whose judgment was clouded by the way she dominated the rest of her world. All of the subs he'd known had been very dominant in their businesses, even their homes. But in the bedroom?

He'd love to know about her orientation—but had no intention of finding out.

She went on trying to convince him she knew. "I like being in control of everything. It's why I plan to be an independent photographer rather than work for someone else. It's also why I chose to apprentice during college to prepare for my career. And—"

Ryder shook his head.

"You don't believe me?"

"Actions speak more loudly than words."

"What kind of proof do you need?"

"*I* don't need to know one way or the other. Just keep your options open in case you ever find a safe and experienced Dom to work with."

Why did the thought of her being with another Dom bother him? She sure as hell shouldn't learn about kink from him. Well, it couldn't hurt to talk about it, he supposed.

"Kink can be fun. My ex-wife and I enjoyed some bedroom kink in our relationship. It can spice things up for sure."

"Only in the bedroom?"

He drew a breath while trying to decide how much he wanted to say about that relationship. "At first. Back when we first began to play, I had no idea how to be a Dom. We tried a few things I'd heard about from the guys I served with, but I was in over my head in no time. Some of my buddies knew about a club in LA where I eventually was mentored by an authentic Dom."

She leaned toward him and propped her chin on her palm. "What kinds of things did you learn there?"

Her wide-eyed innocence had him wishing they'd branched off on an entirely different discussion tonight. How the hell had they gotten onto this subject anyway?

"I don't think you need to know."

"Oh, sorry. I didn't mean to pry if it's hard to talk about her."

Hell, he wasn't finding it difficult to talk about his ex. His feelings for her were long dead and buried. But someone with Megan's curiosity and willfulness might go looking in all the wrong places for the Dom of her dreams. She'd probably wind up hurt, or worse. There were too many asshole posers out there, and it only seemed to be getting worse thanks to the media's clueless and irresponsible reporting.

Which is exactly why I should talk to her. Maybe I can use the opportunity to test her knowledge and make sure her information doesn't get her killed.

"It's not that I can't talk about my ex. I just don't see any point in having this conversation. Save discussion and negotiation for when you become serious about someone."

"Sorry. Just curious." She glanced down at her plate before meeting his gaze again. "You're the first person I've met who actually has any experience in the lifestyle, so I thought I'd ask some questions."

"Everyone's kink is different. Knowing what I'm into probably isn't going to help you down the road. Just promise me you won't do anything stupid like go to a Dom's house for a first date."

"Of course I wouldn't! I'm not even looking for a Dom. I just thought…" She leaned closer to him, lowering her voice to a husky whisper. "I hear there is great freedom in allowing yourself to be restrained by someone you trust. You've been locked up inside your head and your body for so long—"

"Whoa! Being the bottom or submissive isn't *my* kink."

"Have you tried it?"

"Only while being trained to use new techniques or toys. A Dom doesn't try anything that hasn't been tried on him first so he knows what his submissive is experiencing. But that was enough for me to know I'm a Top, not a bottom."

"You know you can trust me. Perhaps things have changed for you since you trained as a Dom."

Had they ever, but the thought of relinquishing control to anyone enough to be restrained, well, no fucking way. "Sorry, Red. You're barking up the wrong tree." Change the focus of this conversation back where it should be. "But I'd bet dollars to doughnuts you're more submissive than Dominant."

"Maybe I just like the idea of playing games in bed and won't care if I'm on the giving or receiving end." She winked at him.

"And just how many times have you *played* in bed with a man?"

Her smiled faded, and she sat back in her chair. "Touché."

Damn, he didn't mean to hurt her feelings.

He was going to kick himself in the morning for this, but at least she'd leave here knowing if she was a Top, a bottom, or maybe even a switch who enjoyed both ends of kink. "If you'd like to try a little experiment—one that doesn't involve a bed—I think we can quickly determine which side of the BDSM coin you're on."

She smiled, eagerness lighting her emerald eyes once more. "What do you have in mind?"

"I'm going to ask you to stand, and I'm going to be behind you." No fear. Perhaps if he ratcheted it up a notch. "I'll want to bind your arms, mostly as a safety precaution in case my guess is wrong about your D/s orientation. Will that be all right with you?"

Damn, did her pupils just dilate? "Absolutely. I'd love to feel what it's like to be tied up."

"Do you mind if I pull your hair?"

"Pull my hair?" The huskiness in her voice told him she was excited by the idea—or was it fear? "Um," her tongue flicked across her lower lip, "it sounds really sexy."

No, definitely arousal. "This isn't about sex. It's about that exchange of power you keep talking about wanting to explore." He waited a moment, but when she didn't respond, he prompted her. "So, yes or no? Would having your hair pulled bother you?"

"I don't know. I haven't had my hair pulled since Patrick tormented me as a kid."

"I'm not going to pull your hair like your brother did. It's simply a means of exerting control over your body."

"Through my hair?"

Jesus, what was he getting into here? She had no clue. Whatever made him want to introduce her to kink in the first place?

"Let's forget all this. I don't think you're ready to find out whether you're Dominant or submissive. The chances of you needing to know are—"

She placed her hand on his. "But I trust you more than I would any other man." She scooted her chair back and stood. "Let's do this. I'm curious now. I want to know." She moved away from the table and turned her back to him. "Do I need to put my hair in a ponytail or something?"

Her long, gorgeous curls covered the top half of her back. He got hard just thinking about winding the long strands around his hand. God forgive him for what he was about to do. He'd do his penance tonight while lying *alone* in bed thinking about her and what might have been if he wasn't so fucked up.

With a sigh, Ryder stood. "No need. Just stand there as you are. Relax a little, though. Do you trust that I won't do anything to harm you?"

She nodded. Hell, she hardly knew him. How could she trust him like that? He didn't trust her that much.

"I need to go get something in the bedroom. I want you to stand here and think about what you've asked me to do. Make sure it's what you want."

"Oh, I'm—"

"I said: Think about it. I'll ask again before we proceed tonight."

Ryder walked down the hall to his bedroom and then into the closet. He pushed the hanging clothes aside until he reached the back corner where he bent down to pick up his toy bag. He'd bought some new things after returning from Fallujah, hoping to resume his relationship with Sherry, but had never gotten the chance to play with them. She'd wanted nothing to do with him by that point.

He lifted the bag and carried it to the bed where he unzipped it. Ah, there's what he needed. He pulled out the forty-foot bundle of solid-braid nylon rope and returned to the dining room where he found Megan standing with her hands at her sides and her shoulders squared as if for battle.

Was she submissive or wasn't she? Her body sent mixed signals. One way to find out.

As he drew near, her body relaxed visibly, rather than growing any stiffer. Perhaps her stance had been one of fear or uncertainty. She really did trust him, for whatever reason. He hoped she'd never put that trust so quickly into the hands of someone who didn't deserve the gift.

He hooked the rope over the back of the chair she had vacated minutes earlier. Drawing closer to where she stood, he placed his hands on her shoulders. She leaned a little closer to him. Wanting to ease her strained muscles before he began, he moved his hands up the sides of her neck, massaging as he went. She relaxed some. When he reached her hair, he splayed his fingers open and slid up both sides of her head as he began massaging her scalp. The spicy scent of her shampoo or perfume assailed his nostrils.

"Mmmm. Feels so good."

"Shhh. Don't say anything. If you need me to stop, though, just say scarlet. That will be your safeword. We can't use red because we'd risk confusion with your nickname."

"You get to use the safeword, too?"

"Yes, Baby. It's for anyone in the scene who needs to put a stop to things."

"Oh, well, I don't want you to stop. But I should point out that just because I like to have my scalp massaged doesn't mean I'm a submissive."

"True. Now try to behave and remain silent unless I ask a direct question. Focus on your breathing. In. And out. Slowly. I want you to get in tune with your body. Listen to it for guidance."

While he hoped she was taking time to prepare herself, he turned, retrieved the bundle of rope, and loosened it, looking for the ends. Standing behind her once more, he divided her hair down the middle and placed half over each shoulder.

"I'm going to bind your arms now. It's purely a safety measure. I don't want you to be hurt. Are you ready?"

"Y-yes."

"Good. Place your hands behind you with the backs of your hands resting on your butt and palms facing outward." She complied, but fisted her hands. "Relax your fingers and stretch them toward the floor. Keep your body—especially your arms, hands, and fingers—relaxed so I can manipulate them as needed. You simply concentrate on your breathing. In. And out."

Her breathing grew erratic, and her arms trembled when he started to apply the rope binding. Ryder circled around to face her, knowing what might help her relax. "Look at me." She met his gaze, and her nervousness was palpable. "Breathe in with me, Baby, and on the exhale release all nervousness and negativity."

Ryder took a deep breath and exhaled slowly, and she was only a second off. "Continue to synchronize your breathing with mine." After several paired breaths, Ryder found himself becoming calmer, too, which surprised him. Apparently, he'd missed being in Dom mode—or Top mode in this case.

Perhaps he missed having control over something—or having someone who trusted him. He gave a mental shrug. Whatever, he enjoyed a sense of oneness with her as they breathed together.

"Now I want you to keep breathing steadily as we have been while I return to standing behind you. Set the pace of our breathing this time, and I will synchronize mine to yours. Cast your gaze to…" He looked behind him to find a focal point. "The rug in front of the fireplace."

When he faced her again, she visibly cringed, and he knew that rug wasn't something she wanted to look at. "On second thought, focus on this spot on the floor." He tapped a place about two feet in front of her, and her gaze followed. "Now breathe."

Resuming his place behind her, he waited for her to begin breathing. When she did, he adopted her rhythm, and began restraining her arms into a dragonfly sleeve. He created the first knot and slipped the rope loops up her arms and over her shoulders, centering the knot between her shoulder blades. Remembering to breathe with Megan, he added a new knot every three or four inches as he worked down her back. Just below the center of her back, he added his first handle, then fashioned two more knots and another handle before tying off her wrists.

Ryder sighed before realizing he was no longer breathing with Megan. To finish off the dragonfly, he needed to run the ropes between her legs and up to her shoulders.

Breathe. In. And out.

He soon was in sync with her again. Before he proceeded, he pulled her hair behind her again and let it hang down her back. It was short enough it wouldn't cover either of the handles, but long enough for him to be able to get a good grip on it.

"Spread your legs a few inches apart, Megan."

He let the ends of the rope dangle and walked around to stand in front of her again. When she started to lift her head, he instructed, "Keep your gaze downward, even if I'm obstructing the place I asked you to focus on now." He didn't want her to see his face in case he lost his own focus while working in close proximity to her sex or her breasts.

Beautiful. She wore a tank top with padded cups. He longed to cup her breasts himself, but when he heard her inhale, he remembered he was supposed to be breathing with her. Grounding himself in their synchronized breaths, he bent and reached between her legs to pull the rope ends quickly through and up to her shoulders where he tucked the right one in until he was ready for it.

As he created the sliding knot on the left, the back of his hand brushed her breast, and he became hard instantly. Her breathing hitched, and he realized having her gaze fixed on his lower body was a bad idea at the moment. Soon she recovered, although the way her lips quivered, he knew she fought to contain her smile.

Ryder stepped up his pace and finished off the tie before walking around behind her again. Slowly and deliberately, he reached for a hank of more than half of her hair and wound it around his fist.

"Listen to your body, Baby. Continue to take slow, deep breaths."

His own body sizzled with pent-up energy. With each twist of his hand, he reined her in, preparing to exert control over her body.

Jesus, I've missed this.

The way she leaned against him told him he probably wouldn't have any trouble with her fighting him. Thankfully, he had the handles on the rope binding in place. If her fight-or-flight reflex kicked in, things could become ugly fast. But judging by how docilely she accepted the restraints, he didn't expect either of them would be hurt in a struggle.

Without warning, he yanked her head back against his chest using one hand on her hair and the other on the arm bindings. For an instant, her reflexes kicked in, and she tried to pull away. Just when he'd begun to wonder if she might be a Dominant after all, her body went limp, melting against his. He grinned.

Submissive to the bone.

"Feel the sensations. Listen to your body."

He continued to hold her, enjoying the feel of her body against his. He just hoped he hadn't unleashed something neither of them was prepared to deal with.

Chapter Twelve

"That's my good girl. Trust me. I won't harm you. Just listen to your body."

Megan's mind had gone blank when he'd pulled her against him, nearly yanking the hair from her head. For a moment, she'd been ready to use the martial arts techniques Patrick had taught her to take him down to the ground. Then her body simply—surrendered. Without any struggle at all.

"Breathe...in...out."

She obeyed as though her body was no longer within her control. Even though he held her in a way that could have been dangerous in the hands of the wrong man, she had no fear. Ryder wouldn't do anything to harm her. She trusted him.

"What are you feeling?"

"I'm not afraid. I feel protected. Safe. Almost euphoric."

"Continue to listen to your body. Trust your instincts. Take another deep breath." She did so, shakier this time from some deep emotion welling up inside.

"Does this mean I'm submissive?"

She heard the smile in his voice. "Yes, I think it does. How does that make you feel?"

"Surprised. A little confused."

"I'm going to release you now. Think you can stand on your own?"

She nodded, but when he began to loosen his grip on her hair, tremors shook her body.

"Shhh. I've got you. Let's just hold this position a little longer, until you're ready for me to release you."

Her heart pounded against his arm. Could he feel it beating?

"Please, Ryder. Don't release me. Show me more."

His hand lowered from her hair, and her knees buckled. He held onto the ropes binding her arms and kept her from falling. "Whoa, there!" He lifted her into his arms. She didn't know where they were going, but didn't care either, as long as he stayed with her. She closed her eyes and leaned against his shoulder.

He laid her down on a mattress. She opened her eyes and stared into his eyes. He seemed as confused as she about what had just happened.

Out of the corner of her eye, she realized she was in the guest bedroom and not his bed. Disappointed and a little afraid he was going to go, she tried to grab for his shirt, but her arms being bound made that impossible. "Don't leave me!"

"I would never leave you alone in bindings." When he began removing the bindings, she knew for certain this experiment was over. "You're going to need to process what just happened, and I won't let you do that alone, either."

Then he wasn't leaving her alone tonight? He met her gaze. "But we aren't having sex. We're both going to remain fully clothed. I need...I want to hold you until you come to terms with that scene in the other room."

Ryder reached down to remove her shoes and then took off his own. He walked around the end of the bed and crawled into the other side where he stretched out and turned toward her.

"Come here, Baby. Let me hold you."

She liked being called baby, which surprised her. She wouldn't have permitted any other man to refer to her that way. She'd always prided herself in being treated as an equal by men. So why did being called *baby* sound so endearing and sexy when he said it?

She blinked rapidly at the sting in her eyes and scooted closer to him. Unable to face him with the threat of tears in her eyes, she turned her back to him, and he spooned her, wrapping his arm around her waist and holding her closer.

His hand moved to her hair, and he stroked it. "What are you thinking?"

"That I'm not going to cry in front of you."

"Thanks for being honest, but if you need to cry, then cry." He stroked her hair, but she refused to give in to tears. "Tell me what you're feeling now."

"That I don't want this moment to end. That I want you to keep holding me this way forever."

"You know I can't do that."

"Can't or won't?"

"Both. A good Dom does no harm to his submissive, and I would do great harm if I let anything grow between us."

"Oh, Ryder. I wish you could see yourself the way I do."

His hand stilled. "How is that?"

"Nurturing, gentle, strong. A warrior who hasn't been able to leave the war behind him yet. Someone who would lay down his life for what's right. A man who—"

"Enough."

"I could go on."

"I figured, but you don't know me well enough to know what kind of man I really am."

"I knew you well enough to trust you in the other room."

"You were foolish to let a near-stranger do that to you."

"I trusted my instincts. You've never done anything to harm me despite a number of opportunities where you could have while we were staying at my brother's condo. Besides, it's not as if you lured me up here or brought me against my will. I was the one who decided we would come up to this isolated house. If I had any inkling you might have nefarious thoughts in mind, do you think I would be here?"

"I imagine there are a lot of dead women who thought the same thing before some serial killer offed them."

"Can we change the subject?"

"That might be a good idea."

Even though she sensed he wanted to distance himself from her, he didn't pull away. The caregiver in him was as strong as the warrior. If only he could lay down his armor for a little while, he might discover a newfound strength and peace.

"Would you…touch me? You already know I like to…pleasure myself. But I want to know what it feels like to have a man touch me there instead."

His body grew stiff, just like the erection pressing against her butt. *Oh, no!* Had she just gone bratty, telling him what to do? She adored the bratty subs in the Shadowlands club she loved reading about, but wasn't sure that's what Doms liked.

"Sorry. I didn't mean to be bratty."

"There's nothing wrong with a sub telling a Dom what she likes. We're still getting to know each other. I think, if I give you an orgasm, we might be treading into an area we shouldn't."

"Taboo?"

"Not by my standards, but we both know this isn't going to continue beyond another day or two at most."

"I'll be okay."

"No. You're not the type who can just walk away from something that intense and move on. I don't want you to have regrets. Besides, if Top knew I was talking with his little sister about these things in the first place, he'd roast my nuts over a fire pit."

"I don't discuss my sex life with Adam—Patrick, either."

"You don't have a sex life."

She elbowed him. "Not for a lack of trying. Why won't you let me decide who I want to be with and when?"

"Because you're too young."

"I'm older than you and your wife were when you got married."

"We haven't known each other long enough. Sherry and I were together for years before having sex or getting kinky."

Okay, enough already. She flipped over and leaned on her elbow as she glared into his face. "Just because I haven't had sex yet doesn't mean I don't have a clue what it involves. I've read a lot of romance novels." When he rolled his eyes, she smiled, undeterred. "You might be surprised that you'd enjoy some of them, especially military romances. But I'm not wet behind the ears when it comes to what happens between a man and woman in bed, any more than I am when it comes to kink. Everyone has to start somewhere."

"You do know that you can have a kink experience without sex."

She pursed her lips. "Well, yes, in theory. But it would be more fun with sex, I would think. I know how excited I get reading about it."

He remained silent for a long, tense moment. "Rule number one—I will engage with you in light kink, but no sex. I will help you explore your submissive side. As you said at dinner, it might help me regain some of the control I've been missing in my life lately."

"I was talking about restraining *you* then."

"Don't even entertain the thought."

Megan grinned. She could hold off on a scene like that. What did she know about restraining someone safely anyway? She had a lot to learn and a short time to learn it.

Time to continue this negotiation. "Define sex."

"Intercourse."

"So you'll touch my clit or my breasts?"

"In a scene, I'll touch anything that isn't a hard limit. I just won't take your virginity. Popping your kink cherry is monumental enough for me."

She couldn't believe how quickly things had evolved from a notion after her encounter with the coyote to negotiating her first scene with Ryder. Despite his protests about not wanting to explore kink with her, he seemed to enjoy it as much as she did.

"When do we start?"

*　　*　　*

Did he want to do this? Hell, yeah, but his wants weren't necessarily what she needed. They wouldn't have more than a few days together before she returned to her world. How would she handle such a short-term relationship? Of course, they could still get together on occasion for a scene—even dinner, drinks, or a movie. He enjoyed spending time with her as a friend, first and foremost.

Ryder pulled away from her and rolled off the bed. "Wait here. I need to get some things ready first."

Disappointment warred with anticipation on her face when he glanced down at her. Maybe he could start building that anticipation to heights she'd never imagined.

"Before I go, you will try the first position I want you to practice."

"Position?" Her voice grew husky, making his cock strain against his jeans.

"Get up from the bed and stand there." While she moved to follow his order, he walked around the bed toward her.

"I want you on your knees while you wait for me."

After a slight hesitation, she reached for the bed and lowered herself to the rug at their feet.

"Hands behind your back."

"Are you going to handcuff me?"

"Jesus, no. Not unless you're into pain. But no worries. I don't even own a pair of handcuffs. All my cuffs are leather."

Her pupils dilated at the word leather.

"Sit back on your heels, back straight and tall, and I want you to stare only at this spot on the rug." His toe showed her where he wanted her gaze, and she assumed the position.

"Very nice. Stay there until I return."

"Yes, Sir."

His cock strained even more at her unwavering obedience. "Who taught you to call a Dom Sir?"

She grinned. "Master Z."

"So you've had some experience with BDSM before?" Why had he thought she was a novice?

"No. Well, not in real life. He's a Dom in a series of books I read. I guess you could say he was my first Dom."

Was he one of the Doms she fantasized about when playing with her Hitachi? She seemed to have learned a lot about protocols from her novels.

He walked down the hall to his bedroom. He'd built this room onto the house, with blueprints provided by Carlos for what he wanted to have in his home someday. Unlike the older parts of the house, this one had a wall of windows, with a French door opening onto a patio where he had installed a hot tub and a sauna.

Before he'd left on this mission the other day, he'd made the pine-log, king-sized bed using the midnight blue and orange Indian blanket Mrs. Chosa had woven. The blanket didn't cover the entire bed, but he liked being surrounded by familiar things in his safe haven.

The bedposts would provide some excellent tie-down points for bondage, but he had no intention of doing that with Megan. Not in this room, or this bed, anyway. He wouldn't be able to stand it when she left as it was, but having his bedroom filled with her memory? Her scent? No. They would make her bedroom their playroom.

He stared at the toy bag on the bed and, with a sigh, opened it again. The first implements he pulled out were a pair of buffalo hide floggers. Fourteen inches. Great for Florentine floggings. Probably not for a beginner, though, so he set them aside.

Damn, it had been so long since he'd negotiated a scene with a new partner, he hadn't even thought to discuss pain levels or her hard limits. They would remedy that when he returned to her bedroom. Next, he pulled out a riding crop. She seemed to like leather. He'd bought this one at a powwow at a pueblo up the road two summers ago.

A package of nipple clamps followed. Too advanced for her, but he grabbed a couple of clothespins instead. Oh, yeah. Her nipples were fucking responsive to the slightest touch or look. He'd have some fun with these tonight, but would eventually advance to the clamps.

He pulled out a few more items and decided her first lesson would be experiencing how a variety of implements made her feel.

She hadn't freaked out when he'd covered her eyes while they'd been hiking. If she consented and he was certain she had no fear, he might blindfold her. An invisible weight lifted off his body. He hadn't had this much anticipation for having fun in a very long time.

No. This wasn't about him having fun, but more about showing her how to have fun. Kinky fun.

Ryder smiled. What god had he pleased so well to have this woman drop into his life to become such a willing and eager partner?

He looked forward to tonight more than he had any other night in a long while.

Chapter Thirteen

Megan knelt, waiting for Ryder to return. She hoped he'd return soon. He would. She trusted him.

Would he ask her to remove her clothes at some point? At least her hysterectomy had been done laparoscopically. Only tiny scars remained from her four surgeries.

She wanted to feel his callused hand and whatever toys he brought to play with rubbing against her bare skin. Her face flushed thinking about what he might introduce her to on their first night.

Her nipples strained against her bra. The thought of him pinching them to even harder peaks made her wet between her legs. Dear God, just thinking about him and what he might do had her near the point of an orgasm. How would she last if he chose to torment her too long?

His footsteps sounded in the hallway, and she straightened her back even more, worried she might have slacked off in maintaining the position he'd asked her to hold. She wanted him to be impressed with her eagerness to please, at least. The thought of disappointing him made her stomach churn.

"Very pretty, Baby. You did well."

Her nervousness dissipated at his words of approval. She met his gaze. "Thank you, Sir."

"Where is your gaze supposed to be?"

"Oh, I forgot!" She stared at the invisible spot on the floor about where he'd indicated earlier.

"It takes time to learn discipline, Megan, but try to concentrate on the few commands I give you. I will try not to overload you all at once."

Those words made it sound like tonight was only the beginning. God, she hoped so.

"Now, I want you to avert your gaze and look at the window."

As she followed his new command, Ryder proceeded to the bed. It was dark outside, but she wasn't asked to look *out* the window, just *at* it. She listened for the sound of chains or metal clanking, but heard nothing. A few minutes later, he pulled the chair from the desk closer to where she knelt and sat down. She started to look toward him, but remembered she needed to wait for instructions.

This submission stuff was harder than she'd anticipated.

"Look at me, Baby."

She turned her head toward him. If he kept calling her Baby, she was going to lose her heart. Red was a fun nickname, but Baby just made her melt.

"Are you feeling any discomfort?"

She brought her focus back. "Well, now that you ask, my knees hurt."

He reached onto the bed and tossed a pillow onto the floor. "Crawl onto the pillow and turn your body toward me when you get back into position."

She complied and waited. He had removed his shirt and donned a leather vest. His chest muscles peeked from between the lapels of the vest, making her want to reach out and see if they were as firm as they appeared to be. His abdominals were just as ripped. The man hadn't let his body go to pot after his service ended.

She waited for him to say something, but he remained silent. His gaze made her aware of her body in ways she never had been before, and she hoped he saw something he liked. Her breasts were tiny, and her waist thicker than she'd like. He couldn't see her hips, but he seemed to enjoy the view when they were down at the Rio Guadalupe wading in the water.

As he continued to stare in silence, she felt her nipples grow hard again. She'd never had a problem with them being so responsive before, but they seemed to react to Ryder at the drop of a hat.

He reached out and pinched them, and she gasped, not expecting such intimate contact so soon.

"Your breasts are beautiful."

Should she answer him? It really wasn't a question or command.

"How would you feel about baring them for me?"

Her stomach flip-flopped. "I…I would like that, Sir."

"Remove your tank top."

She brought her hands forward, not expecting them to be so stiff. How long had she been in this position? Not wanting to disappoint him, though, she grabbed the hem of her shirt and lifted it over her head. Her shirt having the bra cups sewn in, she was bared to him in one fell swoop. The cool air brushed over her skin, and her nipples bunched even tighter.

Once again, he reached out, brushing his knuckles over her bared peaks. "Very nice. I'd like to clamp them. Would that be a limit for you?"

"I'm not sure what my limits are yet. I haven't tried anything. I don't think I like whips or knives." Would he have thought of using his lethal-looking knife on her if she hadn't put that on her list of limits? She shuddered. "Needles would be out of the question. I can't even stand getting shots or having blood drawn."

"What else would be your limit? Would you enjoy being spanked on your bare bottom?"

Not even her parents had spanked her. "I'm not sure. But I could try, and if it's a problem, I'll just say scarlet."

"Good girl. You remembered your safeword to stop. You also can have a word to tell me you need to slow down. Yellow is common. It's easy to remember from traffic signals. Any time you use scarlet or yellow, we'll stop and discuss what you're experiencing and how to proceed—or not."

"Okay."

"Aren't you forgetting something?"

She didn't think so. Scarlet to stop everything. Yellow to slow down. *Oh, crap!*

"Sir! I keep forgetting."

He laughed, letting her know he wasn't annoyed. "You're actually doing better than most newbie subs would."

Without warning, he took her nipples between his index and middle fingers and squeezed harder than before. This time, he pulled her toward him by her nipples. She tried to hold her position until the pain became too much, and she leaned forward to ease the tension.

"Did I give you permission to move?"

"No, but it hurt."

"Why didn't you use one of your safewords?"

"To be honest, I didn't think about them in the moment."

He stood up and walked away, and she thought he was going to end their session. She wanted to plead with him to give her another chance, but didn't want to appear whiny, either.

Soon he returned carrying two spring clothespins. "We'll have to work on getting you to think about using them rather than disobeying my command."

She had no clue how the clothespins were going to help, but at least he was willing to work with her even after she messed up. "I'll try to do better, Sir."

"Thank you. Why don't we test your pain limits? It will help me to know how far to take you."

"Sure."

"Is that how you address your Top?"

"Oh, sorry. I mean, yes, Sir."

"Good girl." He reached out and clamped a clothespin onto her already sensitive nipple. The pressure surprised her, but didn't hurt after the first pinch.

"Does that hurt?"

"No. Well, at first. Now it feels…kind of nice, Sir."

"Thank you for your honesty."

He placed a clothespin on her right nipple, and it grew more swollen. The pressure made them pinch even more, but she tried to smile through the pain. She wanted to please him and not wimp out.

When he reached out and pinched both clothespins harder on her nipples, she bit her lip. Holding them so they wouldn't slip off, he pulled her nipples toward him.

Ow-ow-ow!

He continued to torture her nipples until tears rolled down her face. "Yellow!"

"I wasn't sure you would ever give in. Why did you go beyond your obvious limits?"

"I…wanted to be a good submissive, Sir."

"Don't ignore your body's limits. That will please me more."

Crap. She'd messed up.

"Stand."

He held out his hand to help her to her feet and wrapped his arm around her until he was certain she was steady.

"Thank you, Sir."

"It's a Dom's job to take care of his submissive's needs."

"Well, I appreciate it." She smiled at him.

He walked toward the bed again before coming back to stand behind her. His lips were close to her ear when he whispered, "How do you feel about blindfolds?"

A frisson of electricity ran down her spine at his nearness. "I don't have a problem with my sleep mask."

"How about when you aren't in control of when it goes on or comes off?"

"Well, you blindfolded me on our hike this afternoon with your hands, and I found that…exciting."

"Interesting." Without another word, he placed a cloth over her eyes. It seemed to have an elastic band like her sleep mask, but then he took a scarf or tie or something and placed that over the first blindfold. He really didn't want her to see anything!

He tightened it into a knot at the back of her hair, pulling some of the strands, but she didn't complain. "Too tight?"

"No, Sir. Just right." His hands lowered to her breasts again, and he cupped them from underneath almost reverently.

"Beautiful. Perfect. Now, I think you've worn these long enough for the first time. Prepare yourself."

She had no idea what he meant, but he pinched open the clothespin on the left nipple first. When he pulled it away, her nipple became engorged. She screamed in pain, but he rubbed the nipple with the palm of his hand to quickly disperse the pain. When he reached for the right one and began to pinch it, she tensed.

His fingers stopped just when the nipple began to swell. "Breathe, Baby."

"Please, just hurry and take it off!"

"I. Said. Breathe."

She drew a quick breath.

"Again. Deeper this time."

Wanting him to remove the offending pin as fast as possible, she did so again. He squeezed the clothespin, and once again pain shot from her nipples throughout her chest.

"Crap, that hurts!" His hand brushed the nipple again as he'd done before, and the pain faded.

Ryder cupped her breasts again and placed a kiss on her cheek. "You did well, Baby."

The pain eased even more at his words of praise, and she smiled. "Thank you."

"If we have further sessions together, we'll push your boundaries for pain."

While she couldn't imagine taking any more pain than she had today, often going beyond her limits, the thought of future sessions with him made her happy. "I'd like to have more sessions together, Sir."

"We'll see."

She wanted to groan at those noncommittal words.

He stepped away, and his body heat deserted her. "Now remove your shorts, but leave the panties on."

At least *this* session wasn't over yet. She grinned. "Yes, Sir!"

"And you are to remain silent unless asked a direct question or you need to use your safeword. Is that clear?"

Her heart raced in anticipation of what this night would hold. She would never be the same after this.

"Yes, I understand."

When he saw the lacy thong she wore instead of panties, he probably was going to wish he hadn't given her this command, but she tried not to clue him in to her secret. She only hoped he would enjoy looking at her body as much as she enjoyed his.

Chapter Fourteen

Megan pleased him with her progress. He hadn't been sure he'd remember how to dominate a woman anymore. The last time had been so long ago. While Ryder was stationed at Camp Pendleton in the late nineties, he'd studied the art of Dominance with Jerry Patterson, a Vietnam vet who ran a private BDSM club in Los Angeles. They'd kept in touch until Ryder had been deployed to Fallujah. With his marriage on the rocks after returning, once he'd been discharged, Ryder had headed back to New Mexico and lost touch with Jerry.

Ryder hadn't been the only recon Marine who frequented the club, which he and others deemed to be far enough away from Pendleton and private enough to be as safe as could be expected. Shortly after 9/11, he talked a new roper in his Marine recon unit, Gino D'Alessio, into going up there with him and Sherry. D'Alessio had tagged along a couple other times, too. He'd liked one of the girls who bottomed there. Bianca or something like that.

True, Marines couldn't spend a lot of time in a club like that because, if they'd been caught by an MP, their asses would have been hauled to the brig. But Jerry was a hero to a lot of active-duty and retired Marines, as well as other military personnel. Ryder thought he'd somehow been given a pass from being raided or patrolled by MPs because he was helping a lot of them deal with post-combat issues.

Ryder and his wife had been at Jerry's when he heard the news about what had happened to D'Alessio in Kandahar.

Ryder took a deep breath. He needed to get his head back in the game if he was going to continue this scene with Megan. Besides, he didn't like dwelling on the—

Holy fuck.

Ryder's attention was brought back to the scene with a vengeance when Megan peeled her shorts down her legs, revealing two round globes divided by the thin strap of her thong. He took several deep breaths to ground himself in the scene. If he let his mind stray once more, he'd need to end this scene.

Looking at her beautiful body, he sure as hell didn't want this to end anytime soon. Unable to help himself, he reached out, placed one hand on each cheek of her ass, and squeezed. "Thank you for that surprise, Baby. Any others I should know about?"

"Surprise, Sir? I don't know what you mean."

He slapped her ass with his hand. Firm ass. Jesus, he wanted to take her over his lap and paddle her good, but that position would be more intimate than he cared to go with her. Besides, he needed to initiate her more slowly to the way pain could turn to pleasure.

"You know damn well what you're doing to me, brat."

"Probably no more than what you do to me, Sir. In case you were wondering, I enjoyed that smack on my butt."

Why did he get the feeling they'd just crossed into new territory where they could both find fulfillment, at least for the duration of this scene? For him, he had rediscovered control.

Control over her level of pain and pleasure.

Control over the types of play he introduced her to.

Control over how her body responded to him.

He turned to gaze at the implements he'd placed on the bed. He hadn't given her a chance to choose what she'd like to try. Perhaps being blindfolded, she'd be open to trying things that might have scared her at first glance.

He'd leave the blindfold on.

"We'll do some more impact play on your ass then." He took her by the upper arms. "I'm going to lead you to where I want you. Just relax and trust me."

She moved in the direction he indicated without hesitation. She trusted him so blindly? Of course, that's what he would want in a submissive—but he didn't want any attachment to this submissive beyond a couple of days. He couldn't let her get under his skin, because he'd have to send her home soon.

He sighed.

"Is everything all right, Sir?"

He realized he'd paused longer than necessary. "Yes. I want you to reach out in front of you and grab the iron footboard." She did so, leaning forward until she made contact. "Good girl." Her body was bent over slightly, exposing her ass cheeks to him beautifully. The implements were displayed on the bed before her, but she wouldn't know what he would try on her.

"Remain still."

He returned to the bed and looked at what he'd selected earlier. Paddle, crop, even the belt. Which should he use first? He reached down and picked up the paddle. It was wider than some, which would blunt the worst of the sting. Still, with enough strokes, the wooden paddle should redden her ass nicely. He hoped she enjoyed it, too, because paddling was one of his favorite things.

He wouldn't take her too far their first time. He mainly wanted to gauge her limits for pain, so he returned to the foot of the bed where he set the paddle on her back.

"Oh, that's cold!"

His hand smacked her ass. Man, he loved the feel of his hand on her cheeks. "What were your instructions?"

"Not to speak unless spoken to, unless I needed to use my safeword. I'm sorry, Sir. It just surprised me."

"You can expect to be surprised by any number of things tonight, Megan. You're asking to be taught discipline, and one of the first rules of discipline is to follow your Dom's simple instructions. Is that clear?"

"Yes, Sir." The breathlessness in her voice made him rock hard in seconds.

He grabbed one cheek with each hand and squeezed hard, bringing the blood to the surface. He kneaded and squeezed her ass for several more minutes until she moaned.

So responsive.

Time to see where her limits lay for the paddle.

* * *

Ryder's hand came down in several smacks on each of her butt cheeks. Not hard enough to sting, but her butt soon grew warm. She didn't count the blows because he hadn't asked her to the way some of the Doms in her books did. The spanking stopped, and whatever he had laid on her back a moment ago glided down her back to her butt. Flat and hard, it warmed to her body temperature quickly.

Ryder surprised her with a number of light, quick taps that made her butt grow warmer, too. He paused once more, and she no longer felt the object against her skin until—

Thwack!

A scream nearly spewed from her mouth at the impact, but she caught herself in time and gripped the footboard. What the hell had he hit her with? God, it stung.

Wow, this shit just got very real, very fast.

Thwack!

The first strike had begun to burn when the second hit. Her knuckles hurt from gripping the iron bed frame, and she gritted her teeth to keep from screaming.

Thwack!

He'd returned to hitting the first cheek again. While it stung, this time it became a burn much more quickly.

Thwack!

He laid the offending implement on her back, and his hands rubbed her burning butt cheeks. She wasn't sure if that made them feel better or not.

"How are you doing?"

"O-okay, Sir."

"Would you like this paddling to continue?"

How should I answer? No or hell no?

"Shall I take silence as a yes?"

"Yes, please. May I have another?" God, how cheesy did that sound? She read too many books.

Whatever was on her back remained there, but she felt something small and stingy against her upper thighs and on her already sore butt. It rained four more stinging smacks onto her burning ass, two on each cheek without a pause this time. She blinked and realized her sleep mask was wet with tears.

Crying? Well, this hurt and wasn't exactly what she'd been looking for when she said she wanted to try kink.

When a ninth or tenth blow struck her, harder than any of the others, she screamed, "Scarlet! Scarlet! Scarlet!"

Ryder's hands were empty when he placed them on her burning backside and kneaded her skin. She realized the weight of the first implement was gone from her back. She didn't know or care where either had disappeared to, but wasn't sure touching her burning ass was going to help. When cool air blew on her cheeks, the skin puckered into goosebumps.

"Ackkkk! I don't think that's helping, Sir. God, that burns."

"When did you start feeling the pain was more intense than you wanted?"

Oh, about the second swat.

"Um, maybe after the sixth blow."

"Why didn't you use your safeword then?"

"Because… Well, in my books, the Doms delivered many more blows than that, and their trainees didn't safeword. I felt like a wimp."

She sniffled, realizing the tears were pouring from her eyes harder now, and her mask was soaked.

"I don't want you to compare yourself to anyone else. How many times have I told you to listen to your body?"

"Lots of times." She remembered hearing it at least twice.

He rubbed a cool liquid or ointment onto her ass. "That will take away the sting soon."

"Thank you, Sir."

Sniffle, sniffle.

How much more embarrassing could this night become? What had seemed like fun at first had gone south awfully quickly. If she could just grab a tissue from the nightstand, she could blow her nose rather than risk dripping all over the bed, but she hadn't been given permission to move yet.

Ryder's hands grabbed each of her wrists and pulled. "Stand up, Baby."

She did so, and her butt hurt again from changing positions. He lifted the blindfold and mask from her face, but she refused to let him see her childish tears. His finger under her chin gave her no option but to look at him.

"I can't work with someone who won't tell me when she's reached her limit."

He was giving up on her already?

"I'm sorry. I promise I'll do better. I just didn't expect…so much pain."

"Did you feel any excitement or enjoyment of the pain?"

"God, no! It hurt like hell, and I just wanted it to be over."

He grinned, and she cocked her head. "What's so funny?"

"I think it's safe to say you aren't into pain."

"Without a doubt. But who said all kink had to be centered around pain?" Then again, judging from the implements lying on the bed, she found it hard to think of anything else they could be used for other than to inflict pain. Out of the corner of her eye, she saw a riding crop like one used on horses—was that the second implement he'd used? There also was a leather belt with grommet-covered holes, but she would have recognized that if he had used it. Might be pretty to wear, but she didn't want to feel that across her butt either.

"How does your backside feel?"

She realized the burning had stopped. "Better."

"Good. I think it's time for a little aftercare. We've learned enough for the first night."

Oh, aftercare meant cuddling. Megan smiled. "I'd like that a lot. Sir." She kept forgetting to address him as Sir, but noticed he didn't really call her on it half the time. Maybe he didn't look at her as his real submissive.

He picked up an afghan throw from the bottom of the bed and wrapped it around her. "I think I'd be more comfortable holding you on the couch." Before she had a chance to take a step forward, he lifted her into his arms, and she gave in to the feeling of warmth and caring by resting her head on his shoulder.

Cherished. She understood the meaning of the word she'd read so often in fictional accounts of Dom/sub relationships. Overcome with emotion, she sniffled.

"Poor baby. Rough night, huh?"

She nodded, unable to speak.

In the living room, he set her on her feet and settled himself on the leather sofa before he pulled her into his lap and adjusted the cover over her. His hand stroked her head and down her arm over and over.

"Tell me what you enjoyed about what we did tonight."

"The clothespins. Most of that, anyway. Oh, and when you gave me a scalp massage. God, you give great massages."

"Thank you. Anything else?"

"The blindfold made things interesting. Not knowing what you were going to do increased my excitement."

"Until I started paddling you."

She nodded. "I'm sorry I didn't like it. Is it one of your favorite kinks?"

"I have others to choose from. Don't worry about me running out of kinks to introduce you to. What did you think of the bare-handed spanking?"

"Oh, I did like that. It was just the hard smacks with—"

"I used a wooden paddle first then a riding crop."

"I thought it was the crop, not that I'd have guessed until I saw it lying on the bed." She sat up and met his gaze. "Can we play some more tomorrow?"

His smile helped right her world. "If you'd like to."

"Oh, I'd like that very much!"

"Let's talk a bit more so I can plan a better scene for you. I'm afraid I might have rushed things a bit tonight. I haven't worked with someone so new to kink. Anything else you liked?"

"When you had me bend over and hold the bed. The position was very…suggestive. Erotic. I don't know what to call it."

"You're doing fine. How would you feel about being restrained again, only both arms and legs this time?"

"I like ropes."

"Ropes, chains, cuffs. There are many ways to restrain a person."

She smiled impishly. "I think I'd enjoy that, but it depends on what you plan to do once you have me restrained."

"Do you like being tickled?"

"I'm not sure."

"Scratched?"

"Maybe, just not cut."

"How about various types of sensation play?"

"Like feathers?"

"Sure, that's one type of sensation. There are many others. Ice, chemical play—"

"Oh, I don't want chemicals put on me!"

"You don't even know what I would use. Could be as simple as toothpaste."

"Where would you put that?"

"You'd be surprised what minty toothpaste can do when applied to certain parts of your body. Of course, some Doms use Tabasco."

Oh! She clamped her legs together. "Okay, I suppose we could try something like toothpaste, but you can put Tabasco and other hot sauce on my hard limits list for now."

"The best sensation-play scene would have you blindfolded again and not knowing what I would do—or when and where the various sensations would be applied. Would you trust me enough to do use my best judgment as to what you might like?"

"You always stopped when I admitted I was at my limit."

"That's one way to establish trust in a sub. You do need to be more open with me, though, and not try to tough it out when you really don't like what we're doing. Especially when you're so new to kink. You could get hurt badly by making your Dom believe you wanted more of the same." He stroked her arm soothingly. "Over time, though, you may find that things you once disliked might interest you enough to give them another try."

"I'll try to keep my options open."

He chuckled. "You do that, Red."

Megan rested her body against him and enjoyed having his arms around her. This might be all they would ever have, and if so, she'd come away grateful to him for helping her explore the world of kink in a safe setting with someone she could trust. Maybe someday she'd find a Dominant who wanted to have a sub. If not, she'd have a treasure trove of memories of her time here with Ryder.

Chapter Fifteen

R yder awoke early the next morning and wanted to kick himself from his bed to San Diego for exposing Megan to his baser side last night. She was innocence and sunshine. He, death and destruction.

He glanced at her closed bedroom door on his way to the kitchen. He hoped she'd slept okay. Today, he'd watch for signs of subdrop, this being her first experience.

As he opened the refrigerator door to pull out the ingredients for break-fast, a gunshot rent the quiet morning.

What the fuck?

He ran to the bedroom to check on Megan, but when there was no an-swer, he opened the door to find her slip of a nightgown lying on the bed.

"Megan! Are you in the bathroom?"

No answer.

Her camera case lay open on the dresser. Jesus Christ. She'd gone outside alone.

And all he had to protect her with was his Bowie knife. He didn't even have his boots on, so he ran to the bedroom to retrieve them as well as the knife before running out the patio door. If he snuck up on whoever had fired the shot, he'd have a better chance of taking them down.

But what if he was too late?

Around the side of the house, he crept, heading in the direction of the gunshot.

"Shit, shit, shit!"

Megan.

He followed her voice. Had she been wounded? At least she was alive.

"Oh, God. I can't believe I did that."

Her voice didn't sound like someone under attack. "Megan!" he whis-pered loudly. "Where are you?"

Not bothering to quiet her voice, she called, "Over here! I think I've bagged your lunch."

What the fuck was she talking about? She'd said she couldn't shoot furry little critters. He rounded the sage and rocks to find her crouched high on one of the larger boulders, a sidearm dangling from her hand.

"Are you okay?"

"No. I think my heart's going to pound out of my chest."

No visible wounds. He glanced around to see what she'd shot. Several feet away lay a rattlesnake, squirming slowly, but definitely out of anything resembling its strike position.

"You shot a rattler? Did it bite you?"

"No. I think I scared it as much as it did me. When it started toward me, I freaked out and just pulled out my gun and shot it. It's not dead, though."

He walked over to it and gripped his knife. The bullet had struck the snake right in the head. "I don't think it will be using this body any longer. You're a very good shot."

"Patrick taught me."

He'd have to remember not to get on either Patrick or Megan's bad side. Fuck, if the man knew what Ryder had been doing with his little sister last night…

Offering a prayer of thanks to the rattler for sacrificing its life and for being a brave warrior within its territory, Ryder sighed and bent down. With one swift motion, he chopped off the head and, with another whack, the tail. Despite its appearing dead, he knew rattlers could bite for hours after death.

"Oh, God! Why doesn't it stop moving?"

"It takes a while. Sorry."

"It's not suffering, is it?"

"I can't say, but since its brain has been separated from its body, I don't see how it could. Its warrior spirit has moved on. The body's nerves and muscles cause the postmortem movement. Like when a chicken runs around after you cut the head off."

"So I've heard, but the only dead chicken I've ever seen comes wrapped in cellophane in the supermarket." For a city girl, she wasn't freaking out as much as he thought she might. "I guess I'm going to get to find out for myself if it tastes like chicken or not."

He turned toward her. "You mean you want to eat it?"

"Might as well. Isn't that the Native American way—to eat what you kill?

Besides, this probably will be the last time I'll get to try something like that."

He grinned. The woman was full of surprises.

Then she met his gaze, dead serious. "I'm going to make my time up here an opportunity to try all kinds of new things, Ryder." Her words were more a warning than a statement of fact. "Thanks for last night."

At least she'd dropped the Sir when speaking to him now that they weren't in a scene. Role-playing for fun rather than doing an actual power exchange helped ease some of his guilt over what he'd exposed her to. Then again, even the way she said his given name did things to him. Hell, she could call him shithead and he'd probably get turned on.

"Want to keep the rattle as a souvenir?"

"Um, no, I think I'll pass. I won't need any reminders of what I did."

He glanced over at her and saw tears rolling down her freckled cheeks. Cleaning his knife on some scrub brush for now, he returned it to its sheath and walked toward her.

"You okay?"

"Yeah." She shook her head, negating her words, and he opened his arms for her to come to him. Cradling her, he sat on the rock.

He stroked her soft hair. "Shhh. It's okay. We're going to cook and eat it. The meat will nourish our bodies. If you like, we can do a ceremony over it, thanking it for serving our needs, but I said a prayer over it before I made it safe to handle."

"That's okay. I already told it how sorry I was, just before I—"

"Then it knows."

"You think so?"

"I know so. He's moved on now to other hunting grounds."

She sat up and gazed at him. "We need to do a ceremony like that for you."

He lowered his hand to his side. "What do you mean?"

"A ceremony to let you know that your service is appreciated, but that you need to move on, too."

He glanced back at the snake. "Not the same thing."

"Why not?"

Because...hell, he didn't have an answer, but just knew in his gut this was different.

Gino D'Alessio had been killed in an ambush that left Master Sergeant Montague severely injured. D'Alessio had been deployed to Afghanistan sooner than he was ready, all because Ryder ended up with a severely displaced fracture of his arm while playing football during some down time on Super Bowl weekend in Kandahar. If he'd been more careful or had found a better use of his time, his unit might not have been caught in that ambush. Even so, Ryder would have been there to call for airstrikes in time to avoid the attack.

All my fault.

Jerry had talked him into coming to the club in LA again a couple of days after Ryder had heard the news of the clusterfuck with Ryder's unit in Kandahar. The club's owner mostly wanted to talk with him and help him try to process what had happened. He'd also been one of the first people to reach out to him after the tragedy in Fallujah, but Ryder hadn't wanted him to see what a mess he'd become.

By then, Sherry had moved back to New Mexico and Ryder tried to avoid cities, so he left the Marines and came home riddled with a shitload of guilt to wallow in.

"Hop down." He guided her off his lap and to her feet. "Let's get this snake into some brine. I'm thinking for your first taste of rattlesnake, we'll go with a chili, but it'll take some prep time."

When he retrieved the carcass of the snake, she cringed away from the squirming meat, but didn't scream or run away. Ryder held it to his side, out of her sight, as they walked back to the house.

"How often do you see Carlos?"

"He stops in every now and then. Haven't seen him in a few weeks. Why?"

"Just wondering. You're awfully isolated up here. What if you'd gotten bitten by that snake out there? You could die before someone found you."

There had been times when he courted danger, almost asking for that outcome. Hell, even a few weeks ago, he'd come near to putting an end to his pain. But the idea of checking out that way no longer appealed to him.

Not since meeting Megan. Or maybe it had more to do with having a mission to focus on again. He gave a mental shrug. Whatever it was, he knew he wasn't going to let PTSD rule his life from now on.

"You're right. I'll set up a deal where I check in with him at least once a day."

"You can always call me, too. Two contacts a day, one in the morning, one at night, and then if something happens, you won't be out here as long."

He wasn't sure he could handle being in touch with her by phone every day—and not being able to touch her body, hold her hand, kiss her. Jesus, last night was a fucking mistake he'd have to carry with him the rest of his life.

"Think about it, Ryder. For now, I want to know when my next kink session will be."

"We'll see."

Megan slugged him playfully on the arm. "I wish you'd quit saying that."

"Anticipation is half the journey, Baby."

He couldn't wait for tonight. He'd hate himself again tomorrow, but the thought of not participating in more of her initial journey into submission twisted his gut even more.

*   *   *

Megan knelt on the rug waiting for Ryder that evening. He'd touched her more often today than before. Innocent touches, but each one still sent her reeling. She wanted more. So much more.

Soon they would have their second session. He'd left her waiting here for what seemed like hours but probably wasn't even fifteen minutes.

"Anticipation is half the journey, Baby."

True. Her heart beat faster, and her breath became shallower just thinking about him walking into the room. This time, he'd asked her to remove all of her clothing first. He assured her they would not be having sex, even though she wanted him to be her first lover. But she would settle for the time spent exploring her kinky side. In many ways, it was probably as intimate as having sex would be.

Not that she had any sexual experiences to compare.

Blindfold already in place, she tilted her head in the general direction of the spot he'd directed her to gaze at yesterday.

With daylight gone, the room took on a chill, and she felt her nipples grow hard as an air current passed over her. Where was Ryder?

She couldn't wait for—

"Beautiful, Baby. Thank you."

She smiled. "My pleasure, Sir."

His voice came from near the doorway, but the next time he spoke, he was closer to the bed. "Want to try some new things?"

"Yes, Sir." If only he knew how wet she was thinking about this time together. Maybe—

"Take my hand. It's in front of your breasts." She reached out and made contact with his warm hand. "Stand." She let him help her to her feet. "Hands behind your back again." She complied. "Very nice. Let me inspect you."

Inspection? Would he find her body exciting or lacking in some way? He moved so silently that she hadn't realized he now stood behind her until he spoke once more. "So beautiful. Mine. For tonight, at least."

She went from euphoria at being claimed to sadness because he would only allow her to be his submissive for a short time.

The heat of his body warmed her backside before he wrapped his arms around her and cupped her small breasts. She wondered if his wife's were more ample.

He pinched her nipples. "I love how responsive you are to my touch, my gaze."

She smiled. He liked them.

His lips brushed the side of her neck. He'd instructed her to tie her hair into a top bun tonight. She supposed so he could do things like kiss her neck without a mouthful of hair. When he nipped at her skin, she moaned.

"Nice. Thank you."

She wasn't sure what she'd done to elicit his praise, but his words made her happy.

"Ready to play?"

She nodded.

"Speak. You can't know if I'll see a nod or shake of the head. I need to hear you consent verbally."

"Yes, Sir. Your submissive is ready."

The hands that had been stroking her breasts stopped, and she worried that he hadn't liked her referring to herself as his sub, but she didn't know how else to name it, at least in this moment and this scene.

"We'll explore some more boundaries tonight. See where to set more limits."

A tiny frisson of fear flashed through her mind as she remembered how much the paddling had hurt yesterday, but he cupped her chin and turned her head sideways while remaining behind her. "Remember your safewords?"

"Yes. Scarlet and yellow."

"When do you use them?"

She repeated what he'd taught her yesterday.

"Good. Use them if you need them. Don't wait until your breaking point, and don't compare yourself to anyone else. What's right for you doesn't have to be what's right for anyone else, but it's just as valid."

"I understand, Sir. I'll remember to use the appropriate word if I need it."

"Good girl."

He lifted her into his arms, and she squealed in surprise, but quickly regained her composure. He laid her on the bed. A moment later, he was fitting something on her right wrist. She smelled leather. He manipulated her hand and wrist. Something clicked into place before he slipped his finger between her wrist and the cuff.

"How does that feel? Not too tight?"

"No. Feels like someone holding my wrist."

He stretched out her arm toward the headboard. He seemed to be using rope again. She didn't hear any chains.

"If you feel any tingling or numbness, you're to tell me using yellow at the first sign. Understood?"

"Yes, Sir."

He laid her arm back on the mattress and did the same with her ankle, tying her to the footboard before moving around to the other side of the bed to secure her other hand and foot. If Carlos's grandmother could see how her iron bed was being used, she'd probably flip over a few times in her grave.

Despite being unable to move, the restraints didn't scare her. She trusted Ryder to take care of her, whether they were in a kink scene or walking down the aisle in the grocery store.

He pinched her left nipple, and she soon felt something cold clamping around the peak, growing tighter and tighter. Definitely not the clothespin from last night. He did the same with the other nipple. He tugged on a chain between her nipples a few times, harder with each pull. While it stung a little, she couldn't get over how it excited her, as well. Her clit spasmed with each tug.

"Like that, do you?"

"Oh, yes, Sir." The huskiness of her voice surprised her. She sounded almost sultry.

"Let's see what else you might like."

If he moved, he did so very stealthily. She waited, wondering what he would do next. When he spoke again, he was at the foot of the bed.

"Wiggle your fingers and toes." She did so. "Any numbness or tingling?"

"No, Sir. They're fine."

Instantly, she felt something softly move up the sole of her right foot. She jerked in surprise, but had long ago perfected a mind-over-matter technique whenever someone tickled her feet. Patrick was a terrible tease and loved to torment her as a child. When Ryder moved to the other foot and tried to tickle her, she didn't flinch.

"That's some self-control you're showing."

She wasn't sure if his words were complimentary or if he was sorry he hadn't gotten her to scream. She smiled and decided to take it as a compliment.

Whatever he had used to tickle her feet now traveled up her left leg. What was it? Too light to be his finger. Perhaps a feather? Whatever it was, it continued to make its way up her body. When it reached her upper thigh, she wondered if he'd touch her mound or clit, but he continued to move upward. Anticipating his touch, her nipples grew harder, and the clamps bit into them. She gnawed her lower lip, trying to keep from screaming out. But she didn't really want him to stop. She just needed to regain her self-control.

"Very nice."

The object left her body, leaving her wanting more. She strained upward with her torso, hoping to feel it just a moment longer.

"Lie still unless I tell you to move."

"Y-yes, Sir."

The silence stretched out, and about the time she wondered what he was going to use next, he placed something extremely cold against her clit. "Oh, God!" She jerked away, not caring one whit about composure. She just wanted to get away from whatever he'd put there.

"Lie still and remain silent, unless you want to have another impact session."

She took a deep breath and regained control of herself. Thankfully, she heard what sounded like an ice cube clink into a glass bowl or cup. Maybe he was finished with that torture and would go back to something more pleasurable.

Something sharp poked her side. "Yellow!"

The object was removed immediately. Ryder rubbed the spot and dissipated the pain. "Tell me what you're thinking."

"Was that a needle?"

"Not the kind you're thinking of. I know that is one of your hard limits."

What kinds of needles were there other than the metal ones? Pine needles? No, it was too hard for that.

"If I assure you that I'm not going to puncture your skin, would you like to explore this kink a little more?"

She trusted him. "Can I say yellow again if I need to?"

"Of course. Yellow and scarlet can always be on the table, no matter what we're doing. Even something we've done before without needing a safeword."

"Okay. I'm willing to try again and see if it's something I might enjoy."

"Thank you for trusting me, Megan."

"You've never done anything to make me question your trustworthiness, Ryder. I mean, Sir. I just panicked for a minute."

Chapter Sixteen

Ryder's gaze took in her alabaster white skin. He'd confirmed during their sessions that she did have freckles in places other than on her cheeks, including her upper chest and thighs. Seeing her stretched out on her bed for him, awaiting his touch, made his heart swell with pride. She trusted him. Implicitly.

No conditions.

No hesitation.

No fear.

What a gift to grant him. He didn't know what he'd done to deserve it, but hoped he would never shatter her trust.

He noted several one-inch sized surgical scars on her body and wondered what she'd had to undergo.

Anxious to begin again, he took three African porcupine quills into his hands and positioned them evenly so that he could skim them over her skin with multiple pressure points. They probably were sharper than the needles she feared, but he wanted to see if she might enjoy scratchy sensation play, and he'd never had a chance to try these out.

"Do not move, and you won't be hurt."

Her body stiffened, but she held herself rigid. Taking the quills, he applied the sharpest ends to her skin and raked them down her side hard enough to leave red trails, but not to puncture her. A sharp intake of breath was the only movement she made as her chest rose and fell. He continued down the side of her hip to her leg and then the inside of her thigh where he swirled them around. He watched as her muscles bunched, probably wondering if he'd go near her sex with them, but he lifted them away from her.

"How does that feel?"

"Scratchy."

"Is that a sensation you enjoy?"

"Yes, I think so. I'm just a little nervous. Sorry."

"No need to apologize. You're doing very well and lying beautifully still for me." She smiled briefly before he applied the quills to the inside of her other thigh and made more red swirly scratches. He moved to the outer thigh and hip and up her body until he reached her breast.

"Breathe. Not too deeply, though."

She took several shallow breaths, and he watched the quills poke her skin, but she always stopped inhaling before the quills could cut into her tender skin. "Good girl."

He lifted the quills away from her and placed them on the nightstand to show her later. He'd give her the quills to keep, or toss, because reusing them would be unsanitary. Not that he planned to be playing with anyone else anytime soon.

Only Megan.

With the pointy items gone, she took some deeper breaths. Her nipples remained rock hard. Perhaps he'd left the clamps on long enough. He knew the pain would be greater for her than last night.

Distracted for a moment, he just stared at them. *Jesus, she had gorgeous breasts.* High, firm, perfect—just enough to fill the palm of each hand.

Tonight he wanted to taste them, too. Sitting on the bed beside her hip, he reached up and tugged the chain up and watched her breasts strain. As he pulled beyond her limit, she arched her back. *Oh, that wouldn't do.*

"I'm sorry, Sir! I didn't mean to move, but—"

"No worries, Baby. We'll work on some discipline techniques that will help you to remain still in the future."

"You mean punishment?" She worried her lower lip.

"Some subs see it as a punishment, but I prefer to call it learning discipline. Much as parents train their children to learn right from wrong."

"I'm not a child."

His gaze moved lower to the red curls covering her mound. "No, you certainly are not." He wanted to touch her, but feared she would take it the wrong way and expect more from him than he planned to give.

Better to focus on her breasts. Less intimate. After all, a woman's breasts weren't solely sexual objects. They nurtured babies, too. An image of Megan nursing a baby flashed across his mind.

Whoa. Tonight, Megan's breasts were solely here to bring them both pleasure, well, after he gave her a little pain. He reached out to unscrew the clamp nearest to him.

"Oh, God! That hurts! Shit! Shit! Oh, fuck, fuck, fuck!"

The mashed nipple begged for relief, and he bent toward her to take it between his lips. He sucked the flattened nipple into his mouth and flicked his tongue over it until her squirming and cussing ended, and she relaxed against the mattress once more.

"We're going to have to work on that mouth of yours, too. You cussed like a Marine."

"Well, you would, too, if I did that to you."

He chuckled. "See if you can't control yourself better when I take off the next one." He reached for the clamp—

"Scarlet! Yellow! Take your pick, but please don't remove it!"

He grinned. "Now, this is quite the predicament, Red."

"You'll stop, won't you?"

"Of course. I already have. But you do realize that one of the reasons it hurt more tonight is that the nipple remained pinched longer than last night. And that last night was just a training clamp—a clothespin."

"In other words, I'm screwed."

He grinned, enjoying her sense of humor about the situation. "Pretty much. But I'll wait for you to tell me when you're ready, and I'll help the pain dissipate as quickly as possible as I have each time before."

"With your mouth—and tongue?"

"Yes."

"I did like that part, Sir."

He smiled. "Glad to be of service. Let me move to the other side of the bed so that I can take care of your tender nip as quickly as possible."

"Thank you, Sir."

Still, when he held the clamp in one hand as he began loosening it, she nearly bit her lip until it bled trying not to let out another string of curses. The woman had great potential for becoming a well-disciplined submissive.

She hissed as the blood rushed back into her nipple, and he bent down to minister to it as he had the other. Wanting to reward her for her discipline, his hand lowered to her mound, and he slicked his middle finger in her wetness before bringing it up to her clit. The nub was almost as stiff as her nipple.

"Oh, yes!"

He smiled around her nipple. There wouldn't be time to work with her on orgasm control, so he had no intention of making her ask permission to come.

He let her nipple go with a plop. "Baby, I want you to come for me tonight as loudly as you want."

"Yes, Sir! Oh, please!"

"But we didn't talk about penetration."

"Penetration, Sir?"

"Just my finger, but I wanted to be sure you consented to that before I went that far."

"Oh, I think your finger would feel wonderful right now, Sir."

"Have you used dildoes when you masturbated?"

"No, I mostly concentrated on my clit with the vibes."

The girl knew what she wanted. He chuckled before taking her nipple into his mouth once more. His finger teased the sides of her hood before he moved down her slit to press against her opening. Her virgin opening.

He teased her hole until she relaxed her pelvic muscles, and his finger slipped inside. In and out, deeper each time careful not to rupture her barrier.

The things he'd learned from Carlos, who had gone to school to become a gynecologist after his stint in the Navy.

Not wanting to overdo it, he retreated and returned to playing with her clit.

"Yes, there! I like that best of all."

"I'm sure your clit has had many a workout with your Hitachi."

"Um, yes, Sir, it has. Not nearly so much as since I met you."

He grinned. Jesus, she was so responsive. He wished—

Wanting to get her off and put an end to his torture, he increased the strokes against her swollen clit and sucked harder on her nipple.

"Oh, yes! Yes! Keep doing that! Oh, please don't stop!"

Stopping was the furthest thing from his mind. If they'd agreed to having sex in their negotiations, he'd be on top of her now. Good thing he'd been thinking with his uppermost head then.

*   *   *

Megan felt as though her body would come apart when Ryder let go of her nipple. She started to ask him not to stop when he took her other nipple between his teeth and pulled. Hard. She arched her back and wiggled her pelvis to get the maximum contact with his finger.

Alone in bed with her Hitachi, she had no trouble zeroing in on what gave her the most pleasure and took care of business in no time. Ryder seemed to be prolonging her release. Why didn't he hurry? Couldn't he tell she was near the breaking point?

The heel of his hand pressed against her mound, and his fingers spread her outer lips open. She exhaled the air she'd pent up only to gasp for more when his finger began flicking rapidly against her clit.

"Yes! Yes! Don't stop!" *Please don't stop this time. So close.* Just when she thought she'd fly off the cliff, he slowed again, and his finger stopped touching her clit.

"Ayeeee!" Her body screamed for release. Sweat broke out on her skin, and she felt herself sticking to the sheet. "Please, Sir! This is torture."

His mouth left her breast. "I'm sorry. Would you like for me to stop torturing you, as you call it?"

"Nooooo! Don't you dare stop! But you could go faster, couldn't you?"

"Is the submissive instructing her Dom now in how to grant orgasms?"

This was no time for discussion.

"Please, Sir. Use your incredibly talented fingers and mouth to bring me to a screaming orgasm. Whenever you're ready, of course." There. Did that appease him?

He didn't move. She wished she could see his expression. Had she pissed him off? Would he stop now?

"I see I have a brat on my hands."

Brat? What had she done? Oh, well, perhaps there was a manipulative tone to her words, but she didn't see that she was being all that bratty.

"I need you, Sir. I need *this*. Please!"

His mouth returned to her nipple, and she sighed inwardly, preparing herself to wait until he was ready to give her the orgasm she desired. When he began trailing kisses toward her hip, she wondered what he was going to do next.

The mattress dipped as he put more weight on it and straddled her body, his knees pressing against her sides. They hadn't agreed to make love, but he had been the one reluctant to do so. Would he rid her of her pesky virginity tonight?

He pressed wet kisses against her inner thigh, and she realized he wasn't facing toward her but away from her. That would be an awfully tricky position—

Oh, God! Surely he didn't mean to—

His mouth pressed against her curly mound. She tried to squirm away, but his hands applied pressure to her thighs as his thumbs spread her labia open.

"So beautiful."

Heat suffused her face. He was looking at her—there? She had no words to say until his wet tongue flicked against her clit.

"Oh, no! Stop!"

Why didn't he stop? He continued to play with her clit with his tongue. Oh, yeah. Stop wasn't a safeword. She didn't think she liked this, even though it was anything but physically painful. Should she use her safeword. She really should.

The feel of his tongue on her most secret place felt so delicious, she couldn't bring herself to stop him.

God help her, she wanted this.

She wanted him.

She lifted her pelvis to give him better access, but he pressed her back into the mattress with his hands on her pelvis. His tongue continued to focus its actions on her clit and everything else faded from her thoughts until he began pressing a finger against her vagina, and she nearly writhed off the bed. No! She willed her body to lie still and found that, when she didn't squirm around much, he hit the mark more often.

Maintain discipline.

Be a good submissive—and he will reward you.

His finger entered her vagina again at the same moment when the flicking of his tongue increased against her clit. Involuntarily, her hip jerked upward.

His mouth left her. "Lie still." His firm command had her lowering her butt to the mattress and waiting for him to resume.

"I think you've had enough."

"Noooo! Don't leave me hanging like this, Sir!"

"Remember yourself, Baby Girl."

If ever there was an inappropriate time to call her a baby girl, it was now. Her nails bit into her palms as she fought to keep from saying something that would lead to punishment. Or *discipline* as he liked to call it.

When his tongue lowered to her clit again, she let out a sob of relief. He wasn't going to stop after all. His tongue teased the sides of her clit hood, and he slowly built up the tension once more. As she neared the crest, her thighs began to shake.

Close. So close.

His finger eased inside her again. All thought fled her mind as his tongue flicked hard against her sensitive clit.

Holding her body as still as possible, she let the pressure build slowly until she hurtled over the final hill.

"Oh, God. Oh, God. Ryder, yes, yes, yes!"

Seconds before pleasure turned to pain, Ryder slowed down the motion of his tongue on her clit. His finger slid from her vagina, and she slumped against the wet sheets, drenched from head to toe.

"That was…the best orgasm I've ever had."

Ryder moved, and the motion of the mattress stilled. Without a word, he began removing the cuff on her wrist and then her ankle. She'd been spread eagle so long her muscles ached as she slowly brought them closer to the center of the bed.

She sensed something was wrong, but didn't know what. "Sir, are you okay?"

"Why wouldn't I be?"

He had moved to start releasing her right ankle now. His tone had changed. What had happened? She couldn't wait for him to remove the final restraint and the blindfold. She began shaking, possibly from the cold wet sheet against her body, perhaps from his very real withdrawal.

What happened?

Chapter Seventeen

R yder removed the last of the wrist cuffs. Her explosive response had shaken him to his core. What the fuck was he doing giving her an orgasm like that? He'd just taken this relationship into an area he'd sworn he wouldn't.

Could he then say goodbye in a couple days when she left?

No fucking clue.

He lifted the blindfold from her eyes.

She blinked several times before zeroing in on him. Worry wrinkled her brow, and he bent to kiss the furrows away.

He smiled, but avoided making eye contact again. This woman was too perceptive for *his* own good.

"What's wrong, Ryder? Did I do something wrong?"

Fuck.

"Nothing's wrong, Baby. You came undone beautifully for me. Now, let's get you out of that wet spot." He'd stretched her to the limit by prolonging her release.

Her face flushed, and he helped her to sit up and maneuvered onto her feet. When her knees buckled from the position she'd been in, he scooped her into his arms.

"Why don't you sleep in my bed tonight?"

She reached up and stroked his cheek, smiling again. "Are you sure?"

To be sure she hadn't misunderstood, he added, "I'll take the couch."

"Oh." Her obvious disappointment told him she had expected him to join her. Hell, he was in deep enough without adding sleeping together to his list of sins.

"We need to talk about what happened tonight. But would you like to get dressed first?"

She bit the inside of her lower lip and nodded.

"Think you can stand on your own now?"

Once again she nodded, but didn't say anything. He lowered her feet to the floor near her dresser and watched as she opened the drawer and pulled out a silky looking nightie.

"I'm going to shower first."

"Fine. Meet me in the living room when you're dressed." He looked at her choice of gowns again. "It's chilly tonight. You might want to wear something…warmer."

She shook her head and padded off to the bathroom. He walked into the living room where the blanket he'd wrapped her in last night laid folded on the armrest of the couch. Shaking it out, he placed it next to him and sat while waiting for her.

He sure could use a stiff drink tonight, but wouldn't add getting buzzed to the list of things he'd done wrong around this girl. Her footsteps alerted him to her presence, and he turned to watch her walk into the room, the nightgown clinging to her body and only reaching her upper thighs. Actually, he could see her panties because she'd lifted her arms to towel dry her hair.

"My hair is going to be so frizzy tomorrow."

When she hesitated about where to sit, he held his arm out to her and drew her onto his lap.

"Aftercare?"

"Yeah. We covered a lot of ground tonight. How did you feel about the various sensations I introduced you to?"

"Loved the first one."

"An ostrich feather."

"Oh, that's exactly what I thought. But I hated the ice or whatever that cold thing was."

"I probably shouldn't have placed it right on your clit like that without any warm-up, so to speak."

"I can't imagine anywhere it would feel good."

"You might enjoy having ice rubbed on your nipples sometime."

She plucked at the lapel of his leather vest. "Hmmm. Maybe we can try that tomorrow night."

He tried to tell himself this was for the best for her, but he still wanted to kick himself in the ass for saying it.

"Megan, I'm not sure I can continue to train you."

Her hand stilled. "Is it because I kept talking when I shouldn't and I couldn't keep—"

Ryder placed his index finger over her lips to still her words. "You did everything perfectly for a beginner. I'm the one with the problem."

"I didn't notice any problems, Sir."

He wished she'd call him Ryder—just not the way she'd shouted his name out when she came a little while ago. But technically, their last scene together wasn't over. He needed to talk with her about what he was feeling. Why they needed to put an end to their playtime.

He scrubbed his hand over his face. "I should be drawn and quartered for getting you into kink. We both knew it was temporary, but now I have to worry about what you might do when you go home and start trying to find someone who will continue to train you."

Megan pushed away from him, and from the glare in her gaze, he prepared for incoming fire.

"Who do you think you are? Why do you get to unilaterally decide it's over? I thought the lifestyle was all about communication and mutual agreements."

"It is. But as a Dominant, it's my responsibility to do no harm."

"What if I tell you I have no regrets? You've helped me explore something I've been curious about, but would never have tried with just anyone. Stop trying to be responsible for everything in your world, Ryder. Because some of us can take responsibility for ourselves."

She scooted off his lap and started to walk away before turning around again. He expected tears, but she wasn't finished being pissed with him yet.

"I'm not going to fall to pieces just because we aren't dating when I go back to Albuquerque. I've lived on my own a lot of years without having a man there to take care of me. I never intended for things to go this far, and I'm sorry. You aren't the only one here who's damaged goods, Ryder."

Her lips moved, but he couldn't hear her words. What did she mean damaged? She was fucking perfection.

"I chose the coward's way out rather than suffer."

Wait. What had he missed? Suffer from what? If anyone tried to hurt her, he'd kill them.

Tears filled her eyes now. Jesus, he couldn't tell her he'd zoned out, but how could he unfuck this if he didn't know what the fuck was going on?

He hoped they could at least stay friends. "I don't—"

"You know what?" She didn't give him a chance to respond. "I'm a big girl, and I'm going to be fine whether I continue exploring kink with you or not. That's not who I am at my core. I just thought it would be fun—and it was. Well, until now."

She glanced down, clenching her hands in front of her. He stood and started toward her, but she held up her hand to stop him and his words. "I think I'll head back home in the morning."

Ryder's chest ached at her words, and not just because of what Top would say. "That's not a good idea. We don't know that the danger is over."

"It doesn't matter. Patrick should be home tonight or early tomorrow. If there's any threat, it can be handled under his watch. Besides, I didn't come here because I was afraid of someone hurting me. I just didn't want to see you in so much pain." Two tears rolled down her cheeks. "But if you need to hide out here alone, so be it."

Is that what she thought he did here—hide?

Well, what else would you call it?

And while he tried to convince himself she was the one who needed him, the idea of her going away showed him just how much he'd come to need her here. He'd hoped for at least one more day together.

All the more reason she needed to go home. He couldn't handle long-term attachments to people, not even someone he enjoyed being with as much as Megan. People he loved always came to expect more of him than he was able to give.

This woman deserved someone as strong as she was, someone who would walk beside her and protect her from anyone who tried to harm her. Okay, he'd managed that last part these past few days, not that there'd been any enemies or intruders to fight off.

"Eventually, my shortcomings would have made it impossible for us to have any kind of long-term relationship."

Shortcomings? She was perfect. He was the flawed one. His mind had been so busy processing the fact that she wanted to leave that he'd lost track of the conversation somewhere along the way.

"Megan, there's nothing that would keep me from—"

Shit! What had he been about to say? Loving her? He raked his fingers through his hair and stood up. He couldn't love her the way she should be loved.

"I'll follow you back to Albuquerque tomorrow."

"No need. I'm meeting Patrick at the airport."

He hated seeing her leave.

"Good night, Ryder. And you won't have to sleep on the sofa. I'll just change my sheets and lay a towel on my bed if needed."

She turned and walked away. He didn't bother arguing with her about sleeping arrangements, knowing putting an end to all ties probably would be for the best anyway. Having her sleep in his bed would only complicate matters. He wanted no reminders of her in his bed.

Or his life.

Good luck with that, asshole.

He knew he'd never forget Megan Gallagher no matter how many years passed.

*   *   *

Packing her things took less than fifteen minutes, but she hoped to leave soon after daybreak. No sense prolonging the pain by adding more memories to their time together. She'd already spent too much time with him, revealed too much of herself.

And for what? He hadn't exactly reassured her that having his babies was no big deal. The man would make a good father, teaching his children about the world around them. Images of a little boy or girl with his black hair and tanned skin brought tears to her eyes. She brushed them away.

Ryder had never intended for anything to happen with them beyond these few days. She knew that, so why did it feel as if her insides were being ripped out again?

This was worse than any pain she'd experienced with endometriosis or her hysterectomy, because her heart wasn't so easily repaired. Why had she thought his knowing about her defects might make him see they weren't all that different? Both had unseen scars they hid from the world.

With or without the ability to have babies, he'd pushed her away tonight. Here she'd thought lacking reproductive organs would be the deal breaker in a relationship with a man, but even before he'd known about her defect, he'd been ready to call it quits.

Ryder doesn't want me.

Rather than try to sleep, she opened her laptop and set it on the desk to edit more of her photos. The few images she'd taken of Ryder when he didn't know she was photographing him drew her in. In a number of unguarded moments, he appeared to have been enjoying her company. Sometimes the camera could deceive. A trick of the lighting, perhaps. An unusual angle.

Still, she'd miss those times with him.

Could she settle for friendship with him over not having him in her life at all? Did he even care enough about her to want any contact beyond the morning to come?

"I said, I'm here. I don't make promises I can't keep…"

She'd promised to be there anytime he needed someone to talk with. Would he take her up on her offer if things got rough for him?

When the dawn broke and the light spilled through her window, she closed the computer and placed it in her bag. Picking up her things, she wheeled her suitcase into the kitchen.

Ryder sat at the table, a mug of coffee before him.

He met her gaze. "Good morning."

She couldn't think of anything good about it, other than the coffee. "That smells good." He started to get up. "No, sit. I'll get my own." She set her purse and bags down beside the suitcase.

"Let me fix you some breakfast."

"No, thanks. I couldn't eat anything." The thought of keeping anything down in this room where he'd begun to introduce her to her submissive side would be ludicrous. "I'll just have half a cup, and then I should leave."

"I wish—"

She stopped on her way to the coffee pot and placed her hand on his shoulder. "No regrets. But I promised you once that even if you needed someone to talk with at three a.m., or any time, you should call me. That stands. I'll be there, even if you just want some company." The thought of him doing something permanent to fix a temporary problem scared her. "If you let me down and I find out, I'll kick your ass."

He grinned up at her. "No worries. I've come this far. I'm not going to do anything stupid. Carlos keeps tabs on me, too."

Of course, he had Carlos. He didn't need her. She blinked away the tears before they embarrassed her again and walked up to the counter and poured her coffee. She didn't even pour half a cup. The sooner she drank this, the sooner she could go back to Patrick's. He should be home by now.

She didn't know what she planned to do beyond this summer, but the thought of staying in New Mexico no longer appealed to her. Maybe she'd visit Mom for a while in Chicago. And Adam and Karla might need some help in the coming months. They'd probably love having their own photographer to document their big event.

Whatever she decided, she'd keep busy. No idle time thinking about what might have been.

Chapter Eighteen

R yder sat perched on the red rocks overlooking the valley. The sun was setting behind him, casting a long shadow across the land stretched out below him. The last time he'd come here was with Megan, and her presence remained strong. As the first twenty-four hours of his fasting period came to an end, he prepared his mind for what was to come. Today, he'd looked back over his life, taking inventory while realizing who he needed to seek forgiveness from. The list was long, from his parents to Marcia to Gino and Marc D'Alessio to Sherry and, finally, to Megan.

He'd spent the day deciding what things he wanted to let go of, from the guilt surrounding the losses and injuries of good warriors to his inability to connect with people in a meaningful, lasting way. Tonight, he would come down from the mountain and be immersed in the centuries-old traditions of the purification lodge. Carlos would keep watch over him during his four day and four night vision quest, but in the sweat lodge, he would be joined by other combat veterans, all seeking healing and hope for their world.

The crunch of rocks behind him set him on alert.

"Just me, man. It's time. The sweat leader is ready."

Ryder stood and turned to face his friend. Both wore only a pair of shorts and sandals, even though Carlos wouldn't be going inside the lodge with him. Instead, he'd agreed to stand guard at the door, protecting those inside.

He still remembered the surprise in his friend's voice over the phone two days ago when Ryder called and told him he was ready to participate in the next sweat. His friend had been asking him to do one for years, but Ryder had never deemed himself ready. Perhaps unworthiness was a significant reason for holding back, too.

Finding that a purification lodge ceremony was scheduled for fellow veterans only two days later made Ryder grateful he had gotten his head out of his ass in time to participate. He needed to reclaim his life. He only hoped he would find the answers he needed. He couldn't go on living a shadow life, one in which he kept those he loved at a distance while merely going through the motions of existing.

Hell, Megan's leaving had shown him he didn't do existing all that well, either.

Ryder missed her more than anything he'd lost before in his life. Jesus, he'd screwed things up. Even though he knew she'd be better off without him, damn it, he wanted more in life than to remain alone and in hiding on this mountain. He wanted his life back.

One thing he'd come to realize during this initial day of fasting and reflection was that he really had been screwed up before he enlisted. He needed to forgive and make peace with the father who deserted him and his family, as well as with the mother who had her own problems but at least had continued to provide for him and his sister.

Ryder bent to pick up the water bottles he'd drunk in preparation for the purification lodge ceremony. No beer, coffee, or anything detrimental to his body had passed his lips today. Not even food. Only water. He had been instructed to drink lots of water.

He passed the altar Carlos had helped him construct. It would remain throughout the four days and nights. When he reached Carlos's side, his friend turned in silence, and the two walked side by side down the trail. His friend stood a few inches shorter than Ryder's five-eleven. His stride was long and sure.

The man had been a rock to Ryder for more than two decades. "Thank you, Carlos."

"No need to thank your brother. You'd do the same if I had been the one who had faced combat."

He hoped he would have been there for this man he loved more than any other, even more so than Master Sergeant Montague. He and Carlos had a history, a bond that no one could break. But Ryder was tired of always being the one receiving from Carlos. He wanted to give something back. To do that, he must heal great wounds hidden within.

They drove in Carlos's Jeep to the site the leader had chosen to conduct the ceremony along the banks of the Rio Guadalupe on the pueblo. Ryder's double-sided drum and stick were in the back of the Jeep. He wouldn't use it during the sweat, but planned to take it with him when he returned to the mountain to spend the next three nights. He hoped to make it sing once more.

Drumming spoke to him in spiritual ways other music did not.

Carlos had told him he needed to bring nothing but himself—and a willingness to be mindful and open to whatever happened. Of course, modesty was valued as a show of respect for the Great Spirit and the Relatives, so no one would be nude inside the lodge. And this one would be limited to males only.

After parking in the remote area, they hiked half a mile to the site. Ryder smelled the smoke from the fire before he actually saw the domed lodge, which had been constructed of willow saplings prayerfully cut down on the pueblo. Ryder had helped in its construction yesterday morning, although he hadn't been here when a layer of hand-woven blankets had been placed over the tree trunks. Those had been covered by an Army surplus tarp. A fitting concession to modernize the spiritual ceremony that had once been held under buffalo and other hides.

"Things sure have changed for your people, Carlos."

"Sometimes the more they change, the more they stay the same. The tarp is only a means to an end. The important work is what happens underneath it."

"Well, one thing I know is that I need to change. I don't want to run scared and hide out another day in my life."

"The elders are pleased that you are taking this step. They tell me they have sent many prayers up to the Great Spirit for your healing and peace of mind."

No doubt those prayers had helped lead him here today. "I can be a little dense sometimes."

"True. Stubborn, as well."

Ryder smiled along with Carlos. His friend didn't feed him any bullshit. Knowing The People had been praying for him made him see the need for this ceremony even more.

"They know you respect and understand many of our ways because of the time you spent here with me. You also have provided meat for our community's elderly and sick."

"It's a small way of showing my appreciation. Thank you, Carlos, for being here for me—not just today, but way back when I was a lost and angry kid in high school, too. Honestly, though, providing for others has given me a sense of purpose. I need to be needed. Knowing someone was expecting me to stop by with a freshly dressed rabbit or a mess of fish kept me going on days when I wanted to just put an end to the demons in my head."

"You scared the shit out of me so many times, man."

"I didn't mean to—I just didn't know how to stop hurting. You know your people are my family, too. Ever since your grandmother took me in as one of her own, I've been at peace here. Thank you for giving me this place to stay in after I came back to New Mexico." Ryder clapped Carlos on his bare back. "You saw I was lost and gave me a safe place to regroup."

"I didn't expect you to use this as a hideout, though. As you go through this quest ritual, I hope you will remember some of what you have been taught on the pueblo. No man is an island. These past few years I have feared you becoming another casualty of war. We've lost too many already."

As they neared the fire where the grandfather and grandmother lava stones were being heated, Ryder recognized the fire tender as one of Carlos's cousins and nodded in his direction. In between the fire and the lodge was the altar barrier. Rather than a buffalo skeleton, he guessed this one was of a cow, long bleached by the sun in the desert. At the base of the altar were offerings of sage, sweetgrass, and feathers he and others left during the construction of the lodge.

Most of the other men standing around waiting to begin were strangers to Ryder, and only a couple of them had native features. One looked to be closer to sixty years than forty. He wore a baseball cap identifying himself as a Vietnam vet. The younger men had likely served in more recent conflicts, most since the Gulf War. Like Ryder and Carlos, they didn't wear anything to identify when and where they had served. And yet all were brothers having served their country, most having seen firsthand the horrors of combat.

When the purification lodge leader instructed the nine men to prepare themselves, each man queued up on the tobacco-lined path to the entrance. Carlos, serving as the doorkeeper, explained that the tobacco represented the umbilical cord—and the lodge, the womb of Mother Earth herself.

Before leaving to take his place at the door, Carlos hugged Ryder. "Find your peace, my friend. Use your medicine. Your *verbal* medicine. Don't keep things inside any longer."

Unable to speak from the welled-up emotions, Ryder simply nodded and hoped when the time came to offer his prayer in the ceremony, the words would come.

Soon he stood before the lodge leader, being brushed down with the eagle fan and smudged with burning sage. Ryder bowed in humility to the Great

Spirit and re-entered the womb of Mother Earth following the man before him. Each crawled around the circle from left to right just as the sun moved across the sky and sat cross-legged facing the center pit. The last man to enter was the sweat leader who instructed Carlos to close the flap at the doorway.

The sun had set by this time, and the lodge interior became dark as pitch. The purification ceremony had begun.

*　　*　　*

"You are free to leave at any time if you cannot endure a round," the leader announced. "There is no shame in listening to your body and meeting its needs. If you must leave, speak out 'All my relatives,' and everyone will be asked to move forward to allow you to pass behind them in clockwise fashion to the entrance where I will signal the doorkeeper to allow you to leave."

The leader held the sacred pipe in his hand and filled the bowl with tobacco as he continued. "You may need to leave between the four rounds, as well, and are encouraged to take a dip in the river to revive yourself. Each round will last about half an hour unless we find more we need to talk over. I will explain the significance of each round as we proceed tonight."

After the brief silence where each man was asked to contemplate why he was here, the flap was raised, and the fire tender asked to bring in the first heated stones from the sacred fire. One at a time, a total of seven glowing rocks were placed in the pit that had been dug in the center of the lodge, with the final one being placed in the middle of the others representing the Grandfather. Carlos was instructed to close the flap again. The glowing rocks permitted the men in the circle to make out each other's forms now. Heat reached Ryder swiftly, enveloping him in warmth and taking the chill off the night. Then the leader poured water over the stones, and steam filled the enclosed space.

Wet. Dark. Mother Earth. The womb.

The leader invoked:

Grandfather, Mysterious One,
We search for you along this
Great Red Road you have set us on
each in search of the right path for himself.

Ryder drew a deep breath, momentarily distracted, until he heard:

Give us the strength and the will
to lead ourselves and our children
past the darkness we have entered.
Teach us to heal ourselves,
to heal each other,
and to heal the world.

Overcome with emotion, tears burned the backs of Ryder's eyes.

Shake it off.

Ryder's body shook as he tried to listen to his mother's advice and rein in his weak emotions, but just as he hadn't been able to remain stoic around Megan, he couldn't hide from the Grandfather, Grandmother, or the Relatives, either. A dam burst as a sob broke free, and the Vietnam vet seated to his left, a man he didn't even know by name, placed a hand on his shoulder and squeezed.

Rather than feel a need to hide in embarrassment, the older man's reaching out left Ryder feeling accepted and supported, just as Megan had done when she'd held him as he'd cried in the kitchen a few nights ago.

Spirits invoked, the pipe passed from one man to the next, each one offering up his personal prayer. Some gave their names and told why they had come. Two men asked questions seeking advice on achieving their goals, and the leader answered as best he could before inviting others present to share their wisdom.

Ryder found new understanding and truths of his own in hearing each man's words. All were equals. A sacred band of brothers. Lost souls all seeking to be reborn as the pure beings they once had been before the trials of the world had been unleashed upon them.

When the pipe passed to Ryder, he thanked the lodge leader and the Relatives for this opportunity to be here. "I am grateful to the Great Spirit for bringing me through to this point in my life and hope that I will find the lessons I need to learn from my experiences. But I have hurt many people I loved out of fear and anger over the past several decades. I ask the Creator for guidance and to forgive me for hurting those I love."

A vision of a smiling and radiant Megan swam before his eyes. *Jesus, how he loved her.* She might not be able to forgive him for the way he'd pushed her away, but he would have to ask anyway. She'd brought into his dark world her innocence and joy for living, and he'd stomped on her heart.

Forgive me, Baby.

He passed the pipe to the veteran on his left who held it a long time before speaking. "My name is Joe, and I've spent the last thirty-eight years trying to kill myself with drugs and booze and a lot of other reckless activities. I haven't been able to forgive this country for the way it left us to have to fight our way home, too." Ryder reached over and squeezed the man's shoulder, much as the man had done for him a few moments earlier. Those were dark days in this country. Vietnam veterans still got the shaft from the government sometimes when it came to recognizing combat-related illness.

Joe cleared his throat before continuing. "I have grandkids now. I don't want them to have to go through what I did, and I don't want to screw up their lives by being a bad role model. I'm here to ask God to help me be the warrior I once was and to fight off the enemy—the enemy within."

Ryder hoped the man found his peace. Someday he'd like to be a father, maybe even a grandfather, and he didn't want to shame his family any more than he had already done by shutting them out. When he finished his quest, he wanted to get together with Marcia. He didn't expect to ever know where his dad had gotten to, but could still forgive him and his mom. Some people weren't cut out to be parents.

The round ended, and several men went outside, but Ryder and Joe remained with the leader as the old stones were replaced with new ones. Ryder and Joe asked the leader for more ideas to overcome the darkness in their lives.

In the second round, each man was recognized for his courage, endurance, strength, and other honorable characteristics. Accepting their positive words and prayers helped put his feelings of shortcomings into perspective.

By the time the third round of rocks had been brought in, Ryder became lightheaded as sweat poured from his body. The fast had probably helped to accelerate the process. As the leader recognized knowledge and wisdom and prayed that each man would follow along their paths in all their endeavors, Ryder saw Gino D'Alessio's face before him. The man looked the way he remembered him before his first deployment. Eager. Fresh. Innocent.

Tears welled in his eyes again.

"Forgive me."

"Nothing to forgive. You were there for my brother when he fell. No telling what would have happened if you hadn't been there. Marco needs a keeper." Gino laughed.

Ryder smiled. The brothers had some kind of rivalry going on back when Ryder had known Gino. The first D'Alessio brother he'd met had told him about a woman they'd fought over, but from what Ryder recalled of those nights in the bars in Oceanside, Gino hadn't loved the woman. He'd only wanted to protect his brother.

True brothers. Just like Carlos and Ryder. Ryder wouldn't let anything come between him and his family again, including Carlos.

"Stay strong, brother. Not your fault," Gino said before the vision faded away.

"I will. You, too." He didn't understand what he meant about something not being his fault, but he hoped Gino and Sergeant Miller were at peace in the afterlife.

Deciding to listen to his body, Ryder took advantage of the opportunity to break after this round. Carlos didn't speak to him as he left, but nodded his encouragement. Ryder took a plunge in the river, the water near freezing in comparison to the heat of his skin.

Invigorated, he shook off the water and returned with the others who had left as the fourth and final round began. After being reminded of each of the earlier rounds, the circle was completed with a focus on growth and maturing, from which healing comes.

In conclusion, the leader spoke about how all who walked the earth were related. "What happens to one of us will inevitably impact many others of us."

Ryder saw how his inability to forgive himself for his shortcomings—and even things beyond his control—had made it impossible for him to move on the fulfilling path intended for him in this life.

Ryder prepared to leave the lodge ceremony with a newfound connection with his spiritual side. He'd gone through the motions for years—meditation, nature hikes, time alone in the mountains—but the mental blocks he'd surrounded himself with had kept him from finding understanding and peace within his world.

Crawling out of the lodge, Ryder experienced the sense of being reborn. Just as on the day his mother had birthed him, the future was wide open with endless possibilities. He'd shed the past hurts and mistakes just as he'd shed the sweat from his body.

He would no longer allow shame, anger, and other negative emotions to overshadow everything good in his life. Nothing in life was black and white. No person was all bad or all good.

Before rejoining Carlos for the drive back up the mountain to complete two more nights in his vision quest ritual, he stopped to speak with Joe. After learning the man hadn't chosen to do a vision quest, he knew it was time to say goodbye and told him if he ever wanted to just come and hang out up on the mountain, the door would be open as long as he lived there. He didn't have anything to write his address or number on, but told him to just ask the lodge leader or Carlos. They'd know how to find him.

With a gruff voice and red-rimmed eyes, Joe replied, "Thank you, brother. Same goes for me. Any time. Today's the first day of a new life. Let's make the most out of our new paths."

*   *   *

On the fourth day of his vision quest, Ryder sat cross-legged on the mountain. He'd been in and out of consciousness the past few hours. Spirits of the living and the dead visited him to impart their wisdom, their forgiveness, and their love.

He reached for a bottle of water from the pack Carlos must have left recently, judging from the temperature of the cold water. His friend had watched over Ryder during his quest, ensuring his safety, but they had not met face to face since the night of the purification lodge. Ryder did leave several stones for Carlos in a spot between the house and the ledge where they had agreed upon, letting Carlos know they had a bond as old as the Earth.

Occasionally, Ryder heard chanting and drumming from the valley below where those at the base camp ate, sang, and danced, occasionally using binoculars to check on the three men who also had chosen to undergo vision quests.

But Carlos preferred to watch over Ryder the way it had been done for centuries. Ryder felt safe knowing Carlos was nearby.

A rustling in the brush made Ryder turn to his right, and he spotted the amber-eyed coyote that Megan and he had encountered up here.

"Hello, my brother."

The coyote stared at him, as if measuring his worth. Telepathically, the creature said, "You take life too seriously. You need to find a balance between wisdom and playfulness."

He'd learned firsthand what could happen when people let play take them away from what they should be focusing on. He'd gotten injured playing football in Kandahar, and Gino D'Alessio died as a result.

Shake it off.

He needed to shake off negative thoughts like that. Without speaking aloud, he asked, "Are you my spirit guide animal?"

He'd waited for days for one to appear, the animal that would guide him spiritually on his new path, but none had come.

"No, I'm attached to your female. When will she return?"

He smiled. That made sense, because Megan did embrace both wisdom and playfulness. From what he recalled of the meaning of the coyote spirit animal, being a jokester was one of its main traits.

"You need to lighten up, Ryder. Play a little. Come on."

The day at the Gilman Tunnels, she'd gotten him to play by shedding his boots and socks and wading with her in the freezing-ass-cold Rio Guadalupe. She'd teased him into other playtime, as well, the night they'd first explored her kink side.

But the coyote also represented bringing a balance of wisdom and playfulness together.

The coyote left, and Ryder grounded himself again. He picked up his drum and pounded in a rhythm that mimicked a heartbeat. Just as he and Megan had synchronized their breathing, he matched the drumbeats with those of his own beating heart. As the sun set behind him, a vision floated before him, suspended in air over the ledge, appearing to represent the spirit of the rattlesnake Megan had shot.

The snake's primal energy force lived on, as did those who had been lost to this physical world. Mom. Sergeant Miller. Gino D'Alessio. They lived on in other places in the universe not accessible to Ryder at this time. Forever watching over him.

Carlos's spirit animal was the snake, and Ryder knew more about the meaning behind this one. If indeed the snake was his as well, his future would hold many healing opportunities, change, important transitions, and increased energy.

"Are you one of my spirit guides?"

The snake hovered before him, coiled, its rattle moving while not making a sound.

When the vision began to fade, Ryder called out. "Don't leave. I need to know!"

The crunch of Carlos's boots behind him caused the vision to disappear. "Christ, man, don't move!"

Ryder remained still while a skirmish of some sort ensued behind him. Curious when the struggle ended, he turned in time to watch Carlos take a stick and fling a writhing rattlesnake into the rocks where it slithered to safety for the night.

Ryder grinned, but was too weak to stand on his own. Carlos approached. "That snake was sitting barely a foot away from you. Shit, good thing I came up to escort you back to base camp."

"No worries. It wouldn't hurt me."

Carlos seemed puzzled at first then smiled. "Spirit-animal vision?"

Ryder nodded and returned the smile.

"Not a moment too soon. It's time for the closing ceremony." While some chose to conduct their vision quest alone, one of Ryder's goals had been to make connections with people again, so he had chosen the group approach.

Carlos helped him to his feet, and Ryder brushed off the red dirt from his black shorts. His friend picked up his empty water bottles, stowed them in a bag, and handed it to Ryder. Carlos carried the heavier drum and stick.

"Wait. I have some rabbits for tonight's giveaway." He'd spent time hunting earlier in the day. While he hadn't been as successful as he would be with greater strength, he wanted to present something to the shaman and lodge leader as a small token of what Ryder had received from this experience. He bent to pick up the animals, carrying them by their hind feet.

As they walked along, Carlos said, "We truly are brothers then. Let's go. After the closing, I've got a surprise for you at the house."

Ryder leaned heavily on his brother as they walked down the darkening path to the Jeep. He downed another bottle of water on the way to camp. Once there, everyone gathered in a council circle with those who had maintained the base camp, and the vision seekers took turns sharing what they had discovered.

When Ryder's turn to speak came, he was choked up with emotion.

Carlos wrapped his arm around him, only making it harder. He whispered, "Use your medicine. Your *verbal* medicine."

"I've spent a lot of time letting fear, anger, and guilt eat away at me. First in my childhood and later after returning from the military." He took a deep breath. "My life had become subsistent living. I kept people at arm's length or farther and shunned joy…and love. I've met someone I think could help me become whole again. My prayer is that she will accept my imperfections."

The lodge leader added, "Just as you will accept hers."

Ryder smiled. "Yes. My new path will be one of discovering that being human means there will be nothing perfect. I'll just have to continue to do the best I am able to with the purest of intentions."

Please, Great Spirit, don't let me do anything more to harm Megan.

When all rounds were completed, giveaways were exchanged, and the group feasted on berries, white raisins, corn, and pine nuts, among other natural foods.

All too soon, the time to break down the camp arrived. Ryder tried not to think about this as an ending, though. No, this was the beginning. He had his will to live restored—and the greatest reason of all to live.

He couldn't wait to go see Megan and share what he had learned.

Chapter Nineteen

C arlos helped Ryder into the house an hour later. His friend had remained silent about whatever the surprise was, but Ryder really just wanted to spend a couple of days rebuilding his strength. The vision quest ritual had been both exhilarating and completely exhausting.

"So she told me not to tell you she was here until now. But where did she get off to?"

Megan? Had she returned? Wanting to stand on his own two feet when he saw her for the first time since his revelations, he broke away and placed a hand on a dining room chair instead. Maybe she was in the bedroom. He wished he'd had some time to regain his strength before facing her—and maybe take a shower.

Ryder turned to his friend. "Thanks for everything, man. I can take it from here."

Carlos laughed. "She told me you might not be too eager to see her."

"Oh, I want to see her all right. I've figured out a lot of things that in the last few—"

"Wilson. How are you doing?"

Ryder stiffened when he heard the familiar, yet out-of-place, voice. "Grant? What are *you* doing here?"

"There's something I needed to tell you. About the break-in at Megan Gallagher's."

"Do you know who did it?"

She nodded, and her gaze strayed to Carlos. "I'd prefer to discuss it in private."

Carlos held his hands out. "Hey, I know when I'm not wanted." He turned to Ryder and smiled. "Welcome home, man. We'll talk tomorrow. Get some shut-eye—when you can."

Did he think there was something romantic or sexual going on with

Grant? Well, he'd set him straight tomorrow. Right now, the woman had information that concerned Megan, and he wanted to find out what happened.

They hugged and clapped each other on the back before saying goodbye, and Carlos left the two of them alone. Ryder turned to Grant again. "Want some coffee?"

"No. I can't stay. Just wanted to explain some things."

Ryder pointed to a chair, and they sat across from each other at the table. Grant fiddled with the woven placemat. What the hell was taking her so long?

Had something happened while he was on his vision quest? "Is Megan in any danger?"

Grant met his gaze. "No. She never was. I made sure."

"You? Did Top send you down here to check on her, too?"

Maybe he didn't trust Ryder to get the job done after all.

Shit. Some vote of confidence, Top.

But if Top had known what kind of shape Ryder had been in the night he called, he probably *wouldn't* have relied on Ryder to handle this alone. Hell, more likely, he'd have sent some of his Marines to check on Ryder instead.

"The reason I know Megan wasn't in danger is because…I'm the one who broke into Patrick Gallagher's condo and stole the computer."

Holy fuck.

"Why the hell did you want her computer?" This didn't make any sense.

She glanced down at the placemat and rubbed the bridge of her nose before meeting his gaze again. "Wilson, I've had you under surveillance since soon after you checked out of the VA Hospital. You had me worried for years before that, but try as I may, I wasn't finding you in any databases. It was like you disappeared off the face of the earth. Scared the piss out of me."

Now she made even less sense. "Mind telling me what business it is of yours where I go or what I do with my life?"

She narrowed her gaze. "I made it my business to keep track of you guys ever since Fallujah. You treated me as one of your unit and respected my skills, regardless of the fact that I was a woman."

"What else would we do? You were a member of our team."

"You don't know how it is in some other units. Anyway, since then, I've made it my business to make sure none of my unit becomes a suicide statistic."

She referred to the reports showing an appalling number of American veterans were killing themselves every day. Many were from Joe's Vietnam era, but he knew of more than enough who had served since 9/11 who hadn't been able to fight the demons at home.

But those thoughts were in the past. He wasn't going to let that happen. He had even more people to call who cared about him if things got that dark again. But did she have any fucking clue how close Ryder had come a few times?

"I thought hospital records were confidential."

"I didn't see your records, but I know you did time in the psych unit. I came down here looking for you soon after your discharge. Found Carlos and spoke with him, but he didn't know me from, well, Adam, and wouldn't say anything."

At least he could trust his long-time friend, but he still had no fucking clue what was going on and what it had to do with Megan.

"I met Megan at Top's wedding. We talked that week about a number of things, including how she'd helped her brother deal with his PTS issues."

Maybe Patrick's issues didn't cross over into being diagnosed as a disorder the way Ryder's did. No wonder he functioned a lot better.

"I broke in here and put a camera in your bedroom to keep an eye on you."

He stood abruptly, sending his chair flying backwards. "You *what?* What gives you the fucking right to—"

Her fist pounded the table. "Because I don't want to lose anyone else I care about! I'd do it again in a heartbeat. I don't care if you press charges—or Patrick or Megan, either, for that matter. You have to admit that, when Top put you on this mission to watch his sister, you came back to the living."

He had—but that didn't give her the right to…

Holy fuck! "Which bedroom did you wire?" If she had compromising videos of Megan, he'd snatch her blonde head bald.

"I figured you weren't into a frilly iron bed, so I set it up in the bedroom with the king-sized one."

He relaxed and sat down again, still not sure what to think about having Grant watching what he did in the privacy of his bedroom on a video feed. Lord knows nothing salacious had happened in his bedroom since he'd lived up here.

"You mind telling me why you involved Megan in your crime?"

Her mouth tensed. "Megan struck me as someone who could understand us and know how to deal with the pressures from flashbacks and triggers. I also had a gut feeling that all you needed was for Top to give you another mission and you'd get it together."

"Wait. Top sent you?" He shook his head. "No, Top wouldn't put Megan in danger like that."

"No. He didn't know anything about what I had in mind."

"What if Megan had found you in there? The woman knows how to handle a sidearm. Someone could have been killed." Ryder wasn't so certain Megan would have been the one coming out on the losing side of such an encounter.

"I knew her whereabouts when I went in for the computer. And I kept watch on the house the entire time you were there with her."

Some watch guard he was. He hadn't seen anything out of the ordinary when they came and went from the condo.

"How did you know she'd get in touch with him about the break-in?"

"I didn't, but before I could call him to alert him about a break-in, he called me to ask if I could track down someone near Albuquerque to check on Megan."

Everything had come together better than had happened with many of the five-part Fragmentary Orders issued during his deployments. Had the Great Spirit been pulling some strings for him? Clearly, the one needing rescuing was Ryder, not Megan. Still, that she had been thrown into the middle of Grant's crazy scheme pissed him off.

"Does Megan know about this yet?"

"No, but I brought her computer with me. I think it would be easier for you to take it back to her."

"Easier on you or me?"

She smiled for the first time. "Me, of course."

He ran his fingers through his hair. "Jesus, Grant, I don't want to have to tell her someone I know and once trusted was responsible for shattering *her* trust and security."

Grant flinched and her smile faded, but goddamn it, if she thought he could continue to trust her after doing this, she needed to have *her* head examined by the VA shrinks.

"Wilson, you two are good for each other. I hope you won't hold what I did as a reason to stop seeing her."

At least Top wouldn't blame him for screwing this up. "What did Top say when you told him?"

"Well…"

"You haven't told him."

"I was getting ready to yesterday, but Karla's…having a hard time."

"Shit. He must be beside himself. Does Megan know about his wife? Heck, she might be in Denver now."

"No clue what she knows, but she's still at her brother's in Albuquerque as of this morning. Adam's a private man, though, so don't say anything unless she does."

"I won't. But *you'd* damn well better find a way to fill him in on what you did—and soon. I'm going to get at least one night's sleep before I go to see Megan, but only if you've removed that fucking camera from my—"

"That's where I was when you came in." She placed a small device on the table that had been in her hand all along.

He reached over to pick it up. The thing was as small as a gumball and dusty. Looked like it *had* been there for months, and he'd never had a clue.

He met her gaze. "Grant, trust me on this. Top's going to be pissed as hell that you put his sister in the middle of this crazy-ass scheme. What the hell were you thinking?"

Grant sat back and squared her shoulders, but remained silent.

Ryder didn't want to discuss this any further and stood. "I'm going to bed. You're welcome to stay. Or go. I don't care. But you'd better call Top and come clean before I go to see his sister tomorrow to take back her computer."

This wasn't the way he'd envisioned his first meeting with Megan after his many epiphanies. Already his resolve to leave negativity behind had been cast by the wayside. Before he went down to the city, he'd spend a little time on his mountaintop and refocus himself in where he wanted his head and heart to be before he went anywhere near Megan.

* * *

Ryder's cell phone buzzed, and he looked at the screen. Oh-six-thirty. Adam Montague. Fuck. Why was the man calling him *now*? Had Grant made the call. Or maybe Top had found out what Ryder had been doing while watching over his sister?

In typical fashion, Top skipped the chit-chat and cut to the chase when Ryder answered. "Listen, Wilson, Grant just called and spilled her guts."

Making sure she'd told him the entire truth, he asked, "About what?"

"About Operation Rescue Megan. Or maybe Operation Rescue Wilson is more accurate."

Sounded like he knew. "Yeah. She told me last night. I have Megan's computer and will get it back to her today."

"Have you spoken with Megan yet?"

"No, I'm just coming off a four-day fast and ritual and haven't even been able to process that, much less everything Grant told me last night."

"I'm not condoning what she did—and I'm sure you feel as strongly as I do that something needs to be done to make up for this huge breach of trust. I'll deal with Grant later. I don't know how much you know about her, but I've gotten to know her as a civilian even more so than we did during that brief time in Fallujah. She's impulsive, vindictive, and her moral compass is more than a little twisted. Hell, the woman joined Black Ops after Fallujah to go after the insurgents who killed Sergeant Miller."

And Ryder had been worried about *her* wellbeing on that rooftop? Shit, she'd shown the recon unit even then she didn't crack under pressure.

"Did she find them?"

"She got satisfaction." Top paused a moment. "But one thing remains, if not for Grant, I still wouldn't know you were having trouble. You know the drill. Why the fuck didn't you contact me?"

His chest burned, reminding him to take a deep breath. Whenever any of the Marines who served under Top were discharged, even the ones like Ryder who left after Top retired, they were given his number and told to call him for anything, day or night.

"I've let you down too many times, Top."

"What the fuck are you talking about, Marine?"

"First in Kosovo."

"You were green then. You were always going to fuck up there. That's part of the training process. At least we weren't involved in any combat situations. Everyone came home. It was an excellent opportunity for you and a lot of others to learn how to be better Marines. Hell, we had no clue what was ahead of us back before 9/11."

"True, but I'd been in the Corps for seven years when I screwed up in Fallujah. I should have called for the preplanned strikes and—"

"You also had been given orders—by me—to protect Grant. She never should have been put in the middle of shit like that."

Is that why Ryder had been up there on that rooftop? How could he have forgotten that?

"Together with Doc, you all worked as a team to save Damián's life. I can't thank you enough for that."

Ryder's throat tightened up. "But I got Doc injured."

"I'm not sure anything we could have done would have prevented that clusterfuck or that we could have tried any harder."

Ryder cleared his throat. "Maybe not." He couldn't say any more. He needed to let it go. Move on.

Forgive yourself. It's time to heal.

Apparently, Top could hear volumes through the silence. "Something else twisting your gut?"

He couldn't tell him what Gino had said during the vision quest. The man would think he'd really lost it if he was hallucinating about dead Marines.

"I've had some issues coming to terms with Gino D'Alessio's death. If not for me, he wouldn't have been deployed as a replacement—" Less than a day after his quest and he already wasn't sure how much he'd forgiven himself.

"Not you, too." Ryder didn't know who else he referred to or what he meant. "Listen, Wilson, Gino might have replaced you after your accident—"

"A stupid sports injury. I got sent home for a fucking football game injury."

"Shit happens. Deal with it. But he wasn't there to serve as our FIST. He was half of a scout/sniper team at the time he was killed. The Marine serving as FIST did everything you would have. We just couldn't get any helos in the air until it was too fucking late. There was nothing you could have done to change that fact. The fault lies further up the chain of command, if anywhere."

Really? Ryder needed time and space to process all this intel.

"Easier said than done, but try and let go of the guilt. It just rots your gut." He paused a moment, but Ryder soon learned Top wasn't finished. "Now, hear this. Anytime you're having trouble with what happened in the past, you'd damned well better call me first if you need any kind of help. You got that, Marine? We'll take advantage of every program we can find to get you through it. Hell, we'll go OFP if we can't find a sanctioned program that works. Talk to Doc sometime about what it took to break through to him— not that I intend to repeat that process for you or anyone else if I can help it."

Ryder was afraid to ask for details. Maybe he'd get a chance to talk with Doc again when he went to Denver.

"Actually, Top, I already found some things I think are going to help." Should he mention Megan was at the top of the list? *Not yet.* He wanted to show Top he had his shit together before mentioning any feelings he had for the man's sister. "I just went through a vision quest and purification lodge ceremony here on the pueblo. I already see a difference in the way I handle things."

"Good for you. The Native American tribes can teach the VA a few things."

"I did this outside the VA, but it seemed to help me deal with some things I already had a little screwed up before I even went into the Corps. Issues with my mom and dad."

"Our pasts sometimes bite us in the ass. Trust me. This, I know."

Top had issues, too? Who did he go to when he needed help processing shit? He always seemed to be in control of everything. Maybe no one was immune to having to deal with those dark days. Maybe his wife had helped him. Having someone beside you at those times must be a comfort, even though he'd never forgive himself if he unintentionally did something to hurt Megan during a night terror or flashback. Still, he'd talked with her after some of them, and it really did help.

"Keep me posted. And Ryder, I think we can dispense with our military names. Call me Adam."

"Top…I mean Adam, I'm going to take a ride up to Denver sometime this summer. I'd like to hang out with you guys over some beers sometime and shoot the shit."

"Sounds like a plan. Door's always open for any of my Marines."

"Thanks. I appreciate that."

"Ryder, my best advice: Find a girl, get married, have babies. I highly recommend it." The man's contentment sounded loud and clear through the phone.

Ryder smiled. "Megan tells me congratulations are in order." He grew serious again. "Sorry to hear your wife's having a hard time of it, though." *Damn.* Grant had asked him not to mention that.

"Yeah, and I need to get back to her. Tell Megan we said hi, and we'll call her and Patrick with a full report soon. You be sure to call me if things get— hey, I've got to sign off now." Ryder heard him speaking to someone else. "Kitten, you should be in—"

The call ended, and Ryder was left frustrated that he hadn't gotten up the nerve to talk with Top about dating Megan. Maybe it was for the best. He didn't even know if Megan would want to have anything to do with him anymore. But if the time ever came, he wanted to ask the man for his blessing before he proposed to Megan. She loved her brothers, and he wouldn't do anything to place a wedge between them. They may not want her being saddled with someone as fucked up as Ryder was.

Face to face would be better for that conversation. Perhaps by the time he headed to Denver, he'd know how Megan felt.

Jesus, another city to face.

Maybe he could at least meet with Patrick. Talk about running a Marine gauntlet. But Megan would be worth all that anguish and more.

Ryder pocketed the phone and found himself staring down at the empty bed where she'd slept, realizing at some point in the conversation he'd zoned out and wandered into Megan's room. Not for the first time, either. He even slept in here the night before the vision quest began when he couldn't find peace in his own bed. Just having her spicy scent on the pillow calmed him down. He could close his eyes and pretend she was lying there beside him.

He'd spent a lot of time remembering those two evenings they'd explored kink together. No Dom could ask for a more eager sub. What might have happened between them that last night if he hadn't been running scared?

He'd thrown away the best thing that had ever happened to him.

Jesus, I miss her.

At least now he had a reason to go see her and try to make up for being such a coward. Even if she didn't want to see *him* again, she'd welcome back her computer. Should he call first and make sure she wanted to see him? According to Grant, Megan hadn't gone to Denver yet.

Time for a new mission.

Find a girl, get married, have babies.

Chapter Twenty

M egan adjusted the lighting on the tiny subject in her makeshift studio in
Patrick's condo. Photographing babies was always so bittersweet to
her. This chubby-cheeked angel stared at her with the biggest, bluest eyes as if
she could see through to her soul.

The work didn't feel as fulfilling as it once had. This week, she went
through the motions of shooting babies, recent graduates, and couples
embarking on their happily-ever-after lives together.

Well, at least she'd experienced one of those three monumental events
herself. The others she'd have to give up on.

God, she missed roaming around the land at Ryder's place and discovering nature's surprises. Just walking hand in hand with him as he told her about
the plants and the history and—

Stop dwelling on the past.

With Patrick back in town, she'd decided that tomorrow she'd drive up to
Santa Fe to meet Ryder's sister. Her portfolio was in great shape with the
photos she'd shot at Ryder's. Megan had e-mailed her some of the images, and
Marcia seemed enthusiastic about having some of them displayed in her
gallery. With exhibits in a Santa Fe Plaza storefront, perhaps Megan's new
passion for nature photography could take off.

Not that she would be going back out to Ryder's place for more shots
without an invitation. Fortunately, there were many beautiful spots she did
have access to in New Mexico. If the man chose to remain in hiding, then so
be it. She'd never set out on a crusade to save him.

Oh, but you did. And you failed miserably.

Once she'd returned home from his place nearly a week ago, she realized
he'd gotten dangerously close to breaking down her own self-defense
mechanisms. Their friendship had taken off fast, but their relationship had
changed forever the night she began exploring kink with him. Memories of

the vulnerability she'd felt while restrained that last night washed over her, but in equal measures, she remembered the strength and security she'd experienced. At a single word, he would stop and talk her through her fears, or just stop doing whatever wasn't working for her.

Why had he pushed her away that night? Had he hit a trigger? She couldn't figure out what had happened after he'd given her the most incredible orgasm of her life. Her Hitachi paled in comparison. She'd had no desire to even plug it in since she'd returned to the city. The difference between using the toy to provide her own pleasure and having someone else control and guide her orgasm—well, there really *was* no comparison.

A Harley roared by the condo, and the baby startled then began to fuss. The mother moved to pop in a pacifier, giving Megan the time she needed to regain her focus on this shoot. *Yeah, right.* Thoughts of Ryder were never far from her mind these days and now one of her brother's neighbors had a Harley. Images of the evening she'd ridden up to Gilman Tunnels on the back of Ryder's bike invaded her thoughts. That was where she'd first started to fall in love with him.

Perhaps breaking it off when he did was the right thing. What if they'd had sex? She already had enough carnal memories of the man to make her ache for a lifetime, but making love would have made it impossible for her to put him behind her and move on.

With the baby calm again, Megan took several more shots.

She didn't think she could ever truly move on without talking with Ryder again. *God, I miss him.* She'd promised to be there for him. Would he agree to dinner sometime if she called him? Certainly not here. He hated the city.

After spending time in his world, she wasn't too crazy about city living, either.

What would a future relationship with Ryder look like? Could she settle for being friends? Kink would be out of the question. That had quickly ramped up into something he made clear he wasn't ready for. Although the first night and most of the second, he seemed to be finding as much enjoyment as she was—except that he hadn't come like she had. Her face grew warm remembering his mouth on...

Even if he did decide he wanted her, would that be enough for him? Men who married usually did so because they wanted to have their own biological children. She'd told him she couldn't have kids, and the next thing she knew he was following her home to Patrick's and saying goodbye.

While the mother went to change the baby's outfit, Megan set a new background and props for the next series of shots, and the baby's mother stepped back. "You might shake the rattle in front of her, Mrs. Chynoweth." Megan thought she captured some great shots of the baby's startled expression, followed quickly by the most precious toothless smile.

She couldn't wait to do a photography session at Adam and Karla's the next time she went to Denver. They were experiencing both shock and awe these days.

Megan blinked away the sting in her eyes. *At least they know how lucky and blessed they are.* She intended to become the greatest aunt in the world, living out her maternal instincts vicariously through all of the nieces and nephews Adam and Karla would give her. Maybe Patrick would find a new love, too, and start a family. Anything was possible.

Just not probable for her.

Why had the future without a nebulous husband been so much easier to accept than going through the rest of her life knowing she might have had someone special like Ryder if only she hadn't made her irrevocable decision two years ago? But if not for that surgery, who could say where she would be today or what she'd be doing? Maybe she wouldn't have met Ryder. Even if they couldn't have more than friendship, living without some kind of contact with Ryder would be a great disappointment.

After the photo session was completed, she walked the young mother and baby down the hall toward the kitchen. Megan disarmed Patrick's new security system with the remote, and they walked into the garage. "I'll get those proofs to you within a few days."

"Oh!" The woman startled and held her infant closer to her. Megan turned in the direction Mrs. Chynoweth stared to find Ryder standing beside his Harley in the driveway.

God, he looks beautiful. Her heart pounded with a vengeance. "Hi, Ryder." She barely noticed the mother giving him a wide berth as they passed him to reach their car.

He entered the garage. On closer inspection, she noticed dark circles under his eyes. Had he lost weight, too, even though it had only been a few days since she'd last seen him?

What struck her next, though, was an inner peace she'd never seen before. His eyes no longer held that lost expression she'd noted the first night he'd shown up here. Even his body was more relaxed than before.

"You okay, Red?"

She wished he'd call her baby, which he did when they were more intimate. "Why wouldn't I be?" The man was too perceptive for his own good, so she averted her gaze.

He remained silent. Did he want to continue being her friend? Could they go from such passion back to mere friendship? Ryder needed her more than she needed him, but she hadn't seen him reach out to anyone else during the time they had spent together, either—not his sister or his best friend.

She met his gaze. She'd promised to always be there for him. Maybe that's why he'd come here today. Did he need to talk with her?

"Hey, I'm finished here for the day. Want to have an early dinner in Old Town? I know of a small place that won't be crowded this time of day."

He didn't respond for a long while, but she noticed a tension return to his body that had been absent for a short while. She expected him to say no. Finally, he relaxed again. "Sounds good. We can talk. But first, I have something for you. Wanted to be sure you were home first."

If all they could have was a deeper friendship, then so be it. She could settle for having one small part of Ryder's heart. She wasn't sure that would always be enough, but at least they'd be able to spend time together.

He returned to his Harley and unhooked something attached by bungee cords to the back seat of his bike. When he faced her again, he carried what looked like a desktop computer tower.

Wait. That wasn't just any tower.

She held the door open for him. "Where did you find it?"

"It's a long story. I'll explain over dinner."

He refused to let her carry it, so she showed him the way to her makeshift studio, and he set it on the desk in the corner. From a pouch she hadn't noticed slung over his chest, he pulled out several cords. "I'll have to leave it to you to figure out what goes where."

"I'll take care of it tomorrow. Let's go to dinner. I'm dying to hear this story."

A quarter of an hour later, they were shown by the hostess to a table in a corner. Ryder sat where he could watch both entrances into the room. She had always thought of this place as intimate and cozy. One of the oldest adobe homes in the city, its rooms had been converted into dining areas for the New Mexican cuisine restaurant.

Even though they were the only patrons seated in this room, Ryder's gaze kept darting between the room's two entrances every time a server walked through a door.

She sighed.

"I'm sorry, Ryder. If you'd rather go to the condo, we can make dinner ourselves. Patrick may pop in, but you'll be able to relax more there."

He stared at her as if he wasn't aware of what he'd been doing—or that she'd noticed, perhaps. "I'm fine. This looks like a nice place."

"It has some of the best red sauce in the city. The green's good, too, if you can handle the heat."

"Green's my favorite."

Why didn't that surprise her? Beneath the surface, the man absolutely smoldered. She smiled.

"By the way, I'm going to meet your sister tomorrow to go over my portfolio and put some consignment pieces in her store. Tell me what she's like."

"She's two years older than I am, but I've always felt kind of responsible for her. Our dad left before I was born, and Mom worked long hours at a demanding job. Marcia and I were on our own a lot of the time."

"I'm sorry your mom couldn't be there for you emotionally, although being a single mom has to be one of the biggest stressors in the world."

"Mom made sure we had a roof over our heads and our bellies full. Marcia and I were luckier than a lot of kids."

"I'm sure, but children need both parents. Of course, kids are better off without an abusive parent. Adam probably made out better in life by leaving. But he made himself a new family with Damián and Marc. Who knows? They might have been lost, as well, if not for going into business with him. I know they helped Adam, especially in the years before he had Karla. Judging by all the love in the house for their wedding, I'd say he has an amazing extended-family network set up, too."

"Yeah. I'm learning he cares what happens to us all. What kind of business are they in?"

"We didn't really discuss it much. Some kind of social club in downtown Denver. His wife's a singer there. Until he and Karla moved recently, they lived in the building where the club's located. Not in the safest neighborhood, so I'm sure the decision to move was because of the safety of his growing family... Okay, now tell me how you came to be in possession of my computer."

"Yeah, well, one of the Marines I served with, Grant—I think you said you met her."

"Mm-hmm. At Adam's wedding."

He averted his gaze as if the subject was too painful. "She found out I was struggling and, well, took it upon herself to rescue me."

"I'm lost."

He met her gaze. "No, Megan. I was the one lost. Let me explain what happened." He told her how Grant had broken into the condo and stolen her computer. "After you reported the break-in to him, Adam contacted Grant to see who lived nearby. She gave him my numbers, and he called me in to check on you."

"Wait. I know I'm not supposed to interrupt, but what would she have done if I hadn't told Adam? It was a random thing that he even called that night. Otherwise, I'd have just handled it with the police—and spent the next few nights at a hotel until Patrick came home."

Ryder smiled. "Knowing her, she'd have found a way to make it plausible that she heard it on a police scanner or something. I think he knows she's using her incredible communication skills these days to keep track of his Marine family."

He sobered. "I know this business with Grant is crazy, but it worked. Grant knew Adam would send one of his Marines here to check on you. But she didn't tell Adam what a mess I was at the time. I'm not sure I'll forgive her for putting you in potential danger. If I'd done anything to hurt you... Anyway, Adam called, and I showed up on your doorstep in the middle of the night. You know the rest of the story."

"That's not just crazy, that's *bat-shit* crazy. If I ever come across that woman again, I'm going to give her a piece of my mind." God, what if Ryder *hadn't* been able to handle the pressure? How could Grant risk his wellbeing like that?

"I'm sure Adam's going to have a piece of her hide for putting you at risk like that, knowing as she did that I'd spent time in the psych ward."

"Oh, Ryder, you're only a danger to yourself." She placed her hand over his and squeezed. "I believe everything happens for a reason, though. If I was meant to be the one to help you reconnect with the world again, I'm honored you trusted me enough to allow me to do that."

Their entrees came, interrupting the conversation, and they ate in companionable silence for a few minutes. She still had a dozen questions popping into her head about how all of this had happened, but hadn't enjoyed anyone's company since, well, since she'd left Ryder's place.

She'd suffered such emptiness since then.

Alone.

"I've missed you, Ryder." *More than you can ever know.*

He glanced away, seeming uncomfortable. "I've missed you a lot, too."

Was he just saying that because she had? He'd come to return her computer, so maybe she was reading more into why he was here than he intended. "Maybe we can agree to see each other every now and then."

When he met her gaze, she saw some reluctance. Or perhaps regret. "Sure, Red."

Somehow, she didn't expect him to ever call her for a romantic date. They'd quashed any chance of that already.

Ryder ran his hand through his hair and sat back in his chair abruptly. "Who the hell am I kidding?"

What did he mean? He didn't even want to see her as a friend? That hurt more than his rejection of her being his submissive trainee.

He reached across the table and placed his hand over hers, and she set her fork on her plate, no longer hungry.

"Megan, I'm miserable without you. Yeah, I'd like to be your friend. But I'd like to have something more than that, too." His thumb brushed over her knuckles and sent her nerve endings rushing to the surface.

He does?

Stay calm.

Hear him out.

"What did you have in mind?" Her voice sounded breathless, probably because her heart was pounding all of the oxygen out of her lungs. A significant part of what worked between her and Ryder was their deep level of caring for each other. She wanted something more than kink. What did Ryder want?

"Megan, I can't give you a whole lot other than myself and the love in my heart. I don't know when I'll go off the deep end. I'm sure it'll happen, but I'm working on getting my head on straight. I think I've found something that helps."

She moved her palm upward so she could grip his hand. "I'm glad to hear that."

"Someone, actually. You. My eyes were opened recently. I've got all kinds of possibilities ahead of me, but if I can't have you in my life, they won't be worth much."

"You know I'll be there to help you through whenever I can be."

Ryder stared into her eyes, and the air sizzled around them. "What I'm trying to say…" He ran his free hand through his hair. "Megan, I can't ask you to marry me, yet, but I'd like to see you while I'm working through some things."

Marry her?

He wanted to marry her, despite knowing she wouldn't be able to give him babies? He did remember that monumental detail, right?

Still, she needed to be cautious. Maybe they had moved too quickly—not that she hadn't jumped in feet first and without looking on every important decision in her life. "My time is yours, Ryder. I just want to be with you."

"I can't promise more kink until we're married. That last night," he glanced away, "things went faster than I was ready for."

No kink. "No problem." She could live without kink. It's not like she hadn't lived without it for twenty-six years already.

He met her gaze again. Now to set a few ground rules of her own. "Marriage, if it comes, will be a partnership. Until then, we can have a friendship—with benefits." She waggled her eyebrows and grinned hoping to lighten the moment. "Lots of sexy benefits."

He sighed, as serious as ever. "I'm not going to have sex with you, Megan, until we're married."

She sat back in her chair and pulled her hand away. "Oh."

"It would be selfish of me to ask you to wait for me to get my—"

"Why wait? Why don't we get married now?" Her stomach tied into knots at her words, wondering how he would receive them. "I'm sure Carlos would let you continue to take care of his property as long as you needed a place to live. We could live there until we get our new careers going."

"Look, I need to talk with Adam and Patrick first to make sure there won't be any fallout for you. But I'll make sure they know I'll do everything in my power to keep you safe, take care of and protect you, and love you with every breath I take."

Megan drew a slow, deep breath. "Okay, let me get this straight. You want to marry me—someday—but have to ask Adam and Patrick for permission first?" *Wow—such a gentleman.* Too bad she didn't need either of her brothers to approve of what she knew was right for her life.

"It's the right thing to do."

She moved closer, leaning over the table. "Ryder, if anyone puts the brakes on our relationship, it will be one of us."

"But your brothers understand firsthand the unpredictability of PTSD. They know there could be some bumpy days ahead. Besides, if they don't give us their blessing, it would drive a wedge between you and your brothers, and I won't be responsible for breaking up a family."

"Life is unpredictable, Ryder." Before setting him straight on a few things, she *did* need to make sure he understood what she'd tried to explain last week. No sense in all this talk about marrying only to pull the rug out from under him later.

"Remember what I told you before I left your place?"

He tilted his head. "You said a lot of things. You spoke your truth. I needed to hear it, too."

She shook her head. "No, not that part. I mean, I'm glad you heard that, but I'm talking about my not being able to have babies."

"What?" He acted as though he was hearing her for the first time. How could he have missed something that important? But that night she'd been so filled with emotion, she didn't even remember what she'd said.

Start at the beginning.

"Ever since I hit puberty, I had the most God-awful, painful periods. Two years ago, after having no success with the pill and several unsuccessful surgical procedures, I chose to have a total hysterectomy."

"God, Megan!" He pushed his plate aside, his dinner mostly untouched, and reached for her hand with both of his. "I remember when my mom had one. It took her a long time to get over that. For you to have to face something like that so young—I hope you weren't alone, at least."

"My mom was with me." Did he even know what this meant for her future—*their* future, if they still had one? "You *do* realize this means I can't give you little Ryders or Megans?" A tear rolled down her cheek.

"Oh, Baby, please don't cry. Hell, if the time comes when we want kids, we can adopt. I wouldn't want to bring more kids into this screwed-up world. Someone needs to take care of the ones who are lost."

Megan swallowed hard and let the tears continue to stream unimpeded down her face. He wasn't thinking this through. Never have his own kids? Wouldn't he resent her eventually for depriving him of that? She blinked when her eyes blurred so much she couldn't see him any longer. His face continued to swim before her, but she smiled, trying to be strong. A few more tears escaped. He leaned toward her and reached out with his free hand to brush the tears from her left cheek. Her face leaned into the palm of his hand.

Cherished.

Maybe he meant it. He didn't mind adopting if they wanted children in their lives. She smiled and placed her hand over his. "I will. I do. Whatever the question was—" Thinking back, she realized he hadn't really asked *the* question. He'd only stated what he would do if she said yes, *after* he talked with her brothers. If he didn't care whether she could give him babies—and she couldn't imagine wanting to spend another day without him—what more was there to say? Why wait another minute?

"Ryder Wilson, will you marry me?"

Chapter Twenty-One

R yder stared at Megan a long moment, wanting to make sure he'd heard her right. The expression on her face told him she was awaiting a response. No, he hadn't imagined her question, but had she heard anything he'd said earlier?

"Nothing would make me happier, Megan, when the time is right. Let's give it a few weeks to be sure everyone—"

"Seriously, Ryder, I'm not going to say it again. I don't need my brothers or anyone else to approve my choice of husband."

If he did anything to dishonor her among her family… "Megan, it's not that I need their approval. I just don't want to cause any—"

"If either of my brothers has a problem with the man I want to spend the rest of my life with, then our family would be seriously broken." She squeezed his hand. "Trust me, we aren't any more screwed up than any other family. We don't bite unless you ask nicely—or deserve it."

He couldn't help but grin until the image of Megan biting him sent his thoughts in the wrong direction.

"Ryder, how could they not love you?"

"How can you be so sure?"

"Trust me. Patrick's more worried about whether I'm going to find a man to take over for him and protect me. With my total lack of interest in dating all these years, he probably figures he'll be saddled with me forever." She smiled and signaled for the server to get their check. "But if you need to know you'll be welcomed into the family before giving me your answer…"

Overcome with emotion, he cleared his throat. He'd wanted to be part of a family for a long time. He'd blown it with his mom until it was too late, although he and Marcia still talked. He'd go with Megan to see her tomorrow. He hadn't shown his sister what he'd become since his discharge, but his time of hiding was over. Not that he had conquered his fears yet.

"What if I can't keep things under control?" He didn't have to spell out to her what he meant.

"Then I'll be at your side to hold you, and we'll get through the bad times as well as the good. There's nothing we can't tackle if we're together."

"How can you be so sure? We've known each other less than two weeks. I figured we'd date at least a few weeks or months and see how it goes. I'm thinking about heading up to Denver soon and thought you might want to come along, too. If we wait a bit—"

"Why should we?"

"You mean you want to get married right away?" She had to be the most determined woman on the planet. Damn the torpedoes and full speed ahead. Ryder sighed. Maybe he could talk with one of her brothers before going too far. "Did you say Patrick would be at the condo tonight?"

She scowled. "Are you always this stubborn?"

"I'd call it being practical, Baby. I don't have a house of my own. I don't even have a job."

"Well, I don't have a steady paying job myself, and I'm living with my brother. It will take years for me to make a living at photography."

"It's different for you. But a man should provide for—"

"Don't go there, Ryder. I believe in equality. Besides, I'm not exactly bringing a steady paycheck into this relationship myself."

"It won't be this way forever. I can do anything I put my mind to. I just have to find the right place where my PTSD won't flare up the way it did at the hospital."

"That was right after you got out of the Corps. I'm sure you're going to find something that's perfect for you."

He knew Carlos would let them stay there as long as they needed a place to live. His job was in Albuquerque, and he chose not to live on the pueblo and commute two or more hours a day. Whenever Carlos had wanted to spend time in the mountains, they'd either shared the house or Ryder had used it as an excuse to take an impromptu road trip.

"We'll both survive until we get on our feet, Ryder. I have a trust from my father."

"I don't want to freeload off you." He clenched his jaws. "I plan to work."

"We both will work, but what's mine is yours and yours is mine. I've never touched it because I didn't have a clue what I wanted to do with it. Now we can decide together. The whole world is opening up, Ryder. I can feel it. Without any ties to jobs or property, we can settle anywhere we want. Someplace rural. That would be great for my photography business, too. New Mexico or Colorado—either one is perfect. I promise, though, Chicago is not on my list."

"I never thought about moving out of state."

"We don't have to unless you want to. I think we just need to keep our options open. Have you ever worked on a ranch or farm?"

"No."

"It's something to consider. There also might be maintenance or construction jobs in small towns. We'll talk to Adam when we go up there. I want to help Karla when her mom has to go home. But I'm sure if there are any job opportunities, he'll know about them. He has a lot of connections."

Her optimism became contagious. Among the takeaways he'd learned from his vision quest, sometimes a person needed to make a new start.

"Just don't create obstacles, Ryder. Life has a way of putting enough real ones before us."

"I'm working on changing my tendency to do that."

"That's work enough for now. Give yourself time to heal. We have the rest of our lives together. All I know is that I don't want a prolonged engagement or fussy wedding. I know I'm not getting any sex until that ring is on my finger." She waggled the fingers of her left hand in the air between them. "So let's go to Patrick's and call whoever we think might show up, and we can have a judge or justice of the peace marry us as early as Monday if this state doesn't have a waiting period." She reached under the table for her purse.

What was her hurry? He ran his hand through his hair. "You are one impulsive lady." Their foray into kink the second night they were together made that clear. "Look, it's Saturday. We can't apply for a license until we go to the courthouse Monday. Let's take it one day at a time." A lot could change in two days, although her plan for a small civil ceremony meant fewer people. He wanted his entire focus to be on Megan whenever they started their life together.

At least he'd have a couple of days to get his own head wrapped around the idea of being married. Again. He hoped he'd learned from his mistakes with Sherry. Megan wasn't anything like his first wife, though. She was open, honest, and understood Ryder's issues. In fairness to Sherry, Megan hadn't known the pre-military Ryder only to find herself saddled with a different Ryder after he left the Corps.

Jesus, don't let me fu—

Before he let the familiar negative thoughts filter into his head, he closed his eyes and breathed in positive thoughts. Megan's smile. Her laugh.

He met her gaze, more sure of himself than he had been moments ago. "I love you, Megan Gallagher." *Jesus!* "Do you realize I haven't even told you I love you before this?"

She enveloped his hand in both of hers. "You didn't have to say it for me to know. You said it in so many nonverbal ways. When you reached for my hand as we walked together. The way you made sure I was fed—and very well, I might add—and that I didn't work too long without a break. The massages. Oh, you can just keep doing those. With the way you protected me from dangers, real or perceived. With the way you—"

He held up his free hand. "Okay, okay. I can see you're going to be easy to please, my future wife."

She beamed. "Oh, Ryder, you please me very much. But I also intend to find ways to please you. Not just with kink, although I do want to explore more of that with you when you're ready. I'm sure I'll find other ways, too."

"Oh, Baby, all you have to do is be you. You bring so much joy into my days. I didn't tell you this, but I underwent a vision quest this week and encountered your spirit guide animal."

"Is that like a fetish?"

In the context of the conversation, he knew she wasn't talking about kink. "What do you know about fetishes?"

She smiled. "After my encounter with the coyote up on your mountain and the amazing connection I felt with him, I had to learn more. So I came home and googled coyotes and their special meanings. The Zuni have incredible information online describing all of the different spirit guide animals."

"Very good. Zunis specialize in creating beautiful fetish objects, sometimes referred to as a totem or talisman. It's nothing more than a manmade manifestation of a spirit animal. Small, it can be carried in your pocket for protection or as a reminder of what the guide is trying to teach you."

Megan reached to open her purse and retrieved a carved, Picasso marble coyote with turquoise blue eyes.

Ryder smiled. "I see you've already figured out that the coyote is your spirit animal. He told me so, too. You were more in tune up there than I realized. Oh, and he said he misses you."

"You spoke with him? I envy you having that ability."

"He visited me on the last day of my vision quest ritual. Perhaps we can do the purification ceremony and quest together sometime. I'm sure if you quiet your mind long enough, you'll hear from your spirit guides, not just the animal one but others."

She scowled jokingly. "Are you saying I talk too much?"

He grinned. "I'm saying your mind is very busy. As is your body."

"One of the hardest things for me here in the Southwest was to learn to take things a little slower. We probably keep moving in Chicago just to keep warm. Perhaps you can help me with what you've learned about spiritual matters and the Native American ways."

She shrugged. "Anyway, from what I read online, the coyote shows us that life is unpredictable and uncontrollable. Even when shit happens, it views unexpected occurrences as opportunities, not misfortunes."

She grew introspective for a moment before meeting his gaze again. "You know, I think I should forgive Grant for what she did. If not for her, I never would have met you. Misfortune turned into opportunity—the chance for me to meet you."

While he wasn't there yet, he knew she was right. "One of the things I learned during my quest is that holding on to grudges and bitterness only leads to unhappiness and keeps us estranged from the ones we love."

"Very true." She leaned forward and cupped her chin in her hand. "So did you discover your spirit animal?"

"I did." He knew how she would react and didn't want to tell her.

"Well? Tell me—or is this something we shouldn't tell others?"

He sighed. "No, we can share if we wish. Promise you won't get upset."

"Why would I be ups—Oh, my God! It's the rattlesnake, isn't it?"

"Well, the snake. Yes."

"I killed your spirit guide animal!"

"No, Megan. You can't kill a spirit animal. The one you killed did return to me to let me know he had no hard feelings." Seeing how upset she was, he'd hoped his words might help, but she still seemed distraught. "Megan, he shed this life for another, but he and his brothers and sisters will continue to watch over me." When tears welled in her eyes, he reached out and stroked her cheek with his thumb. "Please, don't cry. Remember, we thanked him for providing food for our bodies and honored him as the warrior he was."

She shook her head, and tears spilled from her eyes. "That's not why I'm crying. Ryder, from what I read, the snake is perfect for you. I even thought of you when I read about it at the Zuni Web site."

"Why do you think so?" He was curious to hear what she'd learned.

She pulled her phone out of her purse. "I can't remember the wording for yours as well as my own, so let me google it again."

He shook his head and wondered if she could live without technology.

"Here it is!" She read aloud, "'The snake is a powerful symbol of our need to discard old ways, patterns, and perspectives. He transforms negative things into something positive.'"

Surprisingly, that definition touched him more than the one he'd remembered. The words rekindled some of the feelings he'd had during his encounter with the rattlesnake on the last night of his vision quest ritual.

"It also says snakes shed their skin, Ryder. They let go of all their negative baggage and start anew."

The backs of his eyes burned. "True." He could barely get the word out and cleared his throat.

In an instant, Ryder knew that during all this talk of marriage and hope for the future, he still wallowed in his negative thoughts of the past and continued to worry that he wasn't good enough for her. He hadn't changed his mindset one bit since the vision quest. Of course, he'd learned in his group therapy sessions at the VA hospital that any behavioral change takes weeks of repetition and reminders before changes happened.

At least now when he became aware of lapsing into old habits and listening to the long-running tapes in his head, as the shrinks called them, he corrected himself. Progress. One step at a time, the lodge leader had advised.

He brushed his thumb over Megan's knuckles. "I can't believe how fast things are moving, but maybe that just means this is right for both of us."

"Ryder, I knew you were the only man for me by day two—and I only took that long because I was so sure I didn't want or need a man in my life, or that no man would want *me*."

"You're the most beautiful woman I've ever known—inside and out. Any man would be proud to have you as his wife."

"Well, I only want one man. You. Say 'yes' and make me the happiest girl in New Mexico."

One thing became crystal clear. As long as Megan wanted him, it didn't matter what anyone else said.

"As long as our witnesses can forever hold their peace, you'll make me the luckiest man in the world come Monday—or whenever the state lets us—by becoming my wife."

Her eyes lit up as her smile broadened. "Really? We can get married by a JP?" When he nodded, she launched herself out of her chair, around the table, and into his lap.

"Oh, I see I can still turn you on after all this time." She wiggled her ass against his erection.

He pinched her butt. "Don't be a tease, Baby Girl. You're supposed to be a virgin."

"Not for long."

"Well, I'd like to walk out of this place with a little dignity, so stop squirming."

What the hell? Sometimes dignity was overrated.

Ryder grabbed a hank of her hair and pulled her backward before he lowered his mouth against hers. She opened herself to him, and his tongue slipped between her lips.

Warm.

Sweet.

Megan.

Her warm breath on his face urged him on. He pulled her hair back to open her mouth wider and deepened the kiss. Their tongues tangled, and her moan made him grow harder. The way she tried to move on his lap told him she felt it. His hand moved to cup her breast.

Jesus.

Needing to regain some control, he released her mouth, leaving both of them gasping for a deeper breath.

"Breathe with me, Baby." Together, they synchronized their breaths, as they had done the night he introduced her to bondage. His connection to her grew stronger than ever.

When their breathing returned to normal, she smiled. "Oh, my! That was... Um, I think I need to pack so we can go home tonight." She glanced around the room, and he followed her gaze to zero in on one embarrassed server who seemed equally interested in not missing the show.

Dazed, he brought his attention back to Megan. "Home?"

"Well, to your place—yours until we're married, anyway."

Hell, no. "With or without your brother's approval, no way are you sleeping at my house until we're married."

"But I spent two nights up there already."

He heard retreating footsteps as the server apparently decided she'd eavesdropped long enough. "That was different. I was on a mission to protect you then. And we know how much trouble we can get into when we're alone together."

She stuck her lower lip out. "You're not going to be an easy man to live with, are you?"

He grinned, and he fought the urge to pull her into his arms and kiss her. "I promise I'll try to be a lot easier after we're married."

*   *   *

Megan gave up trying to tame her hair and pinned a lock of it over her left ear with a barrette to hold it in place. Why were her hands shaking? Thank goodness she hadn't wanted a big wedding. With Carlos as best man and Marcia the maid of honor, the ceremony would be small and intimate. Patrick would record a candid video for Mom, Adam, and others who couldn't be here.

Yesterday, she'd bought a form-fitting, calf-length dress made of white Spanish lace while shopping on the Plaza in Santa Fe after she'd had her meeting with Ryder's sister.

Her future sister-in-law was a hoot and had a keen eye for quality art. Knowing she had liked Megan's work on its own merits without thinking of her as a potential family member gave Megan added confidence in her abilities. No doubt several of her photos would be displayed for sale there from now on, and if they sold, she'd send more to Marcia.

"Sis, are you ready?" Patrick's voice came from the hallway.

"Almost!"

She picked up her handbag and joined him in the hall. Patrick wore a fabulous gray suit. He'd offered to come in uniform, but with this being a civil ceremony, she saw no reason to fuss. How such a handsome man could go without having a woman snatch him up was beyond her.

"Megan, you look beautiful."

She smiled. "Today, I *feel* beautiful because I'm going to marry the man who makes my heart complete."

He shook his head. "I sure hope you know what you're doing. Mom thinks you've gone off the deep end, you know."

"Just wait 'til Mom meets him at Adam's place in a couple weeks. She'll love him, too." She stood on tiptoes, gave him a peck on the cheek, and then wiped away the coral lipstick. "Thank you for not going into typical big-brother mode with Ryder the other night."

"If Adam trusts him with your life, then I know I can."

Marines and their Code. God love 'em.

"I guess we'd better go. Marcia texted me that they're about thirty minutes out from the courthouse. I don't want to keep my future husband waiting."

"You haven't kept him waiting at all, by most wedding standards."

She punched his arm playfully. "You've been listening to Mom. *What harm would it do to wait a few weeks, at least? Get to know him better. Men with combat stress can change at the drop of a hat.*"

"You know what she went through with her first husband."

She nodded.

"I'll try to help reassure Mom that Ryder is trying to change how he responds to his triggers and nightmares. While you were working on your photo edits the other night, Ryder and I had a good long talk."

"Yeah, I was a nervous wreck, worrying the whole time you were going to send him packing for the hills."

Patrick grinned, probably remembering how much fun he'd had intimidating past boyfriends. "Anyway, the vision quest and sweat lodge ceremony he participated in sounds like something I might try sometime."

Megan gave him a hug.

"What's that for?"

"For being a strong Marine who knows when he needs to reach out to others. I'm so glad you found Save a Warrior. I noticed a dramatic change in you when you came home from that experience."

"It's actually spiritually based, like Ryder's vision quest." They broke the hug, and he smiled at her. "You found a good man, Megan. But you know I'm here for you, no matter what. Promise me you'll be a strong Marine sister and you'll let me know if you ever need *anything*."

"I will. But you also taught me how to be strong and take care of myself." She grinned. "Now I think we'd better go."

They walked toward the garage, and once inside, he opened the passenger door of her Ford Escape and gave her a hand up. She'd learned long ago not to even try to open doors for herself around him. As she waited in the SUV, she pulled the vows from her purse and read them over again. The words of her heart for the man who won her heart.

They didn't say a lot on the way downtown. A text from Marcia told her they were in the county clerk's office and could start the process for the license as soon as the bride arrived. Patrick parked, glaring at her when she opened her own door to get out, but went to the back of the SUV to retrieve a large white box.

"Sis, I wanted you to have a bouquet, even if it's a civil ceremony."

She opened the box, revealing the arrangement of pale pink roses and baby's breath. "Oh, Patrick, it's beautiful!" Holding onto the bouquet she wrapped her arms around him. "Thanks so much for being here."

He picked up her camera case. "You know I wouldn't miss it—not that you would have waited for me." She grinned. The man knew her very well. "I've been practicing to use your video camera. Hope I don't mess up recording your big day for Mom and Adam."

"Nothing will mess this up short of my groom being a no-show, and Marcia assures me they're all up there waiting for us." They found the clerk's office, and when she walked inside, she was surprised to see Ryder in his dress blues. He crossed the room to her.

"Breathe, Red," he said as he bent to kiss her, taking her breath away a second time.

"You look even more handsome in your uniform."

"Well, I don't have many occasions to wear it anymore, but I had to today."

"I'm glad you did."

After introducing Patrick and Marcia, they filled out the paperwork and waited to receive the license before walking the few blocks to meet with the justice of the peace.

They informed the JP that they had written their own vows, and the ceremony progressed rapidly to that point. With Ryder's arm brushing hers, Megan didn't hear much until she and Ryder were instructed to face each other. He was prompted to speak his vows first, and everyone else in the room faded away.

With his shaking hands holding her own, he said:

I, Ryder, choose you Megan,

To be no other than yourself,

Loving what I know of you,

Trusting what I do not yet know.

I will respect you as an individual and my partner in life,

and as someone who will help me to grow and heal.

I promise to laugh with you when times are good

and hunker down with you when they are bad.

I will adore, honor, and encourage you.

And I will love you always.

Megan smiled through her tears. Overcome with emotion, she accepted a tissue from Marcia to wipe her eyes before she began her own vows.

The sun smiles on us today, our wedding day,

and how can it not, for our love is stronger than forever.

Our hearts beat together as one.

Ryder, I promise to be a true and faithful partner

from this day forward,

as we face all of life's circumstances together.

In the joys and sorrows,

the good times and bad,

in sickness or in health,

I will always be there for you,

to comfort, love, honor, and cherish you,

today and every day of my life.

They exchanged the rings they had chosen at a unique jewelry store in Santa Fe and promised to live by their vows forever.

After a brief invocation wishing them a happy future, the JP announced, "You may kiss your bride."

"Not yet, ma'am. There's still one thing we must do."

Megan had no idea what he planned until he turned to Carlos, who presented a pottery vase with two spouts and a single handle between them. The tan vase had been painted with corn stalks and other symbols using black and a reddish-orange paint, and then the vase had been glazed.

"This vessel was made by the wife of the shaman who conducted my purification ceremony last—" Ryder's eyes grew misty and his voice broke. Megan took his hands and squeezed them, encouraging him to continue. "—

last week. The shaman prayed a blessing over the water in this vessel last night and again this morning, one that wishes us many happy years as we continue on our earth's journey. The two spouts represent our separate lives and the handle our joining together as one."

Now the tears were in Megan's eyes.

"You will drink first, and then I will drink from the same spout." He held the vase to her and tipped it for her. The water came out a little faster than expected, and she dribbled some. Ryder smiled as he asked her to tip it for himself to drink. Not wanting to mess up his uniform, she lifted it carefully so as not to spill any.

"Now we do the same from the other spout. I will drink first this time." They repeated the process in the reverse order, and she smiled. Ryder took several steps and stood side by side with her. "One more time. This time, we want to try harder than ever not to spill any because it is said if the couple can drink from the vase at the same time and not spill a single drop, good understanding and a cooperative spirit will always be a part of their marriage."

"Oh, we need that!" She winked at him, hoping he didn't think she was making light of the ceremony.

"Among other things. But we are strong and together even stronger. Still, if the Great Spirit will favor us even more with understanding and coopera-tion, we will go far together."

Unable to speak, she swallowed hard and nodded. Ryder brought his head closer to her height—already showing his cooperative spirit—and they placed their lips on the sides of the two spouts. In unison, they lifted the vase slowly until the water first touched her upper lip. She opened wider and drank the holy water. Overcome by an intense emotion she felt a tear slid down her cheek. When Ryder began to turn the vase upright again, she was reluctant to release it, but when she did, not a drop spilled.

Ryder handed the vase back to Carlos before turning to face her again. At least there would be no curse on them for having tears of emotion as far as she knew. But she thought she smelled her daddy's aftershave and knew at least one of her parents witnessed the ceremony today. More tears fell, but she didn't care.

Ryder smiled and turned to face her. He cupped her cheeks. "Megan Wilson, you've done me the greatest honor a man can know. I will work harder than ever to provide for you and be the man you deserve." He bent to kiss her, and she wrapped her arms around his waist, wanting to be as close to him as possible.

When they broke the kiss, she took a deep breath, not wanting to even be a few inches apart from him.

"Today begins the adventure of a lifetime with the man I never even dreamed of finding. Thank you, Ryder. I can't wait to get our journey started." Silently, she thanked her coyote spirit animal—and her brother Adam—for helping her find such an unexpected treasure.

Epilogue

Ryder opened the door to their home. "Wait here while I put our wedding vase in a safe place and stow your suitcase."

He flipped the switch and went into the kitchen where he placed the vase on the counter for washing later. What made it even more special was that the shaman from the sweat lodge had instructed his wife in the creation of this vessel more than a week ago as he prepared for the purification lodge ceremony. He told Carlos he had received a vision of Ryder drinking from a wedding vase just like this one.

The Universe continued to prepare the way for when he was ready to move forward on his life and spiritual journey again.

Ryder carried her suitcase into the bedroom and returned to fetch his bride.

"Your wife's freezing out here at a time when she should be hotter than a recently fired pistol."

Ryder grinned. *Impatient woman.*

He met her outside the door and, without hesitation, scooped her into his arms. She squealed in surprise, although she must have realized by now he was a traditional man. Megan smiled and wrapped her arms around his neck. He bent to kiss her as if he'd never done so before, stealing her breath away. When she shivered, he lifted his head from hers. "You taste better than any nectar on earth, Mrs. Wilson."

My bride.

Her smile warmed his heart, and he carried her across the threshold for the first time as husband and wife. He might just carry her into the house every time. Any excuse to have her in his arms.

When he started to set her on her feet, she hugged his neck even tighter. "I do believe there's one more threshold we need to cross." The smoldering look in her eyes left no doubt what she meant.

He kicked the door closed, turned to click the deadbolt in place while still holding her, and proceeded to his bedroom. *Their* bedroom. This first night would be special. He'd prepared the room for her before leaving this morning for Albuquerque. The waning daylight would make the candle glow perfect. He'd light them while she was in the bathroom to do whatever it was women did on their wedding night.

Not much else he had to do but strip and hang up his uniform.

When they entered the bedroom, he set her on her feet and turned the dimmer switch to give just enough light to see. Turning back to her, he lowered his mouth to hers once again for another taste. His hands stroked down the back of her lacy dress, and he cupped her ass, pulling her against him.

Megan looked so sexy in the form-fitting dress. She'd kept some traditions herself, not letting him see the dress she'd chosen when she and Marcia had gone shopping yesterday. When she walked into the clerk's office, he hadn't been able to keep his gaze off her.

"Before we go to bed, I want us to spend some time in the sauna together. Just one more symbolic way of shedding the past and starting our new life together."

"Just let me get out of these clothes, unless you'd like to watch me strip."

His cock throbbed to life. "Watching might be…enlightening, too."

"Ah, but we're going to turn the tables. First, I get to watch you take off that stud-muffin uniform."

"Hey, respect the uniform."

"Oh, I respect this uniform very much, as well as the man wearing it." She reached up and fiddled with the hook and loop at the collar of his blouse before finally releasing the tight closure. "Man, it's good you didn't have to fight in this thing. No wonder you stand so straight and tall in it." Her fingers moved down to the first gold anodized brass button.

He had no desire to stop or help her, which would bring this to an end sooner than he desired. No, he planned on enjoying tonight at her pace, and if this is what Megan wanted to do, she'd damn well do it. Besides, the smiles she flashed him were not sweet and innocent at all, but sultry and sexy instead. The woman went after whatever she wanted—and she wanted him.

Holy fuck! How did I get so lucky?

For days, he'd worried about tonight, given that he would be her first lover, but as with everything else, Megan just charged in without succumbing to fears.

She'd once said she could tell he would be a gentle lover. No doubt, given how quickly she took to kink, the rough stuff would come later. But tonight, he would be slow and gentle.

Even if it kills me.

*   *   *

Megan worked her way down the line of buttons on the front of his jacket. His white crew-neck undershirt peeked out as she reached the halfway point. Her heart beat harder, and a current seemed to flow through her fingers and up her arms as she touched the uniform in such a personal way. She'd always thought Patrick's uniform looked good on him, but Ryder's...well, as much as she enjoyed seeing him in it, she couldn't wait to see him out of it.

When she reached the white belt and its brass buckle, she squeezed the two ends together and it popped open. She grabbed the belt before it fell and tossed it on the bed and then spread open the jacket. His pecs stretched the white T-shirt.

Gorgeous man. All mine.

No longer able to wait to see his bare chest, she pushed the jacket down his arms. Wanting him to see she could control herself, she carried it over to the closet and hung it up. When she turned, she watched Ryder untuck his undershirt and pull it over his head. The bulge in his trousers told her he was as turned on as she was.

She returned to him and reached for his web belt, quickly opening and dispensing of it as she had done the jacket belt. Next came the hook-and-loop closure, and she reached for his zipper.

He grabbed her hand before she could unzip them. "My turn."

Her breath caught in her throat. The thought of his hands on her made it difficult to breathe. With his index finger, he motioned for her to turn around. Megan tried to move gracefully for him and her stomach dropped when he wound her hair around his fist as he had done their first night in this house. With her nipples peaking, begging for his touch, a strange sensation low in her abdomen left her longing for more.

He lifted her hair and pressed his lips to her neck. She moaned and tilted her head to give him better access.

"Breathe, Baby." His whisper tickled her skin. He twisted her hair and draped it over her shoulder before kneading the muscles in her neck. "Relax for me."

How could she? His touch set her body on fire. Never had she felt so alive. When his hands stopped moving, she drew a ragged breath and waited to see what he would do next.

The sound of the dress's zipper being pulled down and the pressure of his hand against her back sent a shiver coursing the length of her spine that had nothing to do with the chilly air in the bedroom. For the first time, she noticed the candles arranged on every surface in the room except the bed. On the bed were dozens of rose petals.

"My husband is a romantic."

"Your husband is horny. Turn around and strip for me, woman."

She grinned, eager to oblige without his caveman imitation. God, she was going to enjoy every minute in this room with Ryder. There probably wouldn't be a lot of sleeping going on, though.

Imagining some sexy music, she began gyrating her hips and lifted her hands to her hair. She splayed her fingers and shook her hair loose from the twist he'd made. He inhaled deeply.

"I love your scent."

"Thank you. It's the red osmanthus flower probably—rather exotic for us Westerners. Or perhaps the vanilla rum."

The thought of showering with him and having his hands lathering her breasts with her body gel, Forever Red, led to even more fantasies. She already had enough carnal ideas to last them thirty years, give or take—assuming they only had sex once a day, every day.

Somehow she didn't expect them to be that sedate, for the first decade, at least.

A smack on her butt reminded her that he'd asked her to strip for him. She smiled. They weren't doing a kink scene, but the man was forceful anyway. She turned as she grabbed the sides of her dress and pulled the hem up, let it fall, then repeated several times, each time pulling it higher and letting it fall, but never as far as the previous time. When she gave him a peek at her garters, his penis rammed against his fly. Emboldened, she turned her back to him once more and let the hem of the skirt ride up over her hips.

"Holy fuck!"

She grinned. "Like what you see, Marine?"

She'd worn only a G-string with her garter belt, anticipating his reaction when he first saw her out of her dress. Turning again to savor the moment, she saw him rushing to remove his trousers before he'd taken off his shoes. She giggled and let the dress pool at her feet, equally impatient.

The sight of the bulge in his boxers gave her a mixture of excitement and nervousness. What if she didn't do it right? Despite all the books she'd read, none of those scenes came to her now. What should she do?

Help him, of course!

"Sir, would you like me to remove your shoes?"

Megan found comfort in taking the role of submissive with Ryder. When she became uncertain, he could guide her with his instructions. Not that they had negotiated such a scene tonight.

When Ryder sat down on the chest at the foot of the bed, his trousers at his ankles, she knelt at his feet and untied and removed his shoes then his socks. Finally he lifted both legs, and she slid his pants over his feet. Megan intentionally avoided his erection and stood to drape his trousers over the back of the chair much more carefully than she had dispensed with her dress.

Her focus now was on one thing—the bulge in his white boxers. She knelt in front of him once more and reached out to stroke his hardness through his underwear. For the first time, she became a little worried whether he would fit inside her. Her toys weren't nearly this big. Most of her insertable vibes were barely an inch in diameter. Ryder? *Oh, God.*

Her hand shook from a mixture of excitement and nervousness, and Ryder grasped both of them and pulled her onto his lap.

"Tell me what you're thinking."

His enormous erection pressed against the crack of her butt, and no words would come. Ryder cupped her chin and directed her gaze to him. "Afraid I might not fit?"

She nodded.

He grinned. "We're going to take it slowly—and I'm going to use lube to make it as easy as I can on your first time. Remember, there's no rush. We have nothing planned for two weeks except for getting to know each other. Anytime you want me to stop, you just say scarlet, same as in our kink scenes."

"Or yellow if I want you to slow down?"

He pinched her nipple through her bustier, and she lost her train of thought. "You might have to be more specific. In kink, yellow means to stop and talk things out. So if you mean slow down as far as how fast I'm…making love to you, that would require a very different response."

She grinned and relaxed a little. "I can see that might be confusing if we have yellow mean different things at different times. I'll just ask you to slow down if I need you to."

"That should work." His hand cupped her breast. "Jesus, you are so sexy, Baby. And I'm the only man who will ever get to enjoy you."

She leaned against his shoulder and gave him better access to her breasts. He ran his callused thumb over the rim of her bustier, and gooseflesh popped up in his wake. Heat rose from her upper chest into her face. Why did she blush so easily? It only accentuated the fact she was inexperienced.

Megan drew a deep breath and prayed he would let her finish stripping soon so he could touch her skin to skin. When he didn't, she reached up and pulled the cups down below her breasts.

"I like when you touch me there."

"Well, I can see we're already working with a cooperative spirit, because I sure as hell love touching you there." He pinched her nipple, and she gasped, feeling a tension in her groin that made her wish he was touching her there, too.

"Why don't I finish undressing?"

"I'd like that, but first, just a nibble." He lowered his mouth to her nipple and latched on while she grabbed his head to make sure he didn't stop until she was ready. His tongue flicked against her, and she couldn't contain her response.

"Oh, God! Don't stop!"

His chuckle reverberated against her breast. He sucked, hard, and her clit vibrated as if she'd come. He didn't seem to mind her B-cup breasts. Good thing, because she'd never undergo surgery again unless she had to.

With one last pinch, he said, "Finish stripping for me, Baby. I want to see the rest of you again."

She scooted off his lap and unhooked the front of the bustier, one hook at a time. She didn't feel like teasing him, because it would only take that much longer for them to move to the next phase, whatever that was. Sex, she supposed. Despite her fears, she trusted him not to hurt her any more than he'd have to hurt a virgin.

Too bad she hadn't been eligible for the vaginal procedure. Maybe they'd have broken her hymen and rid her of the nuisance.

"What are you thinking about?"

She met his gaze, and her hands stilled momentarily at his words. "Oh, nothing." She unhooked her silk stockings from the garters and reached around back to unhook the belt.

"Be honest with me, Baby. What were you thinking when you got so tense and your face looked so unhappy?"

She stopped moving. Stopped breathing.

Ryder stood and came toward her. "Breathe with me, Baby."

He set the pace, and she soon matched his rhythm, breathing in and out steadily as though one. Slowly, the tension left her body. She met his gaze. "I was just wishing my surgeon had taken care of this long ago."

The look of pain on his face made her wish she'd kept her mouth shut.

"It's going to kill me if I cause you pain."

"Why don't we open a bottle of wine and go sit in the sauna a while?"

"Alcohol and saunas don't mix. You'll dehydrate. But we can head there anyway. Things went a little off plan tonight, although I've enjoyed the hell out of watching you strip for me."

If you expect me to be predictable and follow any of your premade plans…

"Oh, I'm not finished messing with your plans yet."

His eyes smoldered, and Ryder grinned before reaching behind her to finish unhooking the garter belt. "We'll get rid of this, but I'm going to let you wear the G-string. You don't know how sexy it is to me."

Megan smiled. She had a pretty good idea how it affected him.

"I'm going to go get us some bottles of water. You might want to go to the bathroom before we head outside."

She nodded and went to her suitcase to retrieve some toiletries before heading toward the bathroom, wiggling her ass just to tease him a little and try to get her game on again.

"I'm going to make you pay for tempting me like that, Baby."

She glanced back at him over her shoulder. "Promises, promises. Maybe you should grab one of the paddles on your way to the sauna."

*　　*　　*

Ryder shook his head. The woman was going to drive him to drink. The thought of reddening her backside with her wearing a G-string just about had him coming in his boxers. He went outside to turn on the sauna before heading inside to grab several bottles of water from the kitchen. Back in the bedroom, he went to the closet and pulled out his toy bag, setting it on the bed. Opening it, he soon found just what he wanted to use on her sexy ass in a few minutes.

When he heard the bathroom door squeak, he turned toward her, but hid the implement and other items he planned to use behind his back, wanting to keep them a surprise. "Grab four bath towels from the bathroom and wait for me on the patio. The sauna should be ready, but I don't want you to go inside until I do. I doubt you'll be able to last more than ten minutes if you haven't been in one recently."

"I've never been in one."

"Well, then, ten minutes definitely will be our limit tonight. Afterward, we'll jump in the shower."

Her eyes smoldered at the mention of showering together. Good. No need to rush her into bed. Foreplay, whether it culminated in sex or not, was equally enjoyable. They might decide to wait until tomorrow or the next day to make love. Both knew how to have an orgasm without intercourse. Having each stimulate the other would be an incredible experience, too.

After stripping out of his boxers, he grabbed a sleep mask and other items before exiting the bedroom through the open patio door. She stood holding the fluffy towels, and her gaze went to his erection. Her eyes grew wider, and she nibbled her lower lip.

Damn, he needed to relieve her of her virginity as early as possible tonight if she was ever going to relax enough to enjoy sex without worrying about the pain. He made a mental change to his plan and walked past her to the sauna, opening the door.

"When we get inside, lay two towels for us to sit on or the wooden seats will scorch our asses. The other two will be for wiping the sweat off."

He indicated for her to precede him inside. When he joined her, memories of his purification lodge ceremony came to him, but the image of her bare ass cheeks blocked all thoughts of spirituality from his mind.

She arranged the towels and set the others on either side of where they would be seated. He walked over to her. "Close your eyes." She hesitated only a moment. He tucked the items from the toy bag between the folds of one of the towels, and the bottles on either side of them, before standing in front of her. "Are you okay with being blindfolded?"

The hitch in her breathing and pebbling of her nipples told him she probably liked the idea, but he still waited for her response.

"Yes, Sir. I love the blindfold."

He placed it over her eyes and adjusted the elastic behind her head. Her breathing grew shallow, which might be from the intense, dry heat in here as much as from her arousal. He grabbed her hair and pulled it back, and she opened her mouth for him to plunge his tongue inside, mimicking the act that would happen soon. Her hands weren't bound, and she reached up to hold his biceps, more to steady herself than anything, he guessed.

He grasped her ass cheeks and squeezed, alternately kneading them and placing small smacks to prepare them for him. When he pulled away, her mouth was open, gasping for breath. He picked up a bottle and opened it for her, putting it in her hand. "Drink this. All of it."

She took some tentative sips.

"You'll have to be quicker about it if you want the treat I have for you."

She downed the rest of it much as she had done the cognac the night he first met her. He opened and emptied his own bottle before sitting down. Reaching for her hand, he guided her toward him. When she would have sat on the bench, he pulled her face down across his lap.

"Oh!"

"Shhh. You're safe. We're just going to play a little before our shower. Would you like that?"

She nodded.

"Answer me with words."

"Yes, Sir. I like playing with you."

He chuckled. "Your safewords?"

"Scarlet and yellow."

He began warming up her ass with more light smacks before they became harder ones. Her breathy exclamations told him her excitement level was increasing. He reached beside him and pulled out the toy he'd brought to play with her.

* * *

Megan's nose, lungs, and butt all were burning, but for different reasons. Ryder's hand smacking her bare skin made her want to spread her legs wider so he could run his finger over her clit until she came. Her clit and vagina both throbbed, waiting for something to ease the arousal.

Thwack!

Something stung as it hit her left cheek. Definitely not his hand any longer. She squirmed, trying to avoid the blow she knew was coming next, but he placed his hand on her back to hold her still.

Thwack!

"Ow!"

While it didn't hurt like the paddle he'd used before, whatever it was definitely left a sting that didn't go away. Two more smacks of the thing, and she placed her hand over her butt just as the implement came down again.

"Shit! That hurt."

"Remove your hand."

Megan wanted to say no, but that would only prolong her paddling. At least she knew they only had another six or seven minutes inside here before time was up. But he could do a lot of damage in that time.

She moved her hand away, and he spanked her two more times, once on each cheek. Then his hand was rubbing away some of the sting, and she relaxed. Was it over?

His fingers pulled the string of the tiny thong aside, and he skimmed them down her butt crack to her vagina. She wiggled against his hand when he slid a finger inside her. He slipped in easily. So wet. Thank God.

He pulled out and entered her again.

"Just two fingers, Baby. Relax and breathe. Let's try three. That'll be closer to what my cock will feel like inside you."

From what she'd seen, not close enough, but when he pushed inside, she enjoyed the fullness. She pressed back onto his hand. More. She wanted more.

"Eager, are we?"

He pulled out again and slid between her folds to where he teased her clit from its hiding place. She clenched her hands. Her body shook as he played her with his wicked, wicked fingers. *Please, put them inside me again.* He continued to stroke her clit instead, building her to a frenzy of want. Need.

"Stand up." He helped her to her feet and stood as well. "Reach out in front of you. I want your hands holding onto the towels you placed on the bench." She found the towels and gripped them tightly. "Bend over, Baby."

Was he going to paddle her again? Despite the sting, her body hummed with tension. Wet. She waited and thought she heard him unscrewing something. *Fine time to be taking a break for some water.* She still felt hydrated from the bottle she drank earlier and knew she'd be out of here soon. While waiting, she did some Kegel exercises to prepare for the time when his penis would be inside her. She wanted to make it good for him, too.

"So wet for me, Baby." She tamped down a giggle, thinking this wasn't the place for it. He drew her wetness to her clit again. His erection slid along the slit of her sex. Pulling the G-string out of the way, he rubbed his penis up and down her cleft. Whenever he came close to her bundle of nerves, she rocked back on him, wanting more. With his finger stimulating her clit and his penis…well, everything else. She fought to catch her breath.

"Oh, God, that feels good. Don't stop." His fingers increased their strokes. "Oh, yes! There!" He was going to let her come. She was certain of it. "I'm close!"

Oh, God, oh, God, oh, God!

So close. She'd never felt so turned on. His penis pressed against her opening, and she started to pull away, but the hand playing with her clit held her in place. Faster. Closer.

"I can't hold it!"

"Don't hold back, Baby. Come for me."

"Oh, God! Oh, God! I'm coming! Yessssss!"

She crested the peak just as a stinging pain and incredible fullness exploded past her opening, stopping just inside. With his fingers coaxing more and more from her orgasm, it didn't register what had caused the pain until she slowly came down from her climax. Something long and hard slipped from her vagina.

That had *not* been a toy.

Ryder.

When she tried to stand up and turn around, her body began to shake. Her legs folded beneath her, but before she could hit the floor, he lifted her into his arms and pulled off her blindfold. Tears mingled with sweat, drenching her face. Relief and euphoria overcame her, and she tucked her face against the dusting of hair on his chest and wept.

"I'm sorry I hurt you, but I think it was better this way. If you knew when I was going to penetrate you, you'd have just tensed up, and it would have hurt worse."

"I'm okay. I don't know why I'm crying. You were—"

"Come on, Baby. Let's go take a shower."

Outside the sauna, the cool night breeze made her aware of the sweat coming from every pore of her body. He carried her inside quickly, and soon they were in his bathroom.

"Can you stand?"

She nodded, still a bit shaky, although losing her virginity hadn't hurt as much as the paddle he'd used the first night they'd played together.

I'm no longer a virgin. A giggle bubbled up despite her best efforts, and she gazed at Ryder who looked as if she'd suddenly lost her mind.

"Ryder, for someone who says he's never taken a girl's virginity before, you sure are good at it."

"What?"

"I've heard how some men just charge in like bulls with no regard to the woman's body or emotions, but you gave me an incredible orgasm first, which made all the difference."

His body relaxed as though an unbearable weight had been removed, and he smiled. "I'm afraid that's a skill I will have no further use for, Red."

"You'd better believe it." She grabbed his hand. "Now that we've dispensed with that, let's shower. I have a fantasy I want you to fulfill—one of many. But let me rinse off first." She glanced down and saw his penis had shrunk some, but still had flecks of her blood on it.

A little embarrassed to have to ask, she overcame her awkwardness. "Did you come already?"

"No. I didn't want to prolong your pain."

She reached up and framed his face. "If you had any clue what kind of pain I've had down there for more than a decade, you'd know this was *nothing* in comparison. I think we still have a lot of territory to cover tonight, not the least of which is making sure you have at least as many orgasms as I do."

* * *

Ryder didn't know how to respond. She didn't appear to be in shock, but he sure as hell was. He'd tried to combine pain and pleasure for her, but seeing her blood on his cock afterward left him feeling two extremely diverse emotions. He hated that he had caused her pain, but that was coupled with intense pride that she had chosen him to be her first. Even though he thought she was excited and wet enough to take him, he'd used lube to be sure. But nothing could have kept her from bleeding. She didn't seem nearly as upset about it as he was.

It's done. Move on.

God, the feeling of being inside her, even for those brief moments, made him ache to be there again, but surely she'd be a little sore after that.

She set the water to the temperature she wanted, and he followed her inside the walk-in shower he'd installed. The simulated-rain showerhead delivered the best shower ever. Not like being in a real rain shower, but if he closed his eyes…

Holy fuck. Megan had removed the G-string. Her ginger-colored short curls invited him to reach out to seek her clit again, but she moved away.

"I'm sorry. Did I hurt you?"

She grinned. "Of course not. Now, let's wash away all this sweat."

She gave him a bottle with Forever Red on the label, and he squirted some into his hand.

Megan.

Her scent, anyway. Jesus, he needed to keep this in stock for any time she had to be away from him.

Ryder rubbed it between his hands and reached out to smooth it onto her breasts. He probably should have started on her arms or shoulders or back, but damned if she didn't have the sexiest breasts he'd ever seen. He couldn't stop touching them.

She closed her eyes and moaned. When he brushed his thumbs over her tight peaks, she leaned closer to him, and his cock stood at attention once again. Wanting to slow things down, he squirted some more and had her turn around. Starting at her shoulders, he worked his way down her alabaster skin, pausing to pay special attention to her reddened ass. The ping-pong paddle had delivered enough of a sting to give her pleasure—and Megan did respond to spankings and paddlings with pleasure—but not as much as the smaller surface of the wooden paddle he'd used before.

She picked up his bar of deodorant soap and rubbed soap between her hands before turning toward him and covering his chest with the lather. She paid careful attention to his pecs. He saw nothing wrong with equal time, loving her touch on his chest.

When she moved lower, his cock throbbed in anticipation of being stroked. Would she? He leaned back against the wall of the shower to give her full access and let her continue to wash the sweat off him. When she reached his cock, he braced against the wall. She spent a lot of time on him, first with tentative caresses and then with bolder strokes.

When she'd finished thoroughly washing him, she wrapped her hand around his cock and pulled him toward her. He opened his eyes and saw the impish grin on her face that didn't usually bode well. But he didn't care. She led him under the spray of the shower, and together, they rinsed the soap off. She paid special attention to her pubic area. Better for her to do that. He'd been afraid to touch her again so soon.

When they had finished with their shower, she turned off the water and reached outside for two more towels, handing one to him. They dried off, and she kept smiling, making him wonder what she was up to.

"I'm going to have to brush out my hair. Why don't you go open a bottle of wine? I'll join you in bed in a few minutes."

Wine sounded like a good idea. So did her joining him in bed. Maybe it would relax them both a bit. Ryder hung his towel over a hook on the back of the door and headed to the kitchen. He hurried back to the bedroom with his stash and lit every candle in the room to set the mood even more.

Which side would she want to sleep on? They hadn't really discussed it.

Well, if they needed to switch, they could.

Switch sides of the bed, of course. The woman seemed to have a fantasy about tying him down. *That* wasn't going to happen.

After pouring two liberal glasses of wine, he wondered what he should do next. The bathroom door opened. Time had run out.

He turned and watched her face light up even brighter than his candlelight surprise.

"Beautiful! How did I get so lucky?"

With her hair wet, it was a deeper red. Still sexy as sin. She walked into his embrace.

"Baby, I think I could say the same thing."

She lifted her face toward his, and he bent to take her mouth with his. *Mine.* He grabbed a fistful of her long wet curls, and his cock pulsated against her. She reached down to stroke him, as if his cock needed any encouragement. Wanting to prolong the moment, he broke away and reached for the glasses of wine forcing her to release his cock. He didn't want to come in her hand and was perilously close to doing just that.

Before he could propose a toast, she did. "To many decades of exploring what turns us on and to having earth-shattering orgasms." The woman seemed to have a one-track mind tonight.

Not that I'm complaining.

"I'll definitely drink to both." They clinked glasses, and he took a couple swallows of his wine while she downed most of hers gulp after gulp.

"I'm going to have to teach you to savor your alcohol, Red."

She smiled up at him. "I think I need the buzz."

To numb the pain? He stroked her face. "I'm sure it will be gone by tomorrow."

She cocked her head. "What will?"

"The pain."

"Oh, I barely feel the sting anymore."

"Not from your spanking, but…losing your virginity."

"I was *talking* about the paddling. Ryder, I'm telling you, I hardly felt anything else. My virginity is gone. Let's move on." She placed her hands on his chest and nudged him toward the bed. "Of course, there's one way to find out if the pain is truly gone."

After a harder push, he lost his balance and sat down abruptly on the side of the bed where she straddled him, sitting on his erection and wiggling her ass against him.

"I need you to get me worked up again, though."

"You want another paddling?"

She glanced over at his open toy bag. "No, but maybe I could peek inside and see what else might be fun."

"You probably wouldn't know what to do with most of what's in there."

"Then surprise me. Can you do a flogging?"

Could he ever. "One or two floggers?"

Her eyes widened. "At a time?" She grinned. "Two must be better than one."

"That's called Florentine style. Assume the position at the foot of the bed."

In no time, she was ready and waited for him. He drew a deep breath and began swinging the floggers in an attempt to find his rhythm. It had been so long. More confident, he walked over to where she awaited another ass reddening.

He stroked the falls of one flogger down her back to her ass. Gooseflesh raised along her pale skin. Using the other flogger, he caressed her between her thighs. After a few minutes, he took a few steps back and threw the flogger, letting the falls thud against her ass.

"Mmmm. I like that."

He repeated with the other and built up a rhythm as he alternated his throws, raining thuddy blows against her ass. She reddened fast but could be redder. Stepping back, he let the tips of the falls sting her ass as he picked up the pace.

"Ach! Oh, God!"

While her mind told her the sting hurt, her body responded in delightful ways. She began pushing her ass closer to him in anticipation of upcoming blows. After several more minutes, he stopped and walked over to her. He draped the floggers over the footboard and reached between her legs.

Wet. "You liked that, didn't you?"

"Oh, yes, Sir. I really did." Her breathy voice turned him on. "I think floggers are my favorite toy so far."

He chuckled. The list of things she enjoyed continued to grow—and paled in comparison to the list they'd have in a few days.

He pried her hands loose from the footboard before picking her up and carrying her to the bed. He laid her down toward the center and stretched out beside her. His fingers pinched her nipple before skimming over her belly to her mound. After playing with her clit, he slipped two fingers inside her.

She winced, making him worry. Then she smiled and met his gaze. "I hardly noticed it."

"Such a brave one."

"No, your wife is horny. Lie on your back."

He wasn't sure what she had in mind, but rolled onto his back. When she moved to straddle him, he held her waist. "What are you doing?"

"I read on my erotica site that I have more control if I'm on top."

He grinned. "No complaints here." She seated herself over his erection. He throbbed, and she wiggled against him. He reached for the soft curls nestled at the juncture of her thighs, stroking her clit hood with his thumb. When she reached for the headboard, stretching out over him, he lifted his head and took her nipple between his teeth. He tugged at the peak, and she hissed. He repeated with the other one.

"Oh, Ryder. Keep doing that."

"Happy to oblige." He worked her up until she made cute little mewling sounds. Without warning, she lifted herself off and moved one of her hands between their bodies until she grabbed his cock. She guided him to her precious opening.

Before he had time to worry about hurting her, she slammed her body down on him, ramming his cock deep inside her. He watched her face. She winced. He ached for her, but being buried deeper inside her than before made it impossible for him to push her off him. When her features softened, he stopped worrying. She lifted and then slammed herself against him once more.

"Slow is nice, too." She placed her hands on his shoulders and found her rhythm. He reached for her clit and rejoiced in the smile that lit up her face. "Feels good when you come so close to pulling away and then take me inside again.

He closed his eyes and stroked her faster. When she began panting, he grabbed her hips to increase her pace. How'd she get there so fast?

"Keep going, Baby." She pumped up and down on his cock.

Jesus. He wasn't going to last long at this pace.

"Oh, Baby. So hot."

"You, too." He felt her tightening her vaginal muscles, squeezing the life out of his cock. Was she doing it on purpose? *Who cares?*

He needed her to come first, because he wouldn't be able to hold out much longer. "Come for me, Baby. I'll be right behind you."

He fingered her clit, and she began bouncing up and down on his cock even faster.

Come on, Baby. Now. I can't…

Holy fuck!

The orgasm tore through him like flood waters in an arroyo. He filled her just as she screamed her own release.

"Oh, shit! Oh, my God! Yes! Oh, yes!"

He lost track of everything as his cock pulsated within her. It was a long time before he came back down to earth.

"Baby, that was incredible. You're incredible."

"Uh, huh. I think you bring out the wanton in me."

He chuckled as she collapsed on top of him. The feel of her weight on him made him feel like a king.

He stroked her hair. "Megan, I haven't felt like this since…well, in forever, really.

"Like what?" Her voice sounded drowsy.

"Loved. Trusted. Like I finally have found my way home."

"Well, we may have to move from here sometime."

"Not the house, but the sense of belonging I feel only with you. I'm not lost anymore. As long as you're with me, I will always be home."

She pushed herself up on the heels of her hands and smiled down at him. "I love you, Ryder."

"I love you, too, Baby."

She lowered her lips to his in a tender kiss. Both of them were too tired to do anything more tonight.

When she pulled away and met his gaze again, she grinned. "I hear sex in the kitchen is pretty hot. Are you hungry, sweetheart?"

Jesus, help me keep up with her.

What's next?

You'll see Megan and Ryder again in the next installment in the Rescue Me Saga: *Nobody's Dream* (Rescue Me Saga #6), along with Adam and Karla (babies, finally!), and, of course, the main couple in *Nobody's Dream*—Luke and Cassie.

Glossary of Terms
for *Nobody's Lost*

Blouse—term for the upper part of a Marine's dress blues.

Bok choy (sometimes bok choi)—a deep green, leafy vegetable that resembles Romaine lettuce on top and a large celery stalk on the bottom, bok choy is a cruciferous more closely related to cabbage

Bottom—in a BDSM scene, the person(s) receiving the action from the **Top.**

Chiles—New Mexican peppers that are a staple in many regional dishes. The sauce made from chiles can be red or green, depending on the ripeness of the pepper when picked. (The green is the hottest—don't be fooled!) Chopped green chiles also are used in many foods (including bagels). Not to be confused with jalapeño or other hot peppers.

Dom/sub or D/s Dynamic in BDSM—a relationship in which the Dominant(s) is given control by consent of the submissive(s) or bottom(s) to make most, if not all, of the decisions in a play scene or in relationships with the submissive(s) or bottom(s).

Fetish—1) an inanimate object worshiped for its supposed magical powers or because it is considered to be inhabited by a spirit or 2) a form of sexual desire in which gratification is linked to an abnormal degree to a particular object, item of clothing, part of the body, etc.

FIST—Fire Support Team in the Marine Corps (the ones who assess the situation on the ground and call for pre-planned fire support and air strikes)

Fry Bread—a flat bread usually leavened by soured milk or baking powder and then deep-fried in lard, shortening, or oil. Can be topped with honey, jam, or powdered sugar, topped with meat, or eaten plain. Tradition holds it was invented by the Navajo, but it is also popular on the pueblos.

Grunt—term for an infantryman in the U.S. Marine Corps (once derogatory, now more neutral)

Hank—a fistful of hair

Head—bathroom (Navy jargon)

IED—improvised explosive device (homemade explosives, often detonated by vehicles on roadsides in Iraq and Afghanistan)

Jemez—one of the pueblo tribes of New Mexico; also the name for the mountains on the Jemez Pueblo

JP—Justice of the Peace (someone with the legal rights to marry couples in the United States)

Kiva fireplace—The Kiva or Bee Hive fireplace with their distinctive arched firebox door is typical of southwestern design and most often placed in a corner. Historically these Kiva fireplaces were constructed of the same adobe material used to construct the home.

Master Z and Club Shadowlands—a series of popular BDSM-genre books by Cherise Sinclair entitled Masters of the Shadowlands. Z is the owner of Club Shadowlands

MFA—Master of Fine Arts degree

PGR—Patriot Guard Riders, a non-profit group of patriotic motorcycle riders who attend the funerals of the fallen to ensure that protestors cannot disrupt the ceremonies.

PTS or PTSD—Post Traumatic Stress or Post Traumatic Stress Disorder

Safeword—a word agreed upon prior to a BDSM scene that can be used to end (temporarily or completely) a play scene

SITREP—a periodic report of the current military situation

SNCO—Staff Non-Commissioned Officer for those in ranks E-6 and higher, including Master Sergeant rank in the Marine Corps)

Spirit Guide

Subdrop—The temporary depression experienced by submissives/masochists hours or days after intense BDSM play. To learn more about subdrop (and the related Domdrop or Topdrop), I encourage you to read the blog written by one of my editors, Ekatarina Sayanova, explaining this phenomenon at rosesandchains.blogspot.com/2014/02/subdrop-and-domdrop-very-real-phenomena.html.

SUV—Sport Utility Vehicle

Top—1) a nickname for Master Sergeant in the Marine Corps (used only with permission of said Master Sergeant) or 2) the person(s) in a BDSM scene who deliver the action. Also see **bottom**.

USC—University of Southern California

VA—Veterans Administration

Zuni—one of the pueblo tribes of New Mexico; known for making **fetish** animals

Cast of Characters for
Nobody's Lost

Gino D'Alessio—served with Ryder Wilson while training at Camp Pendleton in the reconnaissance Marines unit. His brother, Marc D'Alessio, later served as Ryder's Navy Corpsman in the same unit.

Marc D'Alessio—Navy corpsman ("Doc") in Ryder's recon Marine unit in Fallujah.

Carlos Chosa—friends with Ryder since high school and introduced Ryder to the ways of his tribe on the Jemez Pueblo. Gave Ryder a hand up after Fallujah.

Mrs. Chosa—Carlos's late grandmother whose house Ryder stayed at when learning the Native American ways. Ryder now lives in her house.

Megan Gallagher—half-sister to Adam Montague and sister to Patrick Gallagher; recent graduate with an MFA in photography.

Patrick Gallagher—Megan Gallagher's brother and Adam Montague's half-brother

V. Grant—a Lance Corporal communications specialist who was briefly attached to Ryder's recon Marine unit in Fallujah

Adam Montague (pronounced MON-tag)—Ryder's master sergeant (referred to him as "Top"); Megan's half-brother; married to Karla

Karla Paxton Montague—wife to Adam Montague; singer in the Masters at Arms Club

Damián Orlando—served with Ryder in Fallujah; rides a Harley and is a Patriot Guard Rider

Jerry Patterson—a Vietnam veteran who runs a BDSM club in Los Angeles frequented by several characters in the Rescue Me Saga

Marcia Wilson—Ryder's older sister who lives in Santa Fe

Ryder Wilson—served in the recon Marines with Adam Montague in Kosovo, Kandahar (Afghanistan), and Fallujah (Iraq). Appeared briefly in *Masters at Arms* where he was known as Wilson.

Sherry Wilson—Ryder's ex-wife

Playlist for the Rescue Me Saga

Here are some of the songs that inspired Kally as she wrote the books to date in the series. Because each book isn't only about one couple's journey, she has grouped the music by couple, except for the first one. **Warning**: Possible spoilers if you haven't read the entire series yet!

Relevant to Multiple Rescue Me Saga Couples

Darryl Worley – *Just Got Home From a War*

Angie Johnson – *Sing for You*

Nickelback – *I'd Come for You*

Evanescence – *Bring Me To Life*

Daughtry – *I'll Fight*

Dan Hill – *Sometimes When We Touch*

Trace Adkins – *Semper Fi*

The David Crowder Band – *Never Let Go*

Adam and the late Joni
(backstory in *Masters at Arms* & *Nobody's Angel* and *Nobody's Hero*):

Ed Sheeran – *Photograph*

Sarah McLachlan – *Wintersong*

Rascal Flatts – *Here Comes Goodbye*

Aerosmith – *I Don't Wanna Miss A Thing*

Marc and Angelina
(*Masters at Arms* & *Nobody's Angel, Somebody's Angel, and Nobody's Dream*):

Andrea Bocelli – *Por Amor* (and others on *Romanza* CD)

Sarah Jane Morris – *Arms Of An Angel*

Dean Martin – *Volare*

Dean Martin – *You Belong To Me*

Fleetwood Mac – *Landslide*

Mary Chapin Carpenter – *The King of Love*

Usher – *Scream*

Air Supply – *The One That You Love*

Air Supply – *Goodbye*

Lacuna Coil – *Spellbound*

Air Supply – *Making Love Out of Nothing at All*

Styx – *Man In The Wilderness*

Keith Urban – *Tonight I Wanna Cry*

Paul Brandt – *My Heart Has a History*

Michael Bublé – *Home*

Daughtry – *Used To*

Leighton Meester – *Words I Couldn't Say*

Halestorm – *Private Parts*

And a "medley" of heavy-metal music cited in the acknowledgements of *Somebody's Angel*

Adam and Karla

(*Masters at Arms & Nobody's Angel, Nobody's Hero, Somebody's Angel, Nobody's Lost, and Nobody's Dream*):

Tarja Turunen – *I Walk Alone*

Madonna – *Justify My Love*

Sinead O'Connor – *Song to the Siren*

Rascal Flatts – *What Hurts The Most*

Marc Anthony – *I Sang to You*

Simon & Garfunkel – *I Am A Rock*

Alison Krauss & Union Station – *I'm Gone*

The Rolling Stones – *Wild Horses*

Pat Benatar – *Love Is A Battlefield*

The Rolling Stones – *Under My Thumb*

Gary Puckett and the Union Gap – *This Girl is a Woman Now*

Lifehouse – *Hanging By A Moment*

Leighton Meester – *Words I Couldn't Say*

Air Supply – *Lonely Is The Night*

Beyoncé – *Poison*

Randy Vanwarmer – *Just When I Needed You Most*

The Red Jumpsuit Apparatus – *Your Guardian Angel*

Oum Kalthoum – *Enta Omri* (Egyptian belly dance music)

Harem – *La Pasion Turca* (Turkish belly dance music)

Barry Manilow – *Ready To Take A Chance Again*

Paul Dinletir – *Transcendance*

Creed – *Arms Wide Open*

Aerosmith – *I Don't Wanna Miss A Thing*

Damián and Savannah

(*Masters at Arms & Nobody's Angel, Nobody's Perfect, Somebody's Angel, and Nobody's Dream*):

Sarah McLachlan – *Fumbling Towards Ecstasy* (entire CD of same title)

Johnny Cash – *The Beast In Me*

John Mayer – *The Heart Of Life*

Marc Anthony – *When I Dream At Night*

Ingrid Michaelson – *Masochist*

Three Days Grace – *Never Too Late*

Three Days Grace – *Pain*

Drowning Pool – *Let The Bodies Hit the Floor!*

Goo Goo Dolls – *Iris*

John Mayer – *Heartbreak Warfare*

Three Days Grace – *Animal I Have Become*

Ed Sheeran – *Thinking Out Loud*

The Avett Brothers – *If It's the Beaches*

Leonard Cohen – *I'm Your Man*

A Perfect Circle – *Pet*

Pink – *Fuckin' Perfect*

Edwin McCain – *I'll Be*

Ryder and Megan

(*Masters at Arms & Nobody's Angel, Nobody's Hero, Nobody's Lost, and Nobody's Dream*):

Hard Corps – *The Warrior Song*

Kenny Chesney – *You Had Me From Hello*

Chase Rice – *Ride*

Christine Perri – *Arms*

Adele – *One and Only*

Breaking Benjamin – *I Will Not Bow*

Imagine Dragons – *Demons*

The Goo Goo Dolls – *Notbroken*

Five Finger Death Punch – *Wrong Side of Heaven*

Skillet – *Falling Inside the Black*

Sugarland – *Tonight*

Adele – *Make You Feel My Love*

Adele – *Hiding My Heart*

Deepest Blue – *Give It Away*

Inner Voices – *Baby Girl*

Kenny Chesney – *You Save Me*

Train – *Marry Me*

Blake Sheldon – *God Gave Me You*

Phillip Phillips – *Unpack Your Heart*

John Legend – *All of Me*

Phillip Phillips – *Raging Fire*

Rascal Flatts – *I'm Movin' On*

Luke and Cassie

(*Masters at Arms* & *Nobody's Angel, Nobody's Perfect, Somebody's Angel, and Nobody's Dream*):

Paul Brandt – *I Do*

Keith Urban – *I Want to Love Somebody Like You*

Amanda Wilkinson – *Hearts Open Slowly*

Jamie O'Neal – *Like a Woman*

Ty Herndon – *I Have to Surrender*

Leighton Meester and Garrett Hedlund – *Give In to Me*

Jason Aldean and Kelly Clarkson – *Don't You Wanna Stay Here a Little While?*

Shannon Noll – *Don't Fight It*

Ty Herndon – *I Know How the River Feels*

Tracy Byrd – *Keeper of the Stars*

Brad Paisley – *I Want to Check You for Ticks*

Paul Brandt – *When You Call My Name*

Kip Moore – *Hey, Pretty Girl*

Dustin Lynch – *Cowboys and Angels*

Josh Turner –*Your Man*

Paul Brandt – *Take it Off*

Jason Mraz – *I Won't Give Up*

Rascal Flatts – *God Bless the Broken Road*

John Michael Montgomery – *Hold On to Me*

Dixie Chicks – *Cowboy, Take Me Away*

Keith Urban – *Making Memories of Us*

Bryan Adams – *Between Now and Forever*

Luke Bryan – *In Love with the Girl*

Billy Currington – *Must Be Doing Something Right*

Natasha Bedingfield – *Wild Horses*

Demi Lovato – *Nightingale*

Crowder – *Come As You Are*

Rihanna – *Stay*

About the Author

USA Today bestseller author Kallypso Masters writes emotional, realistic Romance novels with an emphasis on healing using sometimes unconventional methods. Her alpha males are dominant and attracted to strong women who can bring them to their knees. Kally also has brought many readers to their knees—having them experience the stories along with her characters in the Rescue Me Saga. Kally knows that Happily Ever After takes maintenance, so her couples don't solve all their problems and disappear at "the end" of "their" novel, but will continue to work on real problems in their relationships in later books in the Saga.

Kally has been writing full-time since May 2011. She lives in rural Kentucky and has been married almost 32 years to the man who provided her own Happily Ever After. They have two adult children, one adorable grandson, and a rescued dog and cat.

Kally enjoys meeting readers. Check out the Appearances page on her web site to see if she'll be near you!

To contact or interact with Kally,

go to Facebook,

her Facebook Author page,

or Twitter (@kallypsomasters), or

her Web site (KallypsoMasters.com).

To join the secret Facebook group Rescue Me Saga Discussion Group, please send a friend request to Karla Paxton and she will open the door for you. Must be 18 to join.

For more timely updates and a chance to win great prizes, get sneak peeks at unedited excerpts, and more, sign up for her newsletter (sent out via e-mail) and/or for text alerts (used ONLY for new releases of e-books or print books) at her Web site (http://kallypsomasters.com). And feel free to e-mail her at kallypsomasters@gmail.com, or write to her at

Kallypso Masters

PO Box 1183

Richmond, KY 40476-1183

Want merchandise relating to the Rescue Me Saga—and personalized, signed trade paperback books, as well? T-shirts and aprons inspired by scene sin *Nobody's Angel* and *Somebody's Angel*. Or a Ka-thunk!® tee inspired by that feeling Karla gets when Master Adam gives her "the look" or a Dom command. How about a beaded evil stick similar to the one used in *Nobody's Perfect?* New items are in the works, too! With each order, you will receive a bag filled with other swag items, including pens, bookmarks, trading cards (with the original covers of the early books). Kally ships internationally. To shop, go to kallypsomasters.com/kally_swag.

Excerpt from
Hart Attack
by Cristin Harber
(Book Seven in the Titan Series)

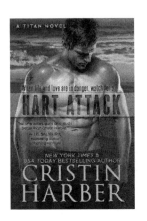

Chapter One

Covered in dirt and squinting against the smoky debris that rained down, Roman Hart growled into his comm piece. "Get me out of here, Rocco."

"Working on it." His team leader barked in the background about a new extraction plan. "Hang tight, Roman. Cash, get a move on, man."

Cash remained radio silent as explosions blasted around Roman. The vibrations killed, his headache raged. Worry churned in his gut that Cash's target was still active, and Roman hadn't heard a word from—

"Would help if I had some eyes." Cash's words drifted through Roman's earpiece.

Good. Still alive. Still throwing digs, not that Roman could help the predicament. Seeing as he was Cash's spotter, this wasn't the greatest situation. Another blast exploded. Roman took a deep breath, not loving the tight spot he'd found himself in, but, even more, hating that they'd come up empty-handed. The ground shook, burning ash floating from the black sky courtesy of some weapons-stealing asshole with a grenade launcher. "Come on, dude. Take out this guy already."

"Gimme a minute…"

Whoever was sending grenades Roman's way was getting closer. Another round of shrapnel and fire rained down. He pinched his eyes closed, waiting.

There was a pause in the blasts, and Roman checked his surroundings. Detonation spots encircled him, basically forming small craters. A few yards right or left, he'd be in pieces. Nothing sounded for more than a minute. His confidence grew that it was almost time to roll.

"You're good," Cash said.

"Took long enough." Roman bolted from his makeshift cover and made his way back toward the team.

"What good is my spotter if he can't say where the hell my target is?"

Roman grumbled. He *had* told both Cash and Rocco where the dude with the bag of grenades was, but at the time, Cash had still been on the move, not ready to shoot, and their team leader was too busy with the flu, trying to keep down his lunch and not bothering to lose his mic. But when Rocco wasn't being sick, he was shouting orders. Dude was good like that.

"Get in, get safe," Rocco muttered.

They had acted on bad intel, gone after stolen codes that could arm an older-than-shit nuke *that had never existed in the first place*. That was, if you read the news reports and believed reporters. Widespread panic had ensued among several foreign governments. Over a weapon that *hadn't existed*. So Titan had been called in. Boss Man stayed at HQ and Rocco led their team on the ground because a stolen nuke and codes trumped the flu. Rocco hadn't balked. They'd hit hard, though they'd hit *wrong*, and were lucky to get out with their asses still intact.

If Roman had to guess, Boss Man was in his element tracking the sources of the intelligence screw-ups.

With the weight of a mission gone wrong on his shoulders, Roman arrived to rendezvous. Winters was already there, Cash seconds later. Silent, they shifted in their boots as though each had the ramifications of the day's fuck-up running through their minds.

Rocco appeared from wherever he'd been bunkered, shaking his head and looking pale, though that probably had less to do with a virus and more to do with a stolen older-than-shit nuke.

"Bad news," Parker's voice came through Roman's earpiece from Titan HQ.

"Don't wanna hear bad news." Rocco scrubbed his face.

"Alright, okay news for now. Tagged their phones with a tracker. Soon as one of 'em makes a call, we're back in business. Roc, Jared's patching through to you."

Rocco switched channels and turned away. Seconds later, his face looked darker. "We've done what can do here. Load up." He stopped, putting his hands on his knees and hanging his head.

Everyone took a step back just in case.

Cash squinted. "Maybe a little R and R is needed before the baby comes."

Rocco laughed harshly. "You think Caterina Savage has any intention of letting the flu in our house? It'd be all, '*ay, Dios mio*. Spray down with Lysol.'" He stood, looking like he was going to lose it again, but then recovered and checked his watch. "Chopper approaching from the southwest in less than one."

As if on cue, the eerily quiet stealth chopper hovered overhead, making ripples in the late-summer air and stirring the dust.

Roman itched to get home. He dug his hand into his pocket and toyed with a small slip of paper at the bottom. Who the hell knew why he kept it, but he did. His fingers had played with it for hours on end, making the thing soften and roll.

"Let's go, boys." Rocco stood back, waiting for the team to load first. He had that look in his eyes, wanting to get home, and that had nothing to do with the flu. Winters and Cash hustled too. They were heading home to their women. It'd been a subtle shift as each of them went down that road. But Roman had noticed.

He thought about the woman who'd shoved the paper into his hand, promising it was only one of the many reasons he'd never get her naked. Thinking about that hissy fit over Chinese takeout, he couldn't help but smile. Beth was something else, and damn if he didn't want her naked and in his hands.

But for now, all he had was a stupid cookie fortune that said *Beware of short life lines*. It made no sense. Especially didn't make sense that Beth was using it as an excuse. Then again, when had she ever had an excuse that wasn't ridiculous? Each one was more absurd than the last, but that was likely because each excuse came with a slew of almosts.

Almost a touch. Almost a kiss. Almost a moment where neither could stop. But they always did.

The girl had a serious set of brakes when it came to him, and man, he loved a challenge. Swallowing her memory, he pulled himself into the chopper. Rocco boarded behind, and then they swayed, lifted, and moved closer to home, closer to her.

Yeah, he wanted her as a distraction from everything nasty that the world had to offer. He looked around, then noticed his serious lack of participation in the general post-mission bullshit as they all stripped gear.

Rocco groaned. "I need my bed."

"Probably what's in your bed," Parker offered from the safety of an ear-piece.

"Ass." But then Rocco rubbed his temples. "You all haven't seen shit till you've seen pregnancy hormones."

Winters nodded. "Second that craziness."

"You two and domestic, parental bliss…" Cash grinned as he unholstered his backup M9 Beretta. "I taught Clara a few counterattack tactics she can throw down in her next game of hide-n-seek."

"Nothing she doesn't already know." Winters smirked at Cash. "Little girl is the queen of the playground. And that has more to do with the defensive maneuvers I taught her than your triangulation tips."

Cash opened his mouth, but Winters shut him down.

"You guys realize how you sound, right?" Roman shook his head. "Little Clara starting a kindergarten militia won't go over well with your wife. Tell me someone knows that besides me."

"I hear ya," Parker muttered. "Mia would kill his ass."

Roman eyed each of them. "Christ. Tell me someone realizes that you're talking about *hopscotch* or whatever instead of how RPGs were flying, Rocco's puking, or Cash taking a tight kill shot. Someone has to think of *something* besides getting home."

For a long moment, no one said a word. Not only was Roman a single guy not whining about missing the same-old day in, day out, but now he'd pointed out that they had lost their damn minds. All of them except Parker. Hell, if those guys weren't careful, they'd all lose their edge.

"Seriously, if you weren't reminded, you'd all get soft."

Winters cleared his throat. "Roman, man?"

"Yeah?" He loosened the straps to his body armor.

"One word."

"And what's that?" He leaned forward, planting his forearms on his knees and shaking his head at the team. "You, my friends, are whipped."

Cash started laughing. Then Rocco.

"What?" Roman narrowed his eyes.

"You can't name that one little word?" Winters leaned back, laughing alongside them. "Ready?"

Cash doubled over. Parker and even Jared chuckled in Roman's earpiece.

"*What?*"

"Beth," Winters said, slapping his leg.

Beth. Roman toyed with the fortune that said he would die early and not get lucky any time soon. She was a headache for him even when he was on mission a continent away. "Nice try, assholes."

But the truth was, soon as he had a chance to see her, Roman would be there, willing and ready to play their game, because it might not be today, might not be tomorrow, but he never lost.

HART ATTACK is available at all major retailers.

New to Cristin's Titan series?

Then be sure to try *WINTERS HEAT* (Book One—currently *FREE*)!

After putting her life on the line to protect classified intelligence, military psychologist Mia Kensington is on a cross-country road trip from hell with an intrusive save-the-day hero. Uninterested in his white knight act, she'd rather take her chances without the ruggedly handsome, cold-blooded operative who boasts an alpha complex and too many guns.

Colby Winters, an elite member of The Titan Group, has a single objective on his black ops mission: recover a document important to national security. It was supposed to be an easy in-and-out operation. But now, by any means necessary becomes a survival mantra when he faces off with a stunning woman he can't leave behind.

When Titan's safe houses are compromised, Colby stashes Mia at his home, exposing his secret—he's the adoptive father of an orphaned baby girl. Too soon, danger arrives and Mia lands in the hands of a sadistic cartel king with a taste for torture. As hours bleed into fear-drenched days, Colby races across the globe and through a firestorm of bullets to save the woman he can't live without.

The *Rescue Me Saga*

kallypsomasters.com/books

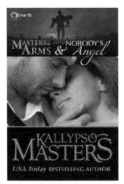

1. Masters at Arms & Nobody's Angel (Combined Volume)

4. Somebody's Angel

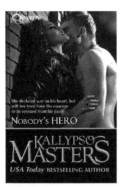

2. Nobody's Hero

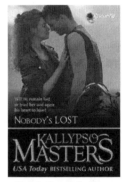

5. Nobody's Lost

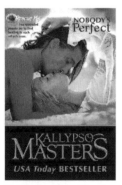

3. Nobody's Perfect

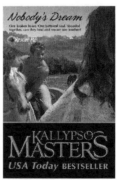

6. Nobody's Dream

26992315R00126

Made in the USA
San Bernardino, CA
07 December 2015